KU-011-934

Laurie Benson is an award-winning Regency romance author, whose book *An Unexpected Countess* was voted Harlequin's 2017 'Hero of the Year' by readers. She began her writing career as an advertising copywriter. When she isn't at her laptop, avoiding laundry, Laurie can be found browsing antiques shops and going on long hikes with her husband and two sons. Learn more about Laurie by visiting her website at lauriebenson.net. You can also find her on Twitter and Facebook.

ACC. No: 05112058

Also by Laurie Benson

Secret Lives of the Ton miniseries

An Unsuitable Duchess
An Uncommon Duke
An Unexpected Countess

The Sommersby Brides miniseries

One Week to Wed

And look out for the next two books
coming soon

Discover more at millsandboon.co.uk.

ONE WEEK TO WED

Laurie Benson

MILLS & BOON

All rights reserved including the right of reproduction
in whole or in part in any form. This edition is published
by arrangement with Harlequin Books S.A.

This is a work of fiction. Names, characters, places, locations
and incidents are purely fictional and bear no relationship to
any real life individuals, living or dead, or to any actual places,
business establishments, locations, events or incidents.
Any resemblance is entirely coincidental.

This book is sold subject to the condition that it shall not,
by way of trade or otherwise, be lent, resold, hired out
or otherwise circulated without the prior consent of the publisher
in any form of binding or cover other than that in which it is published
and without a similar condition including this condition
being imposed on the subsequent purchaser.

® and TM are trademarks owned and used by the trademark owner
and/or its licensee. Trademarks marked with ® are registered with the
United Kingdom Patent Office and/or the Office for Harmonisation
in the Internal Market and in other countries.

First Published in Great Britain 2018
by Mills & Boon, an imprint of HarperCollins*Publishers*
1 London Bridge Street, London, SE1 9GF

© 2018 Laurie Benson

ISBN: 978-0-263-93295-9

MIX
Paper from
responsible sources
FSC® C007454

This book is produced from independently certified FSC™ paper
to ensure responsible forest management.
For more information visit www.harpercollins.co.uk/green.

Printed and bound in Spain
by CPI, Barcelona

For Terry:
To every incredible challenge you've responded
with unbelievable strength. If I could write your
happy-ever-after, I'd leave out all the bad stuff.

Thank you to my wonderful editor Linda Fildew,
my team at Mills & Boon, and my agent
Courtney Miller-Callihan. Hugs to Lori, Mia,
Jen, Harper, Anabelle and Michele, for everything.
Thank you to my family for your love and support.
And thank you to my readers. For those of you
who asked for Andrew's story after you read
An Uncommon Duke, this is for you.

Chapter One

Mayfair, London—1819

There was no mistaking the inviting look in the eyes of the widow as she studied Lord Andrew Pearce across the coffin of her dead husband.

In a stealthy manoeuvre, Andrew shifted his leg and ground the heel of his boot into his brother Gabriel's foot, determined to scuff the impeccable black leather. It would serve him right for dragging Andrew here. In true ducal fashion Gabriel exhibited no reaction, aside from the slight clench of his jaw.

It was all his brother's fault Andrew was being subjected to this. As the eldest, Gabriel had informed his brothers it was their family's duty to pay their respects, even though they all hated the man.

It was the thing to do. It was only proper.

And Andrew was counting the minutes until it was over.

Being this close to a dead body was hard enough, bringing back memories he would just as soon forget. But the attention from the widow of the newly deceased Twelfth Duke of Skeffington in addition to that was making this unbearable.

At nine and twenty, Elizabeth, the Duchess of Skeffington, was only two years younger than Andrew. With her thick black hair, big brown eyes and graceful figure she was considered by many to be a diamond of the first water. However, Andrew wasn't attracted to her. Even knowing she was going to be a very wealthy widow did little to make her any more enticing.

She was a woman who appeared obsessed with rank and prestige. As the brother of a duke, he had experienced his fair share of people who were interested in him only for his family connections. And as a duchess in her own right, he assumed her prejudice against families of lower status was one of the reasons she always seemed interested in him. There were very few ducal families in Britain. Her choices were limited. However, he didn't want a wife.

The Duchess slipped a wayward tendril of black hair over her ear and offered him a shy smile. If Gabriel noticed her attention had been fixed on Andrew since they entered the room, he gave no indication. However, Monty, on his other side, pressed his knee firmly into Andrew's leg. At least one of his brothers was aware of his plight.

'You have our condolences, Elizabeth,' Gabriel said, over the murmur of voices from the other mourners in the ballroom that was darkened with black cloth around the windows.

Her attention finally shifted away from Andrew to Gabriel, and she gave his brother a polite smile. 'Thank you for coming to pay your respects. It's no secret you and Skeffington were on opposing sides on many issues through the years.'

'We were. His death did come as a shock, even with his advanced age. He just addressed the House on Monday.'

Monty tilted his head and eyed the outline of the short thin body lying before them under the shroud. 'Forgive me, but I've not heard what caused his demise. Was he suffering from an illness?' Andrew's younger brother asked.

'He choked on a chicken bone during dinner. The footmen were not able to save him.' It was said with such a calm demeanour, one had to wonder if she had been present to witness what must have been a ghastly event.

Andrew's heart began to pound harder. He knew what it was like to watch someone die. Taking a step back, he looked away from the dead body in front of him and tried to push the memories out of his head. Over the years he had become adept at locking them away, but this was bringing them all back. He should have refused to come today.

As if he realised Andrew was ready to bolt from the room, Gabriel made a move to end the conversation and Andrew's torture. 'Well, I'm sure there are many others here who wish to pay their respects. We will not keep you any further.'

Andrew's sense of unease at being around this much death was starting to lift. Until the Duchess stepped around the coffin and called softly to him as he turned to walk towards the door with his brothers.

He squeezed his eyes shut before turning to face her. 'Yes, Your Grace?'

She gave him a small smile as she started to blush. 'You may call me Elizabeth. We've been acquainted with one another for twelve years.'

'But I'd never presume to be on such intimate terms with you.' It was paramount he stated that, since he had no intention of becoming so familiar with Skeffington's widow.

'But there is no reason we couldn't be now.' There was a hopefulness in her eyes.

He should have pretended he hadn't heard her when she called his name.

'Have you received your invitation to the funeral?' Thankfully she changed the subject when he refused to acknowledge her suggestion. 'The service will be this evening at ten, in St Paul's. Skeffington wished to hold to old traditions and wanted an evening burial.'

It was just like the man not to consider the safety of his mourners. Carriages in London were often robbed while they waited outside churches at night during funerals. Andrew was still uncertain why he had been invited to attend. Gabriel, as the Duke of Winterbourne, was fully capable of representing his family. 'I've received it.'

The gloved fingers on her right hand nervously toyed with the jet beads near her collarbone. 'I know he was not well liked by many in Society, but it would be a shame if there weren't many to offer prayers for his soul. I hope you will be there.'

At least it wasn't customary for the women of the *ton* to attend burial services. He would be safe in the church from her attention. Having someone watch him made him uncomfortable. 'I'll be there along with my brothers.'

She lowered her head and looked at him through her lashes. 'Thank you for calling on me,' she said softly. 'I expect we will see one another soon.'

Did she have to make it sound as if he had called on her with romantic intentions? It was a wake. 'Not too soon. It will be a year before we see one another.' She was newly widowed. The year's mourning period would keep her away from any entertainments he might attend.

She bit her lip. 'Unlike Skeffington, I find I am not all that traditional.'

The walls were closing in. He was feeling like hunted prey and needed to get away from the Duchess and the dead body in the room. 'Well, do have a pleasant day,' he managed to choke out rather inappropriately, before making his way through the crowd of mourners and out the ballroom door.

He was so intent on escaping he almost collided with a woman dressed all in black as he rounded the corner leading to the entrance hall. She let out a soft gasp through the veil covering her face and was able to stop him by raising her gloved hand just before she slammed into his chest. A pleasant floral scent drifted towards him as the black ostrich feather, curling over the front of her black bonnet, brushed against his brow. It was a soft brush, almost a tickle.

Andrew stepped back and tipped his head in a wordless apology before they both quickly went on their way. But after he took a few steps, something made him look back and follow her hurried progress towards the ballroom. Perhaps it was the realisation that he hadn't bothered to notice what she looked like or that she seemed preoccupied and eager to get around him. He couldn't imagine anyone being in a rush to see a dead body.

When he stepped into the entrance hall both of his brothers were waiting for him near the large marble staircase. They resembled matching bookends with their light brown hair, similar features, and black trousers and coats. They both also held the same amused expression as they watched Andrew walk towards them.

Gabriel was fighting back a smile as he turned his attention to adjusting his gloves. 'I see Elizabeth found a way to have a few words alone with you. We were going to leave for White's without you, but decided to wait and see how long it took you to extricate yourself.'

Andrew let out an annoyed breath and rubbed his chin. 'If you both hadn't walked away when she called me, I might have avoided the encounter entirely.'

'She called your name, not ours,' Monty replied with a smirk. 'Who are we to come between you and a grieving widow? Dare I ask what she wanted, or would your answer shock my youthful innocence?'

'You are Mother's least favourite child. She has told me so on numerous occasions,' Andrew replied pointedly. 'Her Grace wanted to know if I'd be attending the burial service this evening. That is all.'

'You don't think she plans on attending, do

you?' Monty asked, appearing aghast. 'She did seem rather interested in you.'

As they made their way to the front door, Gabriel put on his hat. 'She has always appeared taken with Andrew. However, what she finds appealing about him is a mystery to me. Since women in our circle do not attend funerals, I do believe he is in no danger of being cornered behind a pillar in St Paul's tonight.' His mouth twitched with amusement. 'Although, that would be entertaining to witness.'

Charlotte had been hurrying towards the ballroom in Skeffington House, wishing she could have been going anywhere but there, when she nearly collided with a mountain of a man in the corridor. She didn't even have the presence of mind to look at him and offer an apology. The brief incident left her more agitated than she already had been and her stomach started flying around like a bird in a cage. How she wished she was leaving along with him instead of heading towards the room filled with so much death… and so many people who would be expressing their condolences, even if their comments were not directed to her.

Ever since Jonathan had been killed, hearing those sympathetic words would make her queasy, reminding her of the sentiments so many people expressed when they came to call on her for months after her husband's death, making her relive the pain of her loss over and over.

Thankfully, her stomach settled by the time she crossed the threshold of the ballroom which was set for the elaborate wake befitting the oldest Duke in Britain. At the far end of the room was a raised platform where his coffin was laid. Black curtains cascaded around the four corners of the platform from the cornice above, adorned with gilded angels. It was certainly a stately site, although she did find the angels odd knowing the temperament and uncharitable nature of the man lying under them.

Moving past small groups of mourners clustered about the room, she tried to block out the murmur of their voices. The coffin was only a few yards away, with the shrouded body of the Duke. Charlotte had not seen her husband's body to confirm his death. Jonathan's remains were buried in Belgium. The only proof she had were the accounts of what happened to him from his fellow officers and the few personal effects of his that were returned to her. Reaching for the black ribbon around her neck, she clasped the gold signet ring which he had worn that now hung there. The only reason she was here was because her sister needed her.

She spotted Lizzy standing to the left of the coffin, speaking to a well-dressed grey-haired gentleman. As if sensing Charlotte's presence, her younger sister looked up and their eyes met. Lizzy carefully extracted herself from her conversation and hurried towards her. The urgency of her manner made Charlotte feel even more guilty for arriving late.

'I'm sorry I did not arrive sooner, Lizzy. Please do not interrupt your conversation on my account. I know how people like to offer their condolences at a time like this.'

And she would prefer not to hear them.

'It was no bother,' Lizzy said with a careless wave of her black-gloved hand. 'Lord Liverpool can ramble on at times. Skeffington had appointed him executor of his estate. The will stipulates all parties must be present for it to be read and there has been little success in locating his heir. Lord Liverpool was apprising me of the details. Do not look so concerned. I know I will be left in very comfortable circumstances with Skeffington's passing, so have no fear.'

She took Charlotte by the arm to a window overlooking Green Park and wrapped her arms around her in an affectionate hug. The window sash was raised, letting in a breeze which was helping Charlotte breathe as the walls continued to close in on her.

'It's such a relief to have you here, Charlotte. I know you hate London, but Aunt Clara and Juliet are in Paris. They would never have arrived here in time and even if they were here, it's you I really need by my side. Our aunt has never understood me the way you do. And, while our sister means well, Juliet is still so young.' The three Sommersby sisters were always close, but Charlotte and Lizzy were especially dear to each other.

'Juliet is two and twenty. She is not so young any more.'

'But you understand what it is to be widowed.' Charlotte searched her younger sister's face, trying to determine how she was coping with her loss. 'I left shortly after I received your letter, but we had terrible rain which impeded my journey. I know how difficult this can be. How are you faring?'

Her sister waved her hand as if losing her husband was of no true consequence. Which it probably wasn't, to Lizzy. 'It truly is a relief.' She eyed Charlotte's black dress and then studied her bonnet.

Silently, Charlotte began counting down the seconds before her sister voiced her opinion of her ensemble. She got to seven.

'I like your bonnet. The ostrich feather is a nice touch. It's rather fetching. Perhaps I'll have one made for me.' Lizzy wrinkled her brow. 'That isn't four years old, is it?' The concern for liking something that might not be deemed the latest fashion clearly concerned her sister.

'No, I did not have this when I went into

mourning for Jonathan. I bought the bonnet some months ago and added the feather before I left.'

A sense of relief brightened Lizzy's expression. 'You've become quite skilled with trimmings. Had you married a prosperous duke as I had done, and not a third son, you would have no need to alter your bonnets or gowns. You'd simply buy new ones. What do you think of this dress? It's from Madame Bouvier. I'm not certain about the flounces at the hem.'

'It's lovely, Lizzy. Perhaps you'd like to borrow my fichu? I believe that gown was designed to wear with one.'

'Nonsense. I am in a position now to search for a husband. I see no reason to hide the assets God has given me.'

'Your husband has just died.'

'And?'

'He is lying over there.'

Lizzy rolled her eyes. 'Skeffington is dead. He can't see me.'

'But those in attendance can.'

'If one is to catch a husband, one needs to bait them.' She cast a disapproving eye at Charlotte's fichu. 'How I wish you would put away your widow's weeds. I haven't seen you out of mourning attire in years.'

None of her family and friends understood what it was like to have the man you loved ripped from you. When the letter arrived, informing her Jonathan had perished nobly during the Battle of Waterloo, the pain of losing him was more than she thought she could bear. He had been aide-de-camp to Wellington. A man in that position was not supposed to die. A man in that position should have returned from the war and settled with her into a comfortable life. Other men had returned. Why couldn't he?

'For the hundredth time, I will not marry unless I become destitute and I'm forced to do so. The heart isn't capable of falling in love twice in a lifetime and there is no reason to marry if it's not for love.'

The moment the words left her mouth, she wished she could have taken them back. Charlotte had been fortunate to be allowed to marry the man she loved because it cemented an age-old alliance between their families. Lizzy had been ordered to marry a pompous old man for his title. There was no need to remind her of that.

'You always were the sentimental one. Not everyone needs to marry for love. However, I assure you the next time my marriage banns are read in church people will not give me pitying looks. This time, I will see jealousy in their eyes.'

'Why does it sound as if you have already set your sights on the man you'd like to marry?'

'Perhaps I have,' she replied with a broad

smile. 'Which reminds me. You need to go upstairs.' She began pulling Charlotte towards the door by the elbow.

'I assure you I am not in need of a respite. Violet is unpacking my belongings as we speak. I want to be here by your side through all of this, just as you supported me. I know how distressing this can be.'

'Charlotte, do I look distressed?' Lizzy tilted her head. 'I thought not.'

'But I haven't even paid my respects to the Duke.'

'I assure you, he won't miss you. I need you to have Marie get my dress ready for this evening. And perhaps you can go to Lock and Company and purchase me a hat like the one you are wearing. Or you can let me borrow your hat. Oh, please let me borrow yours. The more I look upon it, the more I like it and there probably isn't one exactly like that in the shop.'

'Tonight? Where are you going tonight?'

'I'm going to the burial service.'

Charlotte pulled her to a stop. There were rules and as the oldest Sommersby sister it often fell to her to remind Lizzy of them. 'You can't go,' she whispered sternly. 'It's not done.'

'I'm a duchess. I can be as eccentric as I wish.'

'What of the new Duke? Surely he will not approve of such behaviour.'

'He is not in London to offer any opinion on

the matter. I am going to that church tonight. You can either help me with my arrangements or you can add to the pain this whole event is causing me by trying to thwart me. Either way, I will go.'

Why did Lizzy have to be so stubborn? 'It's too dangerous to travel with the funeral procession through the streets of London at night.'

'I shall have the funeral furnisher arrange armed escorts for my carriage.'

'You don't think it will cause gossip?'

'I am a grieving widow who wants to be with my husband to the very end.' She opened her eyes wide and batted her lashes.

'Lizzy, do you not believe Skeffington is dead? Do you think he will sit up and prove everyone wrong? Is that what this is about?'

'No, of course not. I witnessed his last breath. I even poked him with my fork to be certain. The man is dead. But another man will be at the service and he is the reason I need to be there.' She gave Charlotte a genuine, warm smile. 'Do this for me, Sister. It isn't that much to ask of you, is it? I need to be there.'

Three years separated them in age. They had been very close growing up. Before Charlotte married Jonathan, they had been inseparable. Lizzy raised her eyebrows and smiled again, resembling the young girl who loved to try on Charlotte's gowns and sit on her bed to fix her hair. It was hard not to smile back.

'Will you help me pick out a suitable gown, Charlotte? Please.'

'Very well. I will help you with your plan to attend church this evening. But you must permit me to go along with you. I do not want you to travel alone. Now go back to do your duty as his widow and I will arrange to have a suitable dress ready for you.'

'And your hat? You'll let me wear your hat?'

Charlotte covered her lips to hide her smile. 'Yes, Lizzy. I will let you wear my hat.'

Her sister kissed her on the cheek and squeezed her hand. 'You are the best of sisters. Thank you again for coming to Town to be with me through this. I know how much you dislike leaving your village, however you shall not regret it.'

While Lizzy might have been glad she was here, Charlotte knew her calm and orderly life was about to be disrupted in unknown ways. She could feel it.

Chapter Two

Andrew saw no sense in accompanying the funeral procession to St Paul's and helping to add to the spectacle. His brothers could do that for him. He arrived at the Cathedral after the funeral service had already begun, making his way up the aisle past prominent Members of Parliament and the *ton* to slip into the row his brothers were occupying not far from the altar. Monty covered a yawn as he nodded a silent greeting to him.

It wasn't until the bishop began the eulogy that Andrew shifted his gaze and noticed a black-ostrich plume sway in the front row, across the aisle. He shifted his head and saw the back of a woman wearing a black bonnet like the one he had seen on the woman he almost ran into while leaving Skeffington's house. This wasn't the place for a woman.

'What do you know of the new Duke?' he whispered, tipping his head towards Monty.

'You mean Skeffington's mysterious heir? No one I know has ever heard of him.'

'Nephew?'

'Distant cousin.'

'Married?'

'I would assume he's married or a widower.'

Could he have run into the new Duchess of Skeffington when he was leaving the wake? It might explain why she was in the front of the church now. If they lived in the country they might not know women in Town did not attend burials.

Andrew craned his neck further to try to get a glimpse of the new Duke, but his view was blocked by the rows of mourners. His attention was drawn once more to the back of the black bonnet. If only her face hadn't been covered with a veil, he would have a better idea of what she looked like.

As if the universe had called out to her, the woman turned and scanned the rows of mourners. However, this wasn't the woman Andrew had almost knocked over. It was Skeffington's widow. There was no mistaking her in the dim light of the cathedral with the veil of the bonnet tucked above the brim, revealing her face.

As her eyes locked on to his with the precision of a sniper, Andrew shifted his gaze to the bishop so quickly, it was a wonder he hadn't injured his eye sockets.

* * *

The bishop was telling them not to mourn Skeffington's death, but celebrate the life he lived. Charlotte hadn't known Lizzy's husband very well. He had barely spoken to her when they were in the same room and what he had said could be considered rather dismissing. From the newspaper accounts she had read about him and from Lizzy's letters, he appeared to have behaved that way with most people.

But regardless of what she thought of Lizzy's husband, the bishop was still wrong. There was no celebration in death. It only left intense pain for those who loved them. When Jonathan died on the battlefield, Charlotte died along with him.

Out of the corner of her eye, she saw Lizzy turn around. Softly, Charlotte stepped on Lizzy's slipper, drawing her sister's attention back to the front of the church.

'Why did you do that?' Lizzy whispered harshly.

They bent their heads so the brims of their bonnets were touching. 'You really should be paying attention to your husband's eulogy.'

'The bishop's probably expressing the same thing he did at the house this afternoon when he offered his condolences. Honestly, how many different ways can one talk about death? He probably says the same thing at all his burial services and just adjusts the names. And he is getting paid a tidy sum to say those words.'

'You may find comfort in what he is saying?'

'Do I truly look as though I need comforting?'

'Not exactly, but you could pretend.'

There was a distinct pause to Lizzy's movements. 'That's it. I'll appear the grieving widow in need of comfort.' She dabbed under her eyes with a handkerchief.

'You look as though you have something in your eye.'

'I'm crying.'

'No matter how hard you wrinkle up your face, tears will not flow.'

'Step on my foot.'

'Why?'

'Just do it.'

'I will not. I've already stepped on your foot.'

'Yes, yes, but do it harder this time. It needs to hurt so much, it brings tears to my eyes.'

'I will not help you perpetrate a lie in the house of God.'

'It won't be a lie if you step on my foot hard enough.'

'I will not. Now, stop talking and pay attention,' Charlotte whispered firmly back.

Lizzy turned around once more. And once more Charlotte stepped on her foot.

'I said harder. How am I to cry if you can't manage to maim me?'

'What in the world has captured your attention at a time like this?'

'He's here.'

'Who? The next Duke? If you wish to remain here, I suggest you do nothing to call attention to yourself. He might drag us both back home, which I could understand.'

'Not him. The man I've wanted ever since my first Season, but Father made me marry Skeffington instead. He is the brother of the Duke of Winterbourne.'

Charlotte turned to try to see who her sister was looking at, but the men behind them blocked her view. 'How is it you've never mentioned him before?'

'I did, the night of my coming-out ball, but shortly after that Father told me I'd be marrying Skeffington. I thought I'd lost my chance to marry him, but all this time he has remained unwed. Now I can finally have him.'

Charlotte had tried to convince their mother to speak out against Lizzy's marriage. Their mother would not hear of it. For years Charlotte had suffered with guilt that she could have done more to stop the marriage. She had been newly married herself then and Jonathan advised her not to approach her father on the issue. She had often wondered if she had, would it have made a difference. Whoever this man was, Lizzy deserved him. She deserved to fall in love with that one person who would make her life so much better just by being in it—everyone did.

They were leaving for Charlotte's home in
Cheshire in a few days, so Lizzy could begin
her full mourning period away from the tempting entertainments of London. She was relieved
her sister agreed that, if she remained in Town
reading newspaper accounts of all the balls, routs
and dinners that she was missing, she would be
miserable. Now they had months to spend together again. And when Lizzy returned to Town,
Charlotte was certain there would be no stopping
her sister from trying to win the gentleman who
stood somewhere behind them.

Chapter Three

❦

Four months later...

Andrew stood outside Gabriel's study and knocked on the large mahogany door. There was a time when he wouldn't have had to wait for approval to enter, but since his brother had reconciled with his wife a little less than a year ago, Andrew had got into the habit of knocking. At the muffled sound of Gabriel's response, he turned the handle and walked into the room.

His brother was seated at his massive desk and his attention was on a piece of paper resting on its surface, while he absently ran his fingers through his short light brown hair. Andrew sank into the well-cushioned chair across from him and held back a yawn. Gabriel barely acknowledged him since he was so engrossed in the task at hand. As the head of an organisation that protected the King and Prince Regent, as well as being a Member of Parliament, it wasn't uncommon for Gabriel to be in the middle of something when Andrew entered his study.

After a few more minutes, Gabriel looked up and arched his brow. 'Hell, man, you look awful.'

Andrew had ridden back to London in the early morning hours from Windsor and he hadn't had any sleep. 'I realise I'm not as impeccably attired as you, but I do believe awful is an exaggeration.'

'I wasn't referring to what you are wearing. I was referring to those bloodshot eyes you can't seem to keep open and the shave you desperately need.'

'I'm fine.'

'You need sleep.'

Andrew waved the suggestion away. His leather glove rubbed against the cut on his right hand, irritating it through the bandage. As he removed both gloves, Gabriel's keen eyes focused on the cotton strip.

'How did you get that?'

'A knife fight at Windsor. It's small.'

'How will you explain that one away?'

'I box regularly at Jackson's. There are times I like to bare-knuckle brawl. It's well known. No one questions my scars.'

'You once told Nicholas ladies like men with scars. He was eager to inform me of that bit of wisdom.'

'The ladies I associate with do.'

'However, not the ladies my six-year-old son does. I received word Kempt is now under guard in the Tower. Excellent work bringing him in.'

'It wasn't easy, but it made for an interesting day.' He raised his bandaged hand to show how interesting it had been to capture the would-be assassin of King George. Andrew tilted his head in an attempt to read the papers on Gabriel's desk.

His brother turned the stack over.

'What else do you have for me to do? There must be some interrogation you can use my assistance on or a lead you need me to follow.'

'I have nothing for you.'

That wasn't possible. 'You have nothing or nothing for *me*.'

'Nothing for you at the moment. Enjoy some time to avoid knife fights and pursue your own interests.'

'Knife fights are an interest of mine.'

'Then go find other ones. You've been working for months without stop. When was the last time you spent a significant amount of time simply going wherever the day takes you, doing whatever you want to do?'

'I would grow bored.'

'You might find that you don't.'

'Are you trying to get rid of me?'

'I am trying to ensure you do not drop from

exhaustion or get injured because you have over-taxed yourself.'

'If this is about my hand, I—'

'This isn't about your hand, Andrew. Although, move your fingers so I can be sure it's not seriously damaged under that bandage.'

Andrew shoved his hand towards Gabriel and clenched it into a fist before opening it up and wiggling his fingers. It hurt like hell, but he'd be damned if he'd let his brother know.

'When was the last time you went and visited a friend?' Gabriel asked, pushing his chair away from his desk.

'I went with Hart to the races not long ago.'

'I meant with someone removed from what we do—outside London.'

'Why would anyone want to go outside London? There is more to do here than anywhere else in the world.'

'There are times it's important to disengage from our work and give your mind and your nerves time to settle. You'll be more effective for it.'

'I wouldn't know what to do.'

'Isn't there someone you'd like to see that you haven't because you have not had the time?'

Andrew dropped his head back and stared at the coffered ceiling in Gabriel's study, trying to think of anyone whose company he enjoyed enough to leave London. 'Toby Knightly and I still write to one another. Do you remember him from Cambridge?'

Gabriel nodded. 'Did you not share a room together?'

'We did. He's an out and outer and has been after me to visit him in Cheshire.'

'Then go to Cheshire.'

A sly smile lifted Andrews lips. 'You know there has been unrest in the north.'

'Yes, I know. But you are not going there because of the unrest. You are going there because you need rest and visiting with Toby will be enjoyable.'

'How do you know it will be enjoyable?'

'Hell, man, just go!'

'You will not give me another mission until I take my Grand Tour of the English countryside?' he asked with sarcasm dripping from his voice.

'No, not until I am certain you are well rested.'

'Then you are leaving me no choice.'

'I'm not. I am relieving you of all duties here for a month.'

'A month! That's absurd. A week.'

There was a tick in Gabriel's jaw. 'A fortnight and not a day sooner. Do I make myself clear? You are to completely disengage yourself for fourteen days.'

'This new baby you and Olivia have had has softened your brain. Very well. Since you are not giving me a choice, I shall send word to Toby. I'd prefer not to arrive unannounced at his door.'

Gabriel sat back and smiled. 'Our mother taught you well. She'd be proud.'

'Well, she does like me best.'

'I'm sure that has nothing to do with your grooming habits or your fashionable attire.'

'My grooming habits are impeccable.'

'You need a shave and a haircut.'

Andrew ran his hand through his hair that fell a bit past his collar. 'I like it this length. And no matter what I wear, it will never be up to snuff according to you.'

'I should increase your wages, maybe then you'd see fit to purchase some new coats.'

'I can afford new coats on the income I make from my investments. However, should you see fit to increase my wages, I'll not complain.' He glanced down at the sleeve of his brown coat. 'I like this coat. It's perfectly worn. You make it sound as though I run around London in doublet and hose. I see no difference in the cut of my coats compared to the cut of the ones you wear.'

'No, I don't suppose you would.' A teasing smile was tugging at the corner of his brother's mouth. 'You might find you'd attract a different calibre of women if you didn't consistently look as though you belong in a boxing ring.'

'But I enjoy being in a boxing ring and I'm fine with the calibre of women I attract.'

'Go, Andrew. Give yourself time to rest and release some of that tension.'

That tension was wound so tightly around every fibre of Andrew's being it would never leave him. It had taken hold of him years ago, on a rainy night in Richmond when he confronted his beloved uncle who was holding a gun on Gabriel. Andrew did something that night he never thought he was capable of. He took his uncle's life. Protecting the Crown had a way of changing a man. It had a way of forcing one to lock down emotions that made you vulnerable and allowed you to make the kinds of choices no man should ever have to make.

There was no sense in telling Gabriel that Andrew could move up north and it still would not matter. Andrew would never be without that tension that held down his emotions to enable him to be an effective and efficient operative. He would never live the life of a country gentleman like Toby. No small estate and pleasant wife were in his future. They were distractions he could not afford. He was a man who was always on a mission. To appease Gabriel he would leave, but it would change nothing.

Chapter Four

❦

Settling into the comfortable wing-backed chair, Charlotte accepted a cup of tea from her friend Ann after their walk around the windy garden of Ann's stately home in the Cheshire countryside.

'Thank you again for your invitation to dine here tonight,' Charlotte said. 'Since Lizzy's recent departure, the house seems unusually quiet. One would think I would be accustomed to the silence, but for some reason I'm feeling it rather acutely at the moment.'

'I'm so glad you accepted my invitation,' Ann replied with a smile, pouring tea into her Wedgwood teacup. 'Since Toby invited one of his friends to stay with us, I am grateful for your companionship. Tonight, they went to dine in the village.' She added a splash of milk to her cup. 'You never did say why Lizzy decided to leave. I thought she would be staying longer.'

'She had some estate matters to attend to in

London.' Charlotte was certain Lizzy's hasty departure had more to do with searching out the Duke of Winterbourne's brother before any other woman grabbed his attention than it did with her solicitor, but she was not about to betray her sister's interest in the man.

Disapproval was evident on Ann's face. 'I know Lizzy. She's too social a creature. Do you truly believe she will not attend any entertainments while she is there?'

That was the very concern Charlotte expressed while Lizzy was having trunk after trunk of her wardrobe brought out of Charlotte's house and into her awaiting carriage. Lizzy had always been headstrong. Nothing was going to change that. All Charlotte could do was try to minimise the reactions people like Ann were bound to exhibit at the news. 'It's been four months,' she replied, trying to sound as if that was a perfectly acceptable amount of time to wait before returning to Society.

'Four months is not a year. She should be in mourning for a year.'

'I'm aware of that. However, you can be as unconventional as you wish when you are a duchess.'

'I suppose that is one advantage she had being married to him.' Ann took a sip of tea and stared off into the distance, as if she were considering what it must have been like to be married to such an old man.

'Lizzy has assured me she will just be attending the theatre and going to dinner parties. She certainly will not be marrying until a year has passed.'

The last statement was said more to appease Ann than because Charlotte actually believed it. If the Duke of Winterbourne's brother asked for her hand the day she arrived back in London, she was certain Lizzy would accept, regardless of how close it was to Skeffington's death. If they did get married, Charlotte would finally learn what the man's name was. It was just like Lizzy to identify the man by the most prestigious thing about him and not by his name.

'Everyone always said you three Sommersby sisters were all so different from one another.'

Charlotte shrugged. 'Lizzy is eager to move forward with her life.'

'She isn't the only one who should move forward with her life.' Ann arched her brow and a teasing smile played on her lips. 'Do not roll your eyes. I am simply stating it is time for you to put the past behind you and look towards your future, as well. You are a beautiful, caring woman. Any man would be fortunate to have you as his wife.' She took Charlotte's hand in hers. 'We all know you loved Jonathan. It's a tragedy he never made it back from the war, but you have many years ahead of you to find love again.'

Why was it still necessary to defend her love for Jonathan to the people who professed to care about her? No one fell in love twice in a lifetime. 'That part of my life is over. I am fortunate I do not need to marry again. I do not need excess extravagances like my sister does. I have simpler tastes.'

'I wasn't speaking of your financial situation and you know that. Although, if you were to find a wealthy man, it would not be a hardship.' Ann gave a low chuckle.

They had discussed this before. Nothing would change. 'How long will Toby's friend be visiting? I wish to know how many days of excuses I will need to prepare myself with, should you need more company for dinner.'

Amusement sparkled in Ann's blue eyes. 'He will be staying with us for a fortnight. You certainly cannot find excuses for all of those days.'

'I pray I will be fortunate and the gentlemen will discover they'd much rather dine at home each night and you will not be in need of companionship.'

'I still could invite you to dine with us.'

'And I can then freely decline, knowing you are not sitting all alone with a leg of mutton.'

'It has been rather nice seeing Toby's joy in being with his old friend.'

'Have I met the gentleman before?'

Ann shook her head. 'No. The last time Toby saw him was about six years ago. His name is Lord Andrew Pearce. They attended Cambridge together.' Her eyes widened and she leaned forward. 'I looked for him in *Debrett's*.'

'Please, I beg you, do not tell me of his lineage. I've spent the last four months with Lizzy. I'm convinced she has memorised the contents of that book and freely refers to the people she associates with solely by their most prestigious familial connection. I've had enough of titles to last a lifetime.'

Ann settled back in her chair with a laugh. 'Very well. I'm sure you have.'

'Where does Toby's friend live? Six years is a long time not to see one another.'

'London. Toby has visited him there on a few occasions, however Lord Andrew hasn't had an opportunity to travel this way. I met him for the first time when he arrived this morning. They spent most of the afternoon shooting and this evening they went into the village for dinner. Toby was so eager to spend time with him, I didn't have the heart to tell him they were being rude by leaving me home to dine by myself.'

'What is your impression of Lord Andrew so far?'

'I confess he is not what I expected. I assumed

him to be a rather scholarly type. One who had his nose in books the way Toby does.'

'And?'

'And, he appears to be the type of man one finds in the village on race days or, I imagine, in a boxing ring at the local fair.'

Just as Charlotte was about to reply, the sound of Toby's voice drifted in through the open doorway, followed by a deep rumbling sound that must have been the muffled reply of his friend. Intrigued by the image Ann had painted of Lord Andrew, Charlotte stared at the open doorway to catch a glimpse of him.

Toby came into view first and smiled when he spotted them. He looked neat and tidy with his blond hair cut very short and his narrow frame encased in brown breeches and a cinnamon-coloured wool coat. Then she caught sight of his friend—and her breath caught in her throat. She actually felt it!

He was an imposing-looking man—at least five inches taller than Toby's average height. The cut of his blue coat showed off an impressive pair of broad shoulders and the definition of well-shaped arms. His light brown wavy hair grazed his collar and was a bit longer than was considered respectable, but it suited him and appeared neatly trimmed. His square jaw and the angles to his face would make it very easy to render his image in stone. The flicker of candlelight bounced off the gold buttons on his coat, drawing her attention back to his frame and her gaze dropped to his muscular thighs which were visible through his black breeches, tucked into a pair of topped boots. This was a man who enjoyed sport or rode extensively.

It wasn't until Ann tapped the side of her slipper with her foot that Charlotte realised she must have been staring at him.

'Charlotte,' Toby called out. 'How good to see you.' It appeared the men were heading to another area of the house but her friend, always the perfect gentleman, walked into the room to greet her.

It was taking considerable effort on Charlotte's part to keep her eyes fixed on Toby, which was absurd. The man next to him should not have captured her attention in such a way, but he possessed such an ease of movement, like one who was comfortable in his skin, that it was impossible not to sneak one last glance at him.

Toby gave her a friendly smile. 'I'm so glad you were able to join Ann tonight.'

'It was lovely to receive her note.'

'May I introduce my friend?' he asked, gesturing to the man beside him. 'Lady Charlotte Gregory, may I present Lord Andrew Pearce. Lord Andrew this is Lady Charlotte, a childhood friend of Ann's. Lord Andrew and I are old college chums from Cambridge.'

Lord Andrew took a step forward and gave a respectful bow. Candlelight played through his silky hair. 'A pleasure to make your acquaintance, madam.'

The deep pitch of his voice rumbled through her body. There was no warmth in his eyes or expression, just a keen watchfulness, as if he was studying her, before he turned to Ann and offered another respectful bow.

'I did not expect the two of you home this early,' Ann said, looking pleased with the unexpected encounter. 'I imagine, Lord Andrew, there is little to entertain a man late at night in this part of the country. It must be rather dull, compared to what you're accustomed to.' She turned to Charlotte. 'Lord Andrew is from London,' she informed her yet again before turning back to him. 'Lady Charlotte has a sister who lives in London.' There was a helpfulness to her tone and her eyebrows rose as if she fully expected his attention to shift to Charlotte.

Dear God, was Ann trying to find her a husband? Is that why she had invited her here?

His eyes skirted briefly to Charlotte before he addressed Ann's question. 'While I am partial to London, you do have some well-run establishments here that serve fine food and good ale. That is all a man truly needs.'

Thank heavens, he did not feel obliged to follow Ann's direction and converse with her. If

Charlotte could think of a polite way to excuse herself, she would leave immediately.

'Would you care to join us for tea?' Ann raised her white cup with pink rosebuds. 'A good cup of tea and a seat by the fire are lovely on such a windy night as this.'

The men looked at one another. Whatever silent communication passed between them seemed to indicate Lord Andrew did not object to curtailing their plans to sit with them for a bit. The four wingback chairs made a cosy, inviting group around the hearth, but before the men where close enough to choose a seat, Ann had to open her mouth again.

'You may sit there, Lord Andrew,' she said, gesturing to the chair beside Charlotte. 'And you may sit by me, Toby.' She gave her husband a beaming smile, patting the cushion of the chair beside her.

Charlotte caught the disapproving purse of Toby's lips. Why had she never noticed Ann's lack of subtlety before?

'You never did say why you returned so early from the village,' Ann continued.

'Word was spreading throughout the inn that the roads were getting rather treacherous,' Toby replied, watching Ann retrieve two teacups and saucers from the tea stand beside her.

'Treacherous? But we had been walking in the garden a short while ago. There was nothing to indicate we should be concerned for the quality of the roads.'

'A storm is coming down from the north. After hearing of it while we were dining, I had no interest in having one of our horses injured or being forced to turn back because a tree had fallen and blocked the road, so we ended our dinner early.'

'Did you go to the Swan and Swallow?' Charlotte asked, finding an urge to draw Lord Andrew into the conversation, which had nothing at all to do with the sound of his voice.

But now that his attention was back on her, she once again found it unsettling.

'We did,' his deep voice rumbled. 'Are you from the area, Lady Charlotte?'

'I was raised in Warwick, but now reside here, near the Knightlys. The Swan and Swallow is a fine choice for a man looking for a bit of excitement, more so than the White Hart.'

She felt the stares of Ann and Toby more than saw them, since her attention was fixed on Lord Andrew.

He shifted his body slightly, as if he was studying her just as much as she was studying him. 'And I appear to be a man looking for excitement? I assure you, I came to the country seeking pleasant conversations with my old friend and bucolic pastures for riding. Excitement is the furthest thing from my mind.'

'Then you will be happy you have chosen our sleepy corner of the world. You won't find much to excite you here.'

'Except on a night like this.' His gaze dipped momentarily to her lips, then travelled lower before his eyes locked with hers.

Could he possibly feel what she was feeling, too? Just the sight of him and his voice was making her insides flutter. She didn't like the sensation. It was unsettling to say the least. She tried to look away, but she noticed a small birthmark just under his right eye. It was just a small mark, but it was enough to keep her attention on his hazel eyes, framed with thick dark lashes.

'And what excites you this evening?' she said in a breath, not able to completely gather her voice.

There was a distinct pause while he seemed to taste his own lips. Was he a man who preferred ale or wine with his dinner? Were there remnants of either on his lips?

'The weather is proving enough excitement,' he drawled, leaning back in his chair and startling her out of her musings. 'With tales of carriage accidents, your village has been full of harrowing stories.'

She blinked a few times, recalling the thread of their conversation. Of course, he meant the weather and not being close to her! What a foolish woman she was to assume he was referring to the way he felt meeting her. She had never flirted with a man in her life. She and Jonathan grew up together in a comfortable friendship. They had never flirted with one another.

Would she even know if a man was flirting with her? Apparently not, since she thought Lord Andrew had been—and she had had the unnatural desire to flirt back!

Charlotte took a sip of tea so she wouldn't open her mouth again and make a cake of herself. Thank heavens no one else in the room had any inclination of what she had mistakenly assumed. She needed to leave before she started to blush.

Andrew rubbed the back of his neck. What possessed him to utter a flirtatious comment to the woman beside him? He never flirted with respectable women and didn't recall drinking that much ale with dinner.

It was obvious from the lavender of Lady Charlotte's gown she was in mourning, which made flirting with her completely beyond the pale. And to make the situation even worse, he would guess it was her husband who had passed away based on the gold signet ring she wore around her neck...a very graceful, long neck which was accentuated by the gauzy fichu tucked in the neckline of her silk gown, obscuring any view of what appeared to be enticing cleavage. A few wisps of her wavy black hair had come loose from her upswept coiffure and contrasted sharply against the white fichu. But it was her lips that continued to draw his attention. They were full and rosy. And when she spoke, he was imagining her biting down on those pillowy lips in the throes of passion.

Mrs Knightly cleared her throat and held out a teacup to him. How long she had been sitting like that, he'd rather not contemplate. 'The roads are that treacherous?'

'Quite,' Toby confirmed, his attention on the tea his wife was fixing for him.

'Then Charlotte must stay the night,' Mrs Knightly stated, pouring milk into his cup.

The woman beside Andrew let out the faintest gasp, which stirred his blood.

'Certainly, they cannot be so bad. And I have not brought anything with me. How can I possibly stay?'

Mrs Knightly waved her hand dismissively after handing Toby his tea. 'We are practically the same size. I'm certain I will find things to fit you. If the roads are as bad as they say, it's safer for you to remain here tonight.'

It was apparent Lady Charlotte had no interest in spending the night, and who could blame her after the blunder he had just made. What recently widowed woman in her right mind would want to be near a man who flirted with her?

Lady Charlotte looked to Toby for help. 'Please inform your wife the roads are not that bad,' she practically pleaded, raising her brows high above her green eyes for emphasis.

Much to her obvious displeasure, Toby was no help. 'But you will be heading straight into the storm on your way home. Ann is right. The roads are becoming hazardous with the mud and trees are at risk of coming down. It took us nearly an hour to travel here from the village. You should stay, Charlotte. It is much safer for you, your driver and your horses.'

Not once had she looked at him since their awkward exchange. Could Toby not see that she would rather go out into the stormy night than remain in the same house with Andrew?

'There,' Mrs Knightly stated, appearing rather pleased, 'it's settled. You will stay the night.'

Lady Charlotte placed her teacup on the table to her left, beside the hearth. 'It's not settled. For it to be settled, I need to agree.'

Mrs Knightly took a leisurely sip of her tea. 'Surely you do not want to risk injury. Don't you agree, Lord Andrew? Isn't it safer for Lady Charlotte to remain here until morning?'

Why did she have to drag him into this? He looked at Lady Charlotte, who was blushing while staring wide-eyed at Mrs Knightly. He was such a dolt when it came to respectable women. He couldn't help himself from wanting to spend the evening between the thighs of the enticing widow beside him. Those lips of hers were calling to him every time she spoke, stirring certain parts of his body.

'I said wouldn't you agree, Lord Andrew?' Mrs Knightly reiterated because, apparently, she thought he hadn't heard her the first time.

'Yes, it would be best if you stayed the night.'

In my bed, where I'm certain I can incite more of those gasps.

He cleared his throat. 'As much as I'm sure it's an inconvenience, the conditions were deteriorating by the time we arrived here. They probably have only got worse.'

As if she didn't believe any of them or didn't hear the rain pelting the windowpanes, Charlotte went to the window. It gave him an excellent opportunity to admire her shapely form as she walked across the room. He shouldn't be looking at her. She was a woman in mourning. She was not the kind of woman he should notice in any way. She should be like wallpaper; you're aware it's there, but you couldn't describe it five minutes after you left the room.

To shake himself out of staring, and before she turned and noticed, he looked towards the fire and caught the amused expression of Mrs Knightly.

Taking a drink of tea, Andrew tried to think of an inconspicuous way to let Toby know they should leave the ladies. He had no wish to make Lady Charlotte uncomfortable. Being repulsed by an attractive woman was not something he strived for.

'In the moonlight, you can see how muddy the ground has become,' Lady Charlotte said on a sigh, turning away from the window. She trudged back to her stuffed chair and lowered herself on to the cushion with a defeated expression.

'I promise you will not have to stay here for days. The morning sun will dry out the roads and you will be able to leave by midday,' Mrs Knightly replied reassuringly.

Lady Charlotte reached for her tea. 'I hope that's true.' Her gaze briefly met Andrew's before it skirted to Toby's wife. 'Very well, but I refuse to be more of an imposition than that. I will leave as soon as the conditions improve.'

'You are certainly no imposition,' Mrs Knightly said with a genuinely warm smile. 'We adore having you here.'

Lady Charlotte smiled back at her friend and then glanced once more at him before she took a long sip of her tea. A soft pink flush edged its way up her neck. It was impossible for Andrew not to picture the rest of her body flush with that rosy glow after an enthusiastic encounter in the sheets...or in a carriage...or...

No wonder the woman was eager to leave. She probably knew what he'd been thinking.

As if watching a performance at the theatre, Mrs Knightly let her attention float between Andrew and the woman beside him. The auburn-haired wife of his friend was not very subtle. He was certain Lady Charlotte had not missed her friend's attention.

He looked over at Toby and caught his eye, curious to see if his friend was as eager as his wife to promote a match.

'Lord Andrew and I were on our way to the billiard room,' Toby offered to no one in particular. 'We would hate to impose on your conversation any further, ladies. I'm sure we interrupted some bit of town gossip.'

'But—'

Toby arched a brow, and Mrs Knightly did not continue. At least he had a friend in Toby Knightly.

While he found Lady Charlotte strikingly attractive, he would not pursue her. She was a widow in mourning, not the kind of woman open for a dalliance. Even more importantly, once she was out of mourning a respectable woman like Lady Charlotte would be looking to marry again. With the dangerous life he led, he would not take a wife. And no woman would want to be attached to a man who was capable of doing the things he had done in his life.

Yet he did know he would be thinking about her and those enticing lips when he lay in bed later that night. Now, he would pass the remainder of his evening in the pleasant company of his friend, enjoying a competitive game of billiards and drinking what he hoped to be fine brandy.

'Lord Andrew, it was a pleasure to make your acquaintance,' Lady Charlotte said with what appeared to be an apologetic smile.

Andrew stood and placed his teacup on the table before politely tipping his head to her. 'The pleasure was all mine. If I do not see you before you take your leave tomorrow, I wish you a safe journey home.'

'Thank you, and you as well.'

Strolling out of the room with his friend, he wondered if she was an early riser.

Chapter Five

Charlotte adjusted the blue cashmere shawl Ann had let her borrow the night before as she followed her friends' footman to the breakfast room. Before she even reached the doorway the scent of coffee and bacon drifted on the air. It smelled delicious. At least she would not go home hungry.

There were no sounds coming from the open doorway. Apparently, she was the first one awake and ready to start the day. Dining alone and in silence was nothing new. She had been doing it for years and, considering she was forced to wear this jonquil gown that Ann had loaned her, she really did prefer it that way. No matter what Ann said, Charlotte knew it wasn't possible for her not to have any grey or lavender gowns in the house. Every woman she knew kept mourning clothes on hand for when she needed them.

The footman stopped before the open doorway and stepped to the side so she could enter the room. But when she crossed the threshold her body froze at the sight of Lord Andrew, sitting at the oval table reading the newspaper placed beside his plate of food. Her feet refused to move while she stared at him.

It was early—much too early for a man from Town to be awake. Yet there he was with his head down and his broad shoulders defined by a bottle-green-coloured coat. His head turned slightly as he continued to read, without any indication that he knew she was watching him. She took advantage of his occupied state to study him further and noticed the slightly crooked slope of his nose. It appeared he wasn't even aware his fingers were flicking the upper-right corner of the paper as he read.

A flurry of butterflies circled inside her stomach. She took a steadying breath and forced her legs to move, stepping further into the room. The movement must have caught his attention because he looked up, locking his eyes with hers.

It was impossible to determine if he found her unexpected presence an annoyance, since his expression was unreadable. Regardless of his feelings on the matter, he stood politely and remained that way until she took the seat opposite his.

'Good morning,' he said, sitting down. The deep pitch of his voice settled somewhere near her stomach, sending those butterflies into a frenzy and ensuring she would not be able to eat a thing.

'Good morning,' she replied in return, relieved her voice gave away nothing about the physical effects his presence was having on her. He was just a man. Why was he muddling her senses? His eyes were on her as she searched the room for a footman and realised they were completely alone. This was highly irregular—and highly inappropriate. She turned back to the doorway and noticed the footman had closed the door behind her after she had entered.

'That pot of tea was brought in a few minutes ago,' he said, motioning with his fork to the porcelain pot to the left of her place setting.

She took note of the coffee pot beside him and knew Ann preferred chocolate to tea in the morning. Someone had been notified Charlotte was on her way downstairs. When she looked back at him, their eyes met and she really wished he would go back to reading his paper and ignore her. It had been years since she had been alone in a room with a man, and her stomach did an odd flip. She eyed the bacon and toast on his plate. He had selected crispy pieces of meat, which were her favourites.

'I can recommend the bacon, if you like it rather well done.'

Her stomach still hadn't settled down, and she

gave him a polite smile. 'Thank you, but I find I'm not hungry this morning.'

His brows rose just a fraction while he nodded. They stared at one another for a few moments longer before they both looked away. He busied himself with cutting into his delicious-looking breakfast, and she poured her tea. As she added a splash of milk, Lord Andrew slid the sugar bowl towards her.

'Thank you, but I prefer my tea without.' Charlotte had learned to economise over the years to ensure she would not have to marry again. She no longer had the taste for sweet tea.

'You have my condolences on your husband's passing, Lady Charlotte. I was going to express them last night, but hadn't the opportunity. I assume this occurred recently.'

She shifted uncomfortably in her seat. 'Four years ago.'

There was a slight lift to his eyebrows. She knew most people who met her believed her to be newly widowed due to the half-mourning clothes she chose to wear. It was safer as a widow to be around men dressed in those colours. Unfortunately, she discovered there were certain men who believed a widow out of mourning was a woman who was ripe for seduction. The unwanted advances of Lord Aldrich the week she came out of mourning were enough to make her return to the safety of black, lavender and grey.

The ticking of the mantel clock, the wind rattling the window panes and the occasional popping of the logs in the hearth broke the silence that stretched between them.

Why had she not taken breakfast in her room? She might still have an appetite if she had. Now she was sitting alone with him, drinking tea and watching him eat. Occasionally he would glance at the door as if he, too, was expecting a footman to enter and confer respectability on their encounter. At times her gaze would follow his, mentally willing the closed door to open.

What if he was not attempting to strike up a conversation with her because he thought she was looking for a husband and had set her sights on him? Perhaps Lord Andrew thought she had arranged this with Ann! Where was Ann? Although it was too early for a Town gentleman such as Lord Andrew to be awake, it was not for country folk like Ann and Toby. She closed her eyes and rubbed her brow. Why was Ann torturing her like this?

'Are you well?' he asked, drawing her attention away from what she planned to say to her friend the next time they were alone.

'Forgive me, yes, I am.' She lowered her hand and played with the napkin on her lap. 'I confess, I did believe our friends would be having breakfast here at this hour. Had I known you were dining here by yourself, I would have left you to your peaceful solitude to enjoy your meal and read your paper without having to make polite discourse with someone you do not know.'

After spreading jam on his toast, he lowered his knife. 'I see.'

She couldn't tell if he believed her. She couldn't tell if he thought her to be a widow in search of her next husband. Being trapped alone at breakfast with her would make it a logical conclusion. 'I did not arrive here yesterday evening with a design to meet you. I did not wish to stay last night at all, but was forced to do so by the unfortunate weather and our rather insistent friends. And I did not come down for breakfast with the intention of being alone with you in this room in this compromising situation. It was all done by chance.'

He tilted his head while studying her, but remained silent. *He didn't believe her.*

'I am not a widow with a plan to trap you into marriage. If I were, I would have brought my own clothes last night. Instead, I'm forced to wear this gown that, while lovely, is yellow and I never wear yellow. At least I haven't worn yellow since my husband passed. I can assure you, I would not be sitting across from you shining brighter than the midday sun if my plan was to entice you into marriage.'

She was rambling. Dear God, she wasn't even certain what she had just said. Something about yellow…possibly? Her brain was not working with her mouth. It very well could be from lack of food. That bacon smelled so good, but her stomach was now clenched tight, as if it was trying to tell her that if she ate one bite, she would be seeing it again shortly.

Charlotte shifted her attention from the bacon on his plate to his unreadable expression. She really wished he would say something—anything. Heat was spreading up her neck. She should just excuse herself and return to her room. Or just leave the building entirely—and perhaps the town and county. She rubbed her brow again.

When she glanced over at him, she caught something that looked like amusement in his eyes as he chewed his toast. The shine from the sugar of the jam highlighted his top lip before he licked it off.

Involuntarily, she swallowed. She needed to get away. His presence was having an unsettling effect on her. She stood suddenly, startling Lord Andrew and bringing him to his feet.

'I will leave you,' she said, and before he could reply she turned and walked to the door. When she opened it, she was surprised to find a footman standing outside as if guarding the door.

'Please see that my carriage is brought around in half an hour. I'll leave a note for Mr and Mrs Knightly. I assume they are still abed.'

'I believe so, my lady. I'll see to it directly.'

'Wait,' Lord Andrew called out, holding up his hand and walking towards the doorway with his gaze fixed on Charlotte. 'You cannot leave. It has started to rain again.'

Her head snapped to the window and her eyes widened at the sight of raindrops sliding down the glass panes. She looked at him and had the ridiculous urge to reassure him that she had nothing to do with the rain.

'My lady?' The footman's voice broke the spell from where he stood beside them. 'What would you have me do?'

'Lady Charlotte, the roads have not dried out and we don't know if they are even passable. I think you are forced to remain a bit longer and, since our hosts are nowhere to be found this morning, that leaves it to me to convince you of the sensible course of action.'

That was the longest thing he had ever said to her. 'Why do you…?'

'I would not be able to live with myself if any harm came to you because you fled to prove you have no desire to be in my presence.'

'I'm not trying to prove anything.'

'Then you are simply willing to risk injury to get away from me.'

'Yes. No. I mean…'

His eyebrows flew up and he appeared amused rather than insulted. She really needed to stop talking. She was always completely composed. What was wrong with her? Maybe she was coming down with some unknown illness? That had to be it. She rubbed her brow again to casually see if she had a fever. Thankfully, she didn't appear overly warm.

She motioned with her head for him to follow her as she walked away from the footman back into the breakfast room. When they were at a far enough distance, she stopped and lowered her voice to a whisper. 'I truly am not a widow in search of a husband. I will not be marrying again. I am comfortable in my situation and regardless of what our friends, or rather my friend, might believe, being in my presence will not endanger your bachelorhood.'

He rubbed his lips together and crossed his arms. 'In the event of your previous statements being unclear, you're telling me you haven't arranged to sneak into my bedchamber while I am here and force us into a compromising situation?'

The nerve of the man! 'Of course not!' she whispered back sharply. 'I am not that kind of widow, my lord.'

There was a quirk to his lips, and she realised he had been teasing her. She couldn't help but smile.

He leaned forward again. 'Thank you for reassuring me you have not taken part in hatching a plan to trap me into marriage.'

'I assure you, Lord Andrew, I have no desire to marry you or any other man. Or take part in any type of scandalous activity.'

'I'm relieved to hear it. We are of a like mind. Our firm understanding of the situation makes this a more relaxing experience for both of us.' For the first time he smiled, making him appear quite handsome. His eyes held hers once more before he turned to the footman, who Charlotte had forgotten all about. 'Her ladyship will not be needing her carriage. She will be remaining at Knightly Hall a while longer until the weather improves.'

'Very good, my lord,' the footman replied with a tip of his head. And before either could protest, the man took a few steps back and closed the door on them, once more leaving them alone.

'I do believe your friend has given her staff specific instructions this morning that we are not to be disturbed.'

'I do believe you might be correct in your assumption. I am truly sorry.'

Stretching out his arm, he motioned for them to return to the table. 'It will not be the first time I have been a target because of my bachelor status.'

'There are those who might see our presence in this room together as rather scandalous,' she replied, taking her seat.

He paused before sitting down. 'Do you be-

lieve your friend will make it known in the village we spent time alone like this?'

'Heavens, no.'

The brief sense of panic that flashed in his
eyes cleared and he sat down. 'That's reassuring to hear, because if there were to be a scandal
about me, I would hope it would be a bit more
exciting than just taking breakfast alone with
you.' Lord Andrew's gaze dropped to her mouth.

His teasing made her smile. 'Are you referring to other closed-door escapades?'

'Well, considering the conditions outside, I
suppose one would be forced to remain inside
behind closed doors…unless one was eager to get
wet…outside.' There was a wicked glint in his
eye and a slight curve to his mouth. He arched
his brow, silently challenging her to respond.
There was no lecherous leer to his lips—no in-
timidation with the posture of his impressive
form. He appeared to be a man who enjoyed
playful conversation.

'I've found I prefer a bit of solitude behind
closed doors.'

'Because you simply haven't found the right
company, my lady,' he said with a knowing
smile, making her grin.

'And do you find many people whose company you enjoy, my lord?'

'Surprisingly, not many. I am rather discern-
ing, if you must know. And I much prefer the

company of a single companion to many.' His gaze seemed to penetrate her. 'There is something about devoting your complete attention to one person that I find utterly satisfying.'

Charlotte had not thought about having sex in years. That part of her life was over...and yet suddenly she was imagining what this man's touch would feel like and what it would be like to be the focus of his attentive ministrations. 'Surely your attention wavers a bit.'

Slowly, he shook his head, all the while never breaking their gaze. 'If we are playing in hypotheticals and you are the company I am with, I can assure you that you would have my complete undivided attention. And I would be most eager to engage in any activity of your choosing. Especially if it did involve getting wet.'

It was becoming difficult to take a deep breath. She must have tied her stays too tight this morning. She should end this conversation now. It was beyond improper and she had had no experience in discourse such as this even while she had been married. But his playful safe smile drew her back. 'What a gallant companion you would be,' she replied, 'but I have no wish to cause you any hardship against your will.'

His lips twitched with amusement. 'I would gladly suffer through any hardship for you, my lady. I believe the experience would be most fulfilling.'

The imagine of him filling her made her intimate places tingle. This man was the devil—but she didn't want it to end. She glanced out of the window and gave a dramatic sigh. 'I imagine getting wet outside would be such an inconvenience…hypothetically speaking.'

'If the gardener was present, I would agree.'

She let out a low laugh and pressed her fingertips to her lips to hold in the rest. The corners of his eyes creased as he took a sip from his cup and turned to the window. It was raining harder now, obscuring the view of the gardens.

A flush of heat rose up her neck and she stared down at her empty cup.

'Do not fear I will try to coax you out into the rain, Lady Charlotte. I know your comments were made in jest.'

Did that mean he didn't want to get her wet outside? Why did that notion leave her feeling dispirited? She had never considered having sex outside her bedchamber—at least not before he mentioned it. And if people did have sex outside, where would they have it? Were people really so inclined…not that she was…or ever would be…or would ever be in a position to engage in such an activity…but still, where would one do something like that? She hadn't thought about sex in years. Now suddenly she couldn't stop thinking about it.

'Are you certain you are not hungry?' he

asked, cutting into his bacon, apparently unaffected by their conversation. 'It really is quite good.'

She leaned towards his plate, surveying the crispy pieces. She needed to focus on food, not sex. 'Were they all that well done or just those you have graciously taken?'

He studied the piece on his fork. 'I'd say half were like this.'

It really did smell so good and smoky, and her stomach had settled down. Now it felt as if it would rumble with hunger any minute.

Which it did, to her mortification.

'Are you one of those women who survives on toast and tea? I assure you a hardier breakfast will do you no harm.'

He didn't have to convince her of that. She enjoyed starting the day with something rather robust. She stood and walked to the sideboard. The smoky aroma was so tempting. She selected the crispiest pieces from the china platter along with two slices of fluffy bread and went back to the table.

Lord Andrew had been skimming the paper next to him, but when she sat down he examined her plate with a smile. 'That's much better. I honestly do not know how some women sustain themselves on so little food.'

'I enjoy the taste of food too much to survive on toast and tea, as you so aptly phrased it. You may go back to reading the paper. I will not consider it discourteous, although with the weather as it is, I assume that is not today's edition.'

'It isn't, but I did ask to see any papers that were about. I thought it would give me a glimpse of what has been happening here.'

Charlotte cut into the meat and her mouth began to water. 'I've read the London papers on occasion. I doubt you will find anything of interest to you in those editions.'

'How can you be certain? Copies of the *Observer* are circulated in London and I've read about the unrest due to Parliamentary repression.'

'Are you a Member of Parliament, Lord Andrew?'

'No, I am a mere second son.'

She put her fork down and wiped her lips. He bore no military title. He must be one of the wastrels who spent their days at the gaming clubs and lived off their family's money, while men like her husband gave their lives to ensure he was able to live his life under British rule. 'I would think a man with your title coming from London would have no interest in what happens up here. Unless your interest is purely because you are staying here.'

'I should remind you, Lady Charlotte, although we shared an amusing conversation, you do not know me.'

'This is true. I do not. But famine and unemployment do not seem to be an interesting topic for a privileged bachelor from London.'

She was being rude. She knew it, but was unable to stop. Perhaps her testy emotions with him had something to do with the feelings of desire he was stirring inside her—feelings she needed to forget. To him it was all a game. Meanwhile for Charlotte it was... She wasn't sure exactly what it was, but there was no denying she didn't like him as much now as she had before. It was easier for her to deal with him if she painted him in a poor light.

'And how do you know these things do not interest me?' he asked while wrinkling his forehead.

Jonathan's brothers had never expressed interest in those outside their social circle and the London bachelors Lizzy wrote to her about were only interested in game and drink. 'You yourself said last night that you came here seeking pleasant conversation with your friend and bucolic pastures for riding. The state of the people who have inhabited this area for generations did not draw you here.'

'Like it did Mr Hunt.'

Her spine stiffened. 'Mr Hunt, and men who write for that paper, are champions for a people who could use one. Mr Hunt has done nothing wrong.'

'His speeches on Parliamentary reform have instigated riots.'

'That is not true. He believes if enough of us speak our minds, then change can happen without violence. Violent actions are not the answer to the problems faced by people who live in this area.'

'One could assume with your title, my lady, you would not have an interest in the plight of the common man.'

'I am a widow, Lord Andrew. Famine and financial hardship can appear at my door as well as at the merchants, farmers and factory workers here. What happens to my neighbour down the lane could easily befall me.'

'You could marry again.'

'But I won't. We need equal and proper representation in Parliament. Something we do not have. We need people who will champion our interests there. Do not condemn those who are fighting for their right to feed and clothe their families.'

'I have not spoken of condemning them.'

'But you have strong opinions of Mr Hunt. I saw it in your eyes.' Charlotte had no use for entitled self-centred gentlemen like Lord Andrew. It was probably best she had found out about his true nature. He had her recalling the activities of the marriage bed—activities that were best left forgotten. She hadn't lied to him. She would

not marry again and the less tempted she was
to touch the man across from her, the better off
she would be.

Chapter Six

$\mathcal{C}\!\mathcal{S}\!\mathcal{S}\!\mathcal{S}\!\mathcal{S}\!\mathcal{S}$

Andrew sat back in his chair and watched Lady Charlotte cut into the bacon that had tasted so good a few minutes before. Now, he had no stomach for it. It appeared he'd lost his opportunity to ask her about the unrest in the area since she did not look eager to enter into a genial discussion with him again.

He didn't like the picture she had drawn of him in the brief time they had spoken. He had been enjoying her company immensely before their discussion took a decidedly serious turn. He tried to recall how that happened. There was no denying she had also felt that pull between them. She might deny wanting to go out in the rain and explore each other's bodies, but he knew she had been considering it. Now, if he wasn't mistaken, she thought him an entitled prig.

Instead of turning back to read the papers, he watched her top her toast with strawberry jam. When she delicately licked some of the jam from her finger, Andrew's thoughts drifted to their conversation about the rain…and getting her wet.

He wasn't a man to openly engage in flirtatious conversations with women. It was not something he ever bothered with. Yet there was something about this woman that made his thoughts and words form without his intent and he found he was flirting before he knew it.

She was a combination of beauty and brains, mixed with something he could not name that had him thinking about her more than he should have done last night after he left the drawing room with Toby. For him, that was dangerous. She was a complication he didn't need. His job was to protect King George and the Prince Regent from harm. His duty was above all else. His father had formed the organisation that Gabriel now managed and taught him that having a clear focus on his objective was essential for being effective at what he did. He had also taught him to trust no one and suspect everyone. And Andrew had come to understand how important that advice was.

His Uncle Peter had somehow become radicalised about Catholic emancipation. His beliefs were such that he'd resorted to violence to prevent information from reaching Gabriel. He had killed Andrew's friend Matthew so the agent couldn't deliver his information about a group of extremists in Ireland who had targeted Prinny and he was prepared to kill Gabriel as well, until Andrew stopped him. Andrew had sensed a change in him and had spoken to Gabriel about it before Peter left for his mission with Matthew, but he never considered his uncle would be capable of killing his family and friends. It made him question the character of everyone he met.

Lady Charlotte appeared outraged when he implied Mr Hunt might be fond of violent actions to achieve his goal. But he hadn't been around her long enough to get a sense of her true character. Their discussion seemed to have no impact on her appetite as she ate her toast and ignored him. What a country widow thought of him shouldn't matter. Soon he would return to London. The safety of the Crown was paramount. There were missions that needed his attention. In the meantime, he was helping himself feel productive by looking into any leads he could find about political unrest in the area and searching out the names of people who could be a threat to the Crown. When he left Cheshire, he would not be coming back—and he would never see her again.

Andrew was about to resume reading the paper and pretend she didn't exist when Toby and his wife finally entered the room, followed by a footman. Mrs Knightly did not even try to hide her joy at seeing him sitting alone with her friend.

'How lovely to see you both enjoying breakfast together,' she said, taking a seat beside him at the table.

How long would it take before the woman realised the only thing keeping them in the same room together were those crispy pieces of bacon?

'Did you both sleep well?' she asked, placing her napkin on her lap, as another footman arrived with a pot of chocolate.

'I did, once the thunderstorm had passed,' Lady Charlotte replied, staring pointedly at the footman as he poured some of the fragrant liquid into Mrs Knightly's cup. 'And thank you for insisting I take your shawl. I find it has grown rather cold.' She glanced at Andrew and her expression reinforced the subtle gibe.

'Why did you not instruct them to put another log on the fire?' Mrs Knightly motioned to the footman by the door and that man went about the task. Then she turned to Andrew with a friendly smile. 'I hope your room is to your liking and you slept well.'

He managed not to scowl because of the foul mood he suddenly found himself in. 'It is. The bed is quite comfortable.' There was no sense in elaborating. The comfort of his mattress had no bearing on his sleep. He never slept well.

Toby had settled himself at the head of the

table with a plate full of food. It was a wonder he did not weigh as much as the Prince Regent if that was how much he ate in the morning. Conversely, Mrs Knightly appeared to have no appetite at all, not even for toast.

She glanced from Andrew to Lady Charlotte and then back to Andrew, playing with her cup in its saucer. 'I understand you live in a bachelor's establishment in London called Albany. Are you able to get a restful night's sleep with people coming in and out at all hours there? Lady Charlotte lives not far from here in a lovely home with views of scenic fields. It's quite peaceful there.'

Lady Charlotte put her fork and knife down very deliberately, but kept her attention on her plate.

Andrew was glad Lady Charlotte would not be staying at Knightly Hall long. If he had to continually dodge Mrs Knightly's comments about her friend, it would get exhausting. 'I assure you the noises and disturbances are kept to a minimum. All the gentlemen who have sets there are very respectful of each other's privacy and comfort.'

'Is it true women are not allowed on the premises?'

Mrs Knightly must have interrogated Toby about him. He wondered what else she knew. Due to the secret nature of his work, her investigations on him were not welcome even though

Toby was not privy to that part of his life. He glanced at his friend, who only gave him a slight shrug.

'Yes, that's true. Women are not permitted in the building.'

'What a fine way to ensure no wickedness takes place within its walls. The residents must be all very honourable men, wouldn't you say, Charlotte?'

Lady Charlotte nodded, but her attention was on the contents of her teacup. She really had taken a poor measure of him.

His life was all about nobility and honour— protecting the Crown by sacrificing a life for himself. Regardless of what she thought of him, he knew his life was consumed by noble actions. Hell, one of the reasons he was up here was because ensuring order was so important to him, he couldn't stop.

And why did it even matter to him what she thought?

He had lost his appetite and had no desire to make polite conversation, but he knew he was now forced to sit there until everyone else was finished with breakfast. And by the amount of food on Toby's plate, that could be quite a while. He would just make certain when they all left the room, he would avoid Lady Charlotte for the remainder of her time at Toby's house.

Once the roads were deemed passable she

would be gone. While he had no doubt the Duchess of Skeffington was seeking out his presence in London, he also knew Lady Charlotte couldn't get away from him fast enough. In a few days, he would barely recall the green of her eyes and those soft lips. She would be a faint memory of this trip, if that.

Chapter Seven

Charlotte had successfully put all thoughts of Lord Andrew out of her head when, to her displeasure, Ann had brought up his name while they strolled the grounds of Oakwood House during the annual fair a few days later. It was one event she looked forward to each year when townspeople and the surrounding gentry were invited on to the grounds of the stately home of Mr Ellswith to partake in a day of festivities. The sun was shining. The day was warm. And she had no wish to relive the last time she saw the man.

She strolled with Ann under the trees on the hill overlooking the back of the house, past the stalls with items made by local women and craftspeople. The smell of lamb roasting on open spits mixed with the scent of fresh grass brought back fond memories of her childhood when all three Sommersby sisters would explore their local fair together. She had never attended any fairs with Jonathan. When they were younger, he found them frivolous and, after he entered the army, he preferred to stay away from large crowds.

The excitement and jovial mood of the people around them brought a smile to Charlotte's face as she allowed Ann to pull her along from stall to stall so they could admire the embroidered shawls and gloves, as well as straw bonnets adorned with ribbons and flowers. She made a point of complimenting the work of each woman she spoke to and purchased a lovely pair of lavender gloves embroidered with violets.

She had just picked up a small watercolour of Oakwood House when Ann leaned in closer. 'Have I mentioned Lord Andrew has accompanied Toby here today?'

'You have…twice.'

'Have I?'

'You know you have, Ann.'

'Well, I just want to be certain you know. This will give you time to prepare yourself should you see him.'

Charlotte pulled Ann to a stop and led her by the elbow to a quiet spot in the shade of a nearby tree. 'Prepare myself for what? Has something happened to Lord Andrew?'

'No, however I know something happened between the two of you at breakfast. I've never seen two people not want to speak to each other more than the two of you that morning. I think if it wasn't considered impolite, both of you would have excused yourselves from the table the moment Toby and I walked in.'

'I cannot speak for Lord Andrew, but that is not true of me.'

Scepticism was written all over Ann's face. 'You barely spoke to him.'

'I had nothing to say.'

'You wouldn't look at him and he was sitting directly across from you, even though the night before you could barely keep your eyes off of him when we were sitting by the fire.'

'Have you always paid such close attention to my actions?'

'When those unprecedented actions relate to an eligible man, I do.'

'Please stop. He is a titled bachelor. If he is looking for a wife, he is looking for one who can give him an heir. Obviously after many years married to Jonathan with no child of our own, I am not that woman. I am not able to provide him with a child—or any other man for that matter. So, let us not talk of Lord Andrew and his need of a woman who can provide him with a son.'

'But—'

'No, Ann. We are not going to continue this discussion.'

Her feelings had spilled out in such a rush. It was all so unexpected. She had not considered being unable to have children as an impediment to marrying again. But she had found herself thinking about it the other night. Men of the privileged class wanted sons to carry on the family name and take over their estates when they passed on. Should an unmarried man find out she was a widow without children, he might not pursue her further. However, she had found as soon as she was out of her mourning clothes, that a widow without children was an attractive prospect for a mistress. She was grateful every day that Lord Aldrich had decided not to continue leasing nearby Willowbrooke Manor after she had turned down his offer of protection.

She was about to walk away from their secluded spot and continue shopping when Ann's words stopped her.

'You have never talked with me about any of this before now. I'm sorry. Any man would be a fool to put having children above marrying you. You are a loving and kind woman, Charlotte, and some day a man will see that and fall in love with you.'

Not this conversation again!

'Ann, love does not happen twice in a lifetime. A woman's heart is incapable of loving two men. Most people we know have never even experienced love once. That part of my life is over and I'm doing everything in my power to make certain I do not need to enter into a marriage of convenience just to have a roof over my head. I will not marry again. My marriage to Jonathan was enough for a lifetime.'

Ann took her hand. 'I do not mean to cause you distress. That was not my intention. I adore you and only want you to be happy.'

'I *am* happy. I have friends and family and loyal servants who make my life easier than it could be. I am fortunate that I am able to live a relatively comfortable life.'

Distress knotted Ann's brow. 'Relatively?'

'Compared to Lizzy.'

'Compared to Lizzy we all live *relatively* comfortable lives.'

That had them both smiling at the absurdity of it.

'I never imagined when we were children,' Ann said, 'that Lizzy would live in such grandeur.'

'I think Lizzy would have given up all that grandeur if she could have married the man that she loves.'

'Lizzy is in love?' Ann's eyes grew wide.

She wasn't about to reveal her sister's feelings for the Duke of Winterbourne's brother. She had said too much already. But Ann's eager expression did make her laugh. 'I was speaking in hypotheticals.'

'Oh, yes, I suppose you're right. I'm lucky I fell in love with Toby not long after we were wed. But I do not think anyone would have fallen in love with Skeffington.'

They headed back to the stalls, each considering how they would have reacted to being told they were to marry a seventy-year-old man when they were barely old enough to feel like an adult.

'Lizzy was so much fun to be around when we were younger,' Charlotte mused. 'Do you remember how eager she would be to get into some form of mischief or another?'

'I remember when you were that way as well. I adore being with you, but I think you've forgotten how pleasurable a bit of excitement can be.'

Those sounded like the words Lord Aldrich had said to her when he was trying to coax her into the library during that summer ball. Excitement led to scandal. She was too smart to think one did not go without the other.

Andrew leaned against a tree with Toby, watching the rowing-boat races on the lake not far from Oakwood House. He had often participated in similar races when he was younger during house parties. It was difficult to resist the pull of competition. Even now he was tempted to join in the next race.

Fairs such as this had always been a favourite of his when he was young. He had fond memories of running through them with his brothers and challenging each other to all the games they could. Now, it was an ideal place to overhear rumblings of discontent.

'Shall we see what other forms of entertainment there are?' he asked Toby.

'There's archery for friendly competition. Although friendly competition might be too tame for you.'

Andrew nodded and shoved his hands in the pockets of his coat. That sense of excitement at the chance to best someone in competition ran through his veins. 'How friendly does the competition get?'

'I'm sure the wagers placed here are far less than you are accustomed to, however I always sensed the amount of the wager was never the incentive with you.'

'Anyone can join in?'

'Yes. Men. Women. Young. Old. It doesn't matter. It's all done in good fun.'

'That should make for an interesting experience at least. Will you be joining in?'

'I don't believe so. However, I think I will be betting on you.'

'That's if I decide to compete.'

'You were rather a crack shot with a bow when we were at college, if I recall correctly.'

They made their way up the hill to the front lawn of the house where ten large hay bales with painted targets were facing a large grove of trees. People of various ages stood in the shade, taking turns with the bows and arrows provided. There didn't appear to be an organised competition from what Andrew could see. It was disappointing.

He was about to suggest they get some food since the smell of roasting meat was travelling over the light breeze, but then he spied Mrs Knightly and Lady Charlotte talking with a young man waiting to try his luck.

It was distinctly possible she would give him the cut when she saw him, but instead she met his gaze when the ladies walked towards them. He didn't like the way they'd left things. He didn't like the impression she had of him. But he wasn't sure how to fix it or why it should even matter.

'It is no surprise we are finding you here,' Mrs Knightly said, smiling up at Toby. 'Each year you say you will not compete and each year you do.'

Andrew tipped his hat cautiously at Lady Charlotte and found he was relieved when she offered him a polite curtsy in return.

Andrew turned to his friend. 'You said you would not compete.'

'He says that every time,' Mrs Knightly said, glancing at Lady Charlotte. 'He will probably blame us for his actions.'

'They both coax me relentlessly until there is nothing left to do but compete.'

'Because you are such a fine shot,' Lady Charlotte chimed in.

He had forgotten what a pleasant-sounding voice and accent she had. Especially when she wasn't accusing him of being a thoughtless prig.

'Your skills have improved then?' Andrew asked with good humour.

'They might have.' It might be the ale they had drunk, but Toby appeared quite pleased with himself.

Mrs Knightly brushed a small green leaf off her husband's shoulder. 'Have you the skill, Lord Andrew?'

'I have been told I do.'

'Why so modest now?' Toby sputtered. 'Moments ago, you were boasting how you could beat any of those here.'

'Maybe the two of you should see who is a better shot?' Mrs Knightly offered.

'Do you see how they coax me into this?'

'I spy two bales next to one another at the end of the row that are not being used. We could go there.' Mrs Knightly was quite eager for her husband to compete. It was rather amusing.

As they walked down the row of trees, Lady Charlotte approached Andrew's side. The way she was chewing her lip, he could see she was struggling with something to say.

'Lord Andrew, I feel I must apologise for the way I attacked you at breakfast the other morning. I barely let you speak to defend yourself before I voiced an opinion on you based not on fact but on conjecture. It was unkind of me.'

Her statement took him aback both in its candour and in the act itself. He had thought about her a number of times since she'd left Toby's house and still had trouble recalling how their conversation had turned so quickly. While he was visiting Toby, he saw no reason there should be ill will between them.

'I accept your apology. I believe we both could have comported ourselves better and been more open to listening to the other's views. Was your driver able to navigate the road safely when you were travelling home?'

'He was. Thank you.'

She was walking on the side closer to the trees and a particularly low branch was about to impede her way, so he lifted it for her to walk under.

They approached the shaded area where Toby and his wife were waiting and his friend handed him a bow and a quiver of arrows he had taken from the stash leaning against a tree. Once Andrew had looked over the bow and tested the string, they agreed to shoot three arrows each. It didn't take long for Andrew to win.

The entire time he was competing against Toby, he felt Lady Charlotte's gaze on him. Unlike the times he'd caught the Duchess of Skeffington watching him, with Lady Charlotte he didn't mind. It actually made him stand up taller and take his time to prolong the experience of holding her attention.

Charlotte stood about ten feet from Lord Andrew and watched him shoot arrows into a bale of hay and was mesmerised. His broad shoulders were defined by the brown coat he wore and the outline of the muscles in his legs were visible through his buckskin breeches. When she had walked beside him earlier, he had the faint scent of leather about him, probably from his brown gloves or the topped boots he wore.

With his attention firmly fixed on his target, she felt at ease studying him. The wavy locks of his light brown hair near his collar would occasionally lift in the warm breeze, but nothing appeared to break his concentration. His skill was evident with every arrow he shot, each one landing in the centre ring of the bull's-eye. And the precision of his movements left her transfixed.

As they were about to walk away from the archery area, Lord Andrew called them back. 'Wouldn't the ladies like to try?' He held his bow out to her.

In all the years coming to the fair, she had always enjoyed watching the participants at the archery range, but she hadn't shot an arrow since she was sixteen. She didn't even remember how.

Lord Andrew walked a few paces towards her. 'I assure you it will not slither up your arm like a snake. The bow is harmless. I can show you how to use it, if you are so inclined.'

She tried to school the uncertainty that must have been written on her face before meeting his gaze. Amber flecks in his eyes were visible in the sunlight filtering down on them through the leaves above. As if he sensed her indecision needed a soft push, he pressed the grip of the bow into her palm. He should have released the bow. Instead, his hand slid over hers. The warmth of his skin seeped into hers through the leather of their gloves. They both stood there for a few moments, staring at their hands. She tried to recall the last time a man had touched her hand in such an intimate way and couldn't. All she could seem to focus on was the pressure of his palm.

And his faint scent of leather.

And how she wanted to lean her body into his.

When he released his grip, her hand felt cold in her kidskin glove.

'I haven't shot an arrow in years,' she blurted out. 'My sisters and I were taught and we practised when we stayed in our parents' country home.' Juliet had been the most competitive of the Sommersby sisters. 'I'm not sure I remember how it's done,' she stated, wrinkling up her face as she reconsidered her desire to try.

He extended his elbow to her and motioned to the area set aside for the archers. 'It would be my honour to remind you.'

She told herself the excitement she was feeling was at the prospect of shooting arrows again and not sliding her hand along the crook of his arm as he escorted her to the shooting line. When they stopped at the line and he guided her body sideways, her legs felt weak. The chance of her hitting the target would be hindered by the brim of her bonnet, so she took it off and placed it near her feet.

Lord Andrew handed her an arrow. When she was about to notch it into the string, he stopped her hand and stepped behind her. Tingles ran along her spine.

'Let me show you,' he whispered as his soft breath fanned her hair.

She was so attuned to the feel of his breath and his very masculine presence behind her, it became impossible for her to move. He shifted her hips slightly so she was standing completely sideways to her target and then he guided her arm straight out.

'We can do this one together. Here, do not bend your elbow.'

As she notched the arrow in the string, his hand remained on her arm.

'Now when you pull the string back, remember to keep this arm stiff like a board of wood.

After you are satisfied with your aim, just release the arrow with the tips of your fingers. Do not move your hand. That will keep the bow steady.'

He could have been instructing her how to pluck a chicken. With his deep voice in her ear and warm breath on her neck, Charlotte was having a difficult time not closing her eyes. It felt intimate and clandestine—even though they were in full view of everyone around them. He was asking her something about her aim. Charlotte assumed he wanted to know if she was ready to release the arrow. She adjusted the bow a fraction of an inch as she tried to measure it up against her target.

'You will hit that target.'

It would never be possible to hit anything if he continued to whisper in her ear!

When she let go of the arrow, she expected him to step back—but he did not. Instead, he leaned into her back as the arrow flew and they waited together to see if she would hit the bale of hay. The arrow penetrated the hay bale just at the edge…which was a miracle in itself. She had the strongest urge to hug him. It was an outlandish notion.

Even if she hadn't felt his lips curl into a smile by her ear, she could easily hear the delight in his voice.

'Well done, my lady. I think you're ready to try this without me.' He took a step back.

But she rather preferred doing it with him against her so much more. Did he have to move? Why had she put so much effort into hitting the target on her first try?

'Do you remember how it's done?'

All she could remember was the feel of his strength and warmth behind her. A sigh escaped her lips before she was able to stop it, shortly followed by a warm flush heating her cheeks.

He stepped around to face her while letting out a low laugh. It was the first time she had heard him laugh and it was a wonderful feeling knowing she had amused him.

'Do not sound so defeated. You stated you have not shot an arrow in ages and yet you managed to hit the target on your first try.'

'Because you were guiding me.'

'Because you follow directions well and have good aim. You were the one to line up your target, not me. You were the one to hit it.'

'With some help.'

'Pointers,' he corrected her with a grin. He slipped another arrow out of the quiver slung over his shoulder and held it out to her. 'Are you willing to accept the challenge?'

'I want to hit the centre.'

Approval mixed with admiration shone in his eyes. 'Then tell yourself you will.'

'Is that what you do?' she asked, taking the arrow.

'Whenever I face a challenge, I tell myself I can conquer it.'

'Some challenges cannot be conquered.'

'If you believe that, you will never hit your target.'

Closing her eyes, she took a deep breath. The scent of dirt and grass filled her lungs.

I will hit the target. I will hit the target.

'Imagine it happening in your head.'

She glared at him and notched the arrow. 'Shhh.'

Carefully, she took aim and then closed her eyes once more, trying to channel his concentration and confidence into her.

I can do this.

She released the arrow and peeked out of one eye.

When the arrow struck firmly in the centre of the target, she let out a squeak of joy. Allowing the bow to fall from her hand, she launched herself at Lord Andrew.

He wrapped his strong arms around her waist and lifted her so her boots were inches off the ground.

'I did it! Did you see? I did it!'

By his expression, he seemed to be as pleased as she was.

And if those around them hadn't seen, they did now with the spectacle she realised she was making. People nearby applauded her accomplishment and called out words of praise.

'That was a crack shot, Charlotte,' Toby exclaimed from the shooting area beside them, where he was instructing her beaming friend in the skills of archery. 'I think Andrew should give me a few pointers before I decide to shoot next.'

Her feet were back on the ground, but she barely felt the earth beneath her boots because Lord Andrew had yet to release her from the circle of his arms. His rounded biceps felt hard under the soft fabric of his coat and she moved her hands to take measure of the curves. This was not a man who spent his time all day playing cards. This was a sporting man. No wonder he was so good at archery with arms like this.

It felt safe in his arms.

It felt exciting in his arms.

It felt...

Emotions knotted inside her, as Charlotte shifted her attention from his eyes to his lips. But before she was able to admit what she wanted, he dropped his arms and took a step back. The cool air struck her hot skin, sending a shiver up her spine.

'Well done, my lady,' he said with an approving smile and a bit of a rasp to his voice. 'You've conquered your own challenge.'

The arrow was solidly embedded into the hay bale and she wished she could have taken it home so she could remember this moment—remember the feeling of accomplishment coursing through her. And remember Lord Andrew Pearce.

She shot four more arrows which all hit in or near the centre of the hay bale before she sadly relinquished the bow and picked up her bonnet.

'Thank you for encouraging me to do that,' she said to Lord Andrew as she watched him prop the bow against the tree and slip the strap of the quiver over his neck.

'It seemed a shame to miss an opportunity that probably doesn't present itself very often. I find when I challenge myself, I feel the most alive.'

She never thought about activities that way, but she supposed he was right. Excitement was still humming through her body, and she almost felt giddy. The feeling was foreign, but wonderful.

'It's a pity they did not award you some prize for an accomplishment such as yours,' he said. 'Then you could walk around the fair and enjoy the accolades of those around you.'

'*I* know I hit it and feel a sense of true accomplishment. That is all that matters to me. I shall remember that for a long time.'

Lord Andrew tipped the brim of his hat to her. 'Then I am especially pleased I suggested it.'

'It probably sounds foolish to you that such a small accomplishment has brought me such joy.'

It was suddenly embarrassing to look him in the eye. One would think she had just come out and this was her first Season.

'No challenge that is faced and conquered is a small accomplishment.'

She looked up at him and it was hard to look away.

But then suddenly he strode to the edge of the firing line and held up his hand. 'Halt,' he shouted in a commanding tone, raising his hand to indicate all the archers should stop shooting.

The people assembled lowered their bows.

Heavens, what was he going to do? An uneasiness crept around her stomach as she became afraid he was going to announce her accomplishment and embarrass her.

'This will only take a few moments,' he yelled out again, striding towards her target and then pulling out the arrow she had launched successfully. When he was safely back to the firing line, arrows began to fly across the grassy field once more.

He stopped before her and presented the arrow to her in both his palms. 'Your prize, my lady.'

Hesitantly, she took the arrow he had very kindly retrieved for her. It had been a long time since someone had done something so thoughtful. 'Thank you. You placed yourself in peril to get this for me. There was no guarantee those archers would not have seen you as a moving target for a more challenging sport. Quite a few appear rather pickled.'

The corner of his mouth tipped up, and he adjusted his glove. 'I had every confidence I could have dodged them if they had tried.'

Charlotte narrowed her eyes at him and tilted her head. 'Are you always this confident about everything?'

He gave a slight shrug. 'I suppose I am. If I want to do something, then I believe I can.'

'And you always do what you want?'

His gaze fixed on her mouth and he licked the centre of his top lip. 'Within reason. Some things I'd like to do require consent.'

The air was growing thick again and she was fighting the urge to step closer to him. 'And you always ask for consent when necessary?'

He lowered his voice. 'Always. I'm an honourable man and asking for consent can be quite a pleasurable experience.'

Her brow wrinkled while she tried to imagine how exactly asking for consent could be pleasurable.

'Ah, my lady, I find I wish you and I were alone.'

She found herself unusually flattered by his interest—and in agreement with his statement, although she would never admit it out loud, even completely to herself. 'We are outside now. I believe you did mention something about being outside.'

It was satisfying to see her teasing words surprise him, as he lowered his head and rubbed his jaw. He peered at her through his lashes. 'But we are not alone without anyone about to overhear our discussions or judge our actions.'

'Or gardeners tending to shrubbery.'

There was a wicked glint in his eyes. 'Especially gardeners tending to shrubbery.'

She wanted to ask him where he thought people went if they wanted to be alone outside. Could it be accomplished at a fair like this? Not that she would do that. Not that she wanted to. And yet, his wicked expression had her wondering if those were the looks he would give her right before he lowered his head and kissed her.

Chapter Eight

The only thing stopping Andrew from asking if he could kiss her was the very public venue they were in. In seconds his body was fighting his conscience with need.

There was this soft floral scent floating around her. It was somewhat familiar, but he couldn't place where he had smelled it before. When he was standing behind her, with his nose close to her hair, the scent was driving him mad.

He had wanted to slide his arms around her and feel the weight of her breasts in his cupped hands. He wanted to skim the tip of his nose along her graceful neck before trailing kisses up to her ear. With whispers, he wanted to tell her how he thought about taking her against one of the nearby trees until they were both weak and fulfilled. He looked into her eyes with a need so great, the rest of the world seemed to fall away.

Until Toby slapped him on the back and brought him to his senses.

'Well done, old boy. That was a capital suggestion of yours inviting the ladies to have a go with the bows and arrows. I don't know why I'd never thought to suggest it before.'

Lady Charlotte looked away and adjusted the white fichu by her neck, pulling it gently away from her skin. It appeared he wasn't the only one who was in need of a dip in the lake.

'You were wonderful, Charlotte,' Mrs Knightly said, beaming at her friend's accomplishments. 'Much better than I. It was lovely to see you enjoying yourself so much.'

'I have Lord Andrew to thank for his skilled direction,' she said, offering him an almost shy smile.

'Nonsense. The accomplishment was all your own.'

It was getting harder to look away from her again, until Toby cleared his throat.

'Shall we see what else is of interest here today?' his friend asked, offering his arm to his wife and heading off down the path to the house.

There was only one thing here that interested Andrew and she was standing beside him with her hands clasped behind her back.

Andrew tossed a guinea to one of the servants standing not far away guarding the bows and arrows from theft. 'For the lady's prize,' he clarified, motioning with his head to the arrow she held in her hand.

They followed Toby and his wife as they made their way towards the house along the grove of trees that arched above them from either side. The smell of roasting meat drifting towards them was something Andrew could focus on while he tried not to think about how badly he wanted Lady Charlotte. He had noticed the curve of her waist and shapely bottom when he was adjusting her body to improve her shot. Now he was having trouble thinking of anything else.

'Have you had the opportunity to sample any of the food today?' she asked, moving aside to avoid being trampled by a group of children running past them.

'I have not, although the smells coming from beyond the house have been tempting me all day. Do you know what it is they are cooking?'

'They are roasting lamb and pig on open spits, and I agree the smell has been making me hungry since they started to cook them. It was wonderful to wander through the stalls and do some shopping while delicious smells wafted around you.'

'You almost make it sound as if the food is your favourite part of the fair.'

'Almost? The food is my favourite part.'

They both shared a friendly laugh while he enjoyed her candour.

'I would say the food is mine as well, but I confess I am too competitive by nature. Sport has always held my interest.'

She glanced across at his arm. 'And what sport interests you aside from archery?'

'Here? At the fair?'

'Or back in London. I would think you were not singular in your enjoyments.'

He enjoyed many things—many he shouldn't mention in the company of a refined lady even if she had been married. 'I am partial to boxing when I'm home.' He regularly went a few rounds each week and was a silent partner in one of the finest boxing establishments in London, doing well for himself reaping in the financial gains. 'I find it does wonders to help quiet my mind with the mental focus needed to win.'

'Do you win your matches often, my lord?'

'Some would say I'm very skilled at the sport.'

'What would you say?'

'I would say I'm attempting not to appear a braggart.'

Her gaze dropped to his arm again before she looked towards the ground and smiled. 'Have you followed the sport for a long time?'

'Since I was at Cambridge. We would often sneak away from college when news of a nearby match circulated amongst the students.'

'Had you been there to watch Tom Cribb fight Tom Molineaux?'

Hell, this woman was perfect!

'How is it you know of Cribb and Molineaux?'

A touch of sadness crossed her features before she gave him a small smile. 'It was all you would hear about from the men at the time. They talked about it for weeks. My husband was disappointed he was only able to read about it in the papers.'

'I travelled with my friend Hart to see it. Nothing would have stopped us.'

'Were the crowds really as large as were reported?'

'If memory serves, I remember hearing fifteen thousand showed up to witness it and it certainly felt as though you were standing in a crowd that large that day.'

'Any other sports strike your fancy?'

'I ride most mornings, although in London it's usually to clear the cobwebs from my mind and not to race. I think I just enjoy the morning air.'

'There is something about the morning air that is magical. I like to go for early walks, after settling things with my housekeeper for the day. I find early morning activity helps shore me up for the tasks I have to do each day.'

By the time they reached the food stalls, she knew more about the superficial parts of his life than most people of his acquaintance. It wasn't that she was nosy and asked too many questions, it was that she was engaging and they had common interests. And she was very easy to talk to.

They joined their friends in sampling the roasted lamb and pork, each vying for the crispiest pieces they could get, and sat at a table on the terrace of the manor house, drinking lemonade and ale under the clear blue sky. He had forgotten how much cleaner the air was outside London.

His purpose in accompanying Toby here today was to gather intelligence about the area and assess the threat to the Crown. His mind was itching to be put to good use and his instincts were to search for threats no matter where he was. Gatherings such as this were useful because they brought together various classes of people and the more people drank, the more vocal they would become.

While Andrew and his party sat discussing the merits of various taverns and inns in the area, two gentlemen at nearby tables began arguing, shifting everyone's attention to them. One of the gentleman, who was sitting directly behind Lady Charlotte, became so animated Andrew shifted his chair closer to Mrs Knightly in order to get Lady Charlotte out of harm's way. She became startled when, without warning, he tugged the legs of her chair with her in it across the stone floor, closer to him.

'Forgive me,' he said into her ear, so she could

hear him over the men shouting, 'I want to be sure no harm comes to you.'

'I appreciate the gesture, but may I suggest the next time you warn the lady first of your plan before almost pulling the chair out from under her. I assure you her heart will thank you for it.'

She managed to make him smile while all his senses were attuned to the argument. The disagreement was about a particular gentleman who represented the area in the House of Commons. There was a time and place for heated debate. On the terrace of that man's house with guests close by was not one of them, in Andrew's opinion. Finally, the companions of the man furthest from them convinced him to leave before they came to blows.

When the commotion had settled down, Andrew leaned towards Lady Charlotte. 'Who were the two men arguing?'

'Mr Repton is seated closest to us. He is the apothecary in the village. The other gentleman was Mr Charles, a gentleman farmer who owns an estate in a nearby village.'

She rolled her eyes and said Mr Charles's name on a groan, leaving no doubt she was not fond of the man.

'You do not care for Mr Charles?'

She glanced back at the short, robust fellow around Andrew's age, laughing with his friends as they walked away. 'The man is a toad. He is one of those who believes violence will promote the action that you spoke of the other morning. I have witnessed the man kick a poor defence-less dog until a number of us implored him to stop before he killed it. And he regularly is in-volved in brawls with strangers in his village. He is someone I purposely avoid.'

He should walk around and learn more about Mr Charles. But part of him did not want to leave the side of the woman to his right—who now, thanks to his quick action, was sitting so close to him their knees were touching under the table.

With the end of the argument and the storm-ing off of Mr Charles, Andrew's senses were softening and his body was not strung tight in anticipation of a violent outburst. Now his body was consumed with the heat radiating from the leg pressed against his.

There was just something about Lady Char-lotte. He wasn't about to court her. He barely knew her—and marriage was a complication his covert life did not need. However, she was ach-ingly tempting, and he was imaging being alone with her on the terrace, laying her down on the table, lifting up her skirts…

'Wouldn't you agree, Lord Andrew?'

The use of his name by Mrs Knightly had broken into his thoughts of the woman beside him. He looked up from his tankard of ale and all three of his companions were looking at him with expectant expressions. It was Lady Charlotte who came to his aide.

'I believe Lord Andrew would agree animals do indeed get startled by fireworks, which is unfortunate, however there is a pleasurable excitement that runs through one's body when they explode in the sky. I will stay to watch them, Ann, even if you and Toby decide to return home before they begin.'

She really had noticed his mind was elsewhere with a detailed explanation like that. He knew she understood his silent thank you, when she gave him a hint of a conspiratorial smile.

'Should you wish to remain, I will stay to see you arrive safely home when the fireworks have finished,' he offered, knowing it wouldn't be a hardship to spend the evening with her.

'You are very kind, I would not wish to impose on you.'

'It is no imposition, I assure you. I enjoy fireworks just as much as you do.'

'There will be drunken revelry all over,' Mrs Knightly needlessly advised him. 'Do make certain she reaches her home without incident.'

She pointedly eyed his tankard, which he placed on the table and pushed away to show he would not be in his cups at the end of the evening.

'I will take great care with her ladyship's safety.'

Lady Charlotte tipped her head to him. 'I do appreciate your offer to see me home. It is not far.'

'It would be my honour.'

Chapter Nine

By the time the sun started to hang low in the evening sky, Charlotte felt a certain sadness that the day was nearing an end. Walking through the fair with Lord Andrew and her friends had brought her more joy than anything else had in a long time. There was something about Lord Andrew's sense of adventure and encouragement that had them all trying things they normally would never have.

As she bade farewell to Ann and Toby with Lord Andrew by her side, she could feel the glances from some of her neighbours as they looked him over. He cut an impressive form with his height and broad shoulders, but it was more than that. Lord Andrew Pearce possessed a commanding presence, the likes of which she had never witnessed before. It was in the way he carried himself. There was a confidence without arrogance that she found intoxicating.

When he strode around the grounds of the house, one could easily assume it belonged to him with his comfortable manner and skill in country pursuits. She hadn't questioned him about his family. It was not her place and he didn't seem interested in sharing it with her. Soon he would be gone and back in London. Their association would end. Who his father was had no bearing on their interaction.

They stood side by side, watching a man juggle flaming torches near the house in comfortable silence. She glanced over and caught the calculating gleam in his eye as he watched the torches fly up and down.

'I know you have every confidence in your abilities,' she said, 'however, the salve I use for burns is at my home and I have no desire to go and fetch it.'

His lips rose in that now familiar smile and he eyed her sideways. 'I am merely trying to determine how he does it. From what I can gather there is a rhythm to it.'

'Do you always study things that closely?'

'When I'm intrigued by them, I do.'

'And the risk of setting yourself on fire is intriguing?'

'Determining how *not* to do it is more the thing.'

He could set her body on fire with just a mere look, which was unprecedented. He didn't even have to say anything. She hadn't experienced that before. Not even with Jonathan. How was it possible she was imagining the feel of this man's lips on hers, when they barely knew one another?

The sky was beginning to turn pink. Or maybe that was her. Heat spread up her neck to her cheeks.

He leaned in, close to the edge of her bonnet, and lowered his voice to a deep whisper. 'Whatever it is you are thinking, it has you blushing.'

She gave him a chastising glare. 'A gentleman should not comment on a woman's blush. And how can you even notice it in this dim light?'

'The kind juggler has provided me with enough light to see it and I am so glad he has.'

'Perhaps you should consider not mentioning it again.'

'Perhaps you should consider telling me what you were thinking.'

'I am holding a rather sharp arrow, my lord,' she teased.

'And I'm holding an image in my head of what I'd like to do with that sharp tongue of yours.'

If another gentleman had said those words to her, she would have slapped him. However, Lord Andrew's comment didn't feel threatening or leave her feeling as if she needed to scrub her body with soap. His deep whispered suggestion had her imagining kissing him and sliding her tongue over his, knowing the taste of his lips.

'What are you thinking, woman? You're practically crimson.'

'You need to stop talking to me and go back to analysing how you can become the world's finest torch juggler.'

His low-throated laugh had her reluctantly smiling.

'Very well, I will leave you to your thoughts, but if I require burn salve later tonight, I shall lay the blame at your door.'

When servants came out from the house and began lighting the torches that lined the gravel path around the back formal garden, Charlotte and Lord Andrew discussed where they thought it would be best to view the fireworks.

'I will be happy to escort you to the terrace, if you so wish,' he offered.

She was not fond of the close scrutiny of the local gentry. If they were able to sneak away, they could watch the fireworks in peace. 'There is no need for us to watch from up there,' she said. 'I know a pleasant spot on a hill near the woods that lead to my home. There were years I had no inclination to be around crowds of people and I would watch them from that hill.'

For two years after Jonathan was killed, Charlotte preferred to avoid the overly kind conversations with people in the village she barely knew. It seemed there were those people who wished to say they were friends with a Waterloo widow—

as if it were a badge of honour or something to be admired. For those two years, Charlotte watched the fireworks far removed from everyone else.

'If that is your wish, I am happy to oblige. You know this park better than I and I will defer to you.'

They stole away from the house as people began to head towards the terrace and made their way to a small copse. Normally she had to walk slower since Ann's legs were shorter than hers, but Lord Andrew also possessed a long stride and they kept a comfortable pace with each other through the secluded wooded area leading up to the hill. The moon was now high in the darkening night sky and a few puffy clouds were drifting along.

'We should hurry,' she said, clutching her prize arrow and lifting her skirt up to better climb the hill.

He held his hand out to help her, but she shook her head. She had grown accustomed to managing for herself. When they reached the top, they stood under a cluster of oak trees and surveyed the vista before them. The hill was higher than Oakwood Hall, giving them a direct view of the stately stone house with its lower windows illuminated like points of light. The glowing torches, placed behind the house, looked like rows of tiny sticks and gave a visual marker for how far the formal gardens stretched. The eve-

ning was unseasonably warm. Around them fire-
flies speckled the air with their own show of
light and crickets chirped in the distance.

'I commend your choice of location,' he said,
looking out towards Oakwood Hall. 'This is a
spectacular view.'

'I am glad you approve. It really is lovely, even
without the fireworks exploding. I like to walk
and my home is not far. One day, I decided to
travel off the footpath and explore.'

'Ah, an adventuress.'

She knew he must have said it in jest. There
wasn't an adventuresome bone in her body…not
any more—not for a very long time.

He looked around the grassy ground and then
at her lavender gown. 'You will ruin your dress
if you sit.'

'We can always stand, or you can sit if you
wish. Standing will not be an inconvenience to
me.'

By the crease in his brow it was evident he
was not happy with either suggestion. 'Would
you be scandalised if I removed my coat?'

She hadn't seen a man in his shirtsleeves in
more than five years. The idea of seeing him in
such an intimate fashion sent a rush through her
body. 'No one is here to judge what is proper. If
you are so inclined to remove your coat, I will
not protest.'

He peeled his coat off. There was no other

way to describe it and it left Charlotte transfixed by his unintended seductive movement.
Once more she marvelled at the way he was so
comfortable in his skin. His movements weren't
studied and yet they had a profound effect on her.

Shaking out his coat, he laid it on the ground
so the silk lining was facing the grass. 'There,'
he declared, seeming quite pleased with himself. 'That should protect your gown from ruin.'
Without even a glance her way, he sat down,
stretched his long legs out in front of him and
crossed his ankles. When he finally looked up
at her, she managed to close her mouth before
he noticed.

Nothing. Nothing prepared Charlotte for the
sight of Lord Andrew looking as if he were
at home away from prying eyes. In his shirtsleeves—in the moonlight—the linen of his shirt
hugging the curves of his biceps, giving Charlotte a better idea of what he would look like
without his shirt and waistcoat. She had never
felt more feminine in all her life. He was so much
bigger than she imagined…and broader…and—

'Have I soiled the lining of my coat so you
could remain standing all night?'

How could he expect her to sit beside him
while he looked like that and carry on a conversation? Was he mad?

He patted the area next to him. 'I realise I

have never been here before, but I do believe the fireworks will be happening behind you.'

As if divine providence stepped in, she heard the first one launch. She turned to see sparkles of white and gold fill the sky in the distance.

'Come and sit, or you will miss all of it.'

She took a deep breath and lowered herself to the ground cover he had graciously provided for her. They were less than a foot apart.

'You can release that arrow now,' he suggested, nodding towards her hand. 'I assure you I will not pinch it from you.'

Her knuckles were probably white under her kid gloves from how tightly she was clutching it in her hand. It took an effort to release it and place it next to her.

Lord Andrew let out a low laugh. 'I notice you placed it on your other side.'

His good humour was helping to relieve some of the tightness she was feeling throughout her body.

'I thought it best not to tempt you by placing the arrow between us.'

'The arrow isn't what I find tempting.'

Was he feeling it, too? Her gaze dropped to his lips just as a giant boom reverberated through the hills. They both turned towards the house to see more colourful lights shoot into the sky and crackle apart.

'I'm thinking about kissing you.' He said it in

such a matter-of-fact way, as if the idea would not set her body aflame—as if the idea of kissing this practical stranger would be a common occurrence.

Charlotte had only kissed one man in her life. She never thought she would want to kiss another—until now. Now she wanted to know what his lips felt like against hers. She wanted him to wrap her in his arms where she would feel desirable and cherished. And she wanted to know if his kiss could be enough to end the desire running through her body.

He placed his gloved finger under her chin and gently guided her face so she was looking at him. The scent of leather filled her nose. There was no amusement in his expression. No cavalier bravado. Just an intensity that made her believe if he didn't kiss her right then, they both would burn up like a piece of char cloth.

It was becoming hard to breathe and if he did in fact kiss her there was a good chance she would lose consciousness from lack of air. But if he didn't kiss her...

She licked her lips to appease the need of feeling his lips on hers.

He swallowed hard. Almost hesitantly, he untied her bonnet and put it aside. Gently, he wrapped his fingers around the back of her neck, pulling her closer, and he lowered his head. She closed her eyes and his lips faintly brushed hers. They were soft, yet firm, and she wanted more.

One of them, or maybe it was both, deepened the kiss until Charlotte was lying on her back with her arms around his neck and he was over her, propped on his elbows. Her body began to ache between her thighs. The knowledge that she was privy to the intimate way this man tasted was driving her to know more. He broke their kiss to nip at her lower lip before kissing across her jaw and down her neck. At the hollow near her shoulder, he started to softly suck her skin while he unbuttoned her spencer and caressed her breast. Charlotte had never expected to feel this way again. A soft moan escaped her lips, ecstasy and agony combined.

She had this surprising craving to get closer to that strength that seemed to radiate from him, so she unbuttoned his waistcoat and slid it over the curves of his shoulders. The outline of the muscles of his chest felt solid through the thin linen of his shirt, making her feel soft and feminine. As he kissed down to the swell of her breasts and pulled the fichu from the neckline of her gown, it was impossible not to run her fingers through the soft strands of his hair.

'Charlotte, you have me aching for things I should not have. Cannot have.' His hot breath scorched her skin.

Her Christian name on his lips did funny

things in her chest. They were both breathing rapidly as if they had just run up the hill they were on and her entire focus was on how good he was making her feel.

'Can we...?' He let out a strangled breath before releasing one of her breasts from her stays and sucking on her nipple.

The feeling was intense. She dug her nails into his back, through his shirt, as her head dropped back.

She knew she was moaning. She should be mortified. Ladies never made a sound. Her mother had instructed her of that on her wedding day. But there was no way she could stop herself. His hardness pushed into her leg. Apparently, her moaning was not making Andrew uncomfortable.

She knew they should stop, but every inch of her body was screaming not to. Suddenly he threw himself on to his back beside her with a groan. While his chest rose and fell on shaky breaths, he draped his arm across his eyes. Air wasn't entering her lungs smoothly either and staring at his forearm, with the outline of masculine veins and muscles, was not helping.

Finally, he lowered his arm and turned towards her. 'Forgive me. I shouldn't have—'

She placed her finger against his smooth lips. 'I didn't say stop.'

'But—'

'I would have told you to stop if I'd wanted that.'

Her burning desire was reflected in his eyes.

'I want to be inside you more than anything.' His voice was deep and husky.

She wanted him just as much. She wanted all that masculine intensity wrapped around her. Just looking at him now was making her feel like the most desirable woman in the world. For the first time in years she felt wet between her thighs and she recalled their conversation over breakfast. Pressing her fingertips to her lips, she tried to hold back a laugh.

He appeared affronted. 'Before my body explodes like those fireworks from frustration, do you care to tell me what is so amusing?'

'We are outside.'

He looked around as if silently acknowledging the obvious.

'No gardeners are about.'

His brow wrinkled, then a sly smile crossed those delicious lips. 'So it would seem.'

'It isn't raining.'

'No, it is not.'

She chewed on her lip. 'But it is wet.'

Now a devilish look was in his eyes and his lips curled up some more. He turned fully on his side and propped his head in his hand. He hadn't exaggerated when he said he would give her his undivided attention. Being under this much attention from a man like him could be addictive.

'Truly?'

Charlotte nodded and felt the heat spread across her cheeks.

Slowly, he tugged off his left glove—finger by finger—with his teeth. 'I think it's rather unfair of you to keep all that wetness to yourself.'

Looking at his ungloved hand she had a fairly good idea what he had in mind. Could she allow him to touch her? She chewed her lip. A slight breeze blew across her stockings. He was gathering up her skirt with his fingers and stopped mid-thigh. Leaning over, he placed his lips on the shell of her ear. 'Would you like me to touch your leg, Charlotte?'

She would never have this again. She would never again feel a man's touch on her body. Never was a long time. 'If you're so inclined,' she uttered on a breath.

The tips of his fingers skimmed up her calf and over her knee. 'Shall I continue?'

She swallowed. How far would he go? 'If you wish.'

The pads of his fingers slid along her thigh. His touch was light and teasing, and stopped near her hip. 'Continue?'

Just the thought of his fingers sliding against her was making her heart race faster. It had been so long. She knew how good it would feel. It was just his fingers that would be touching her. She moved her legs a few inches apart and nodded. But instead of touching her between her thighs, he skimmed his fingertips back down to her knee, and she licked her suddenly dry lips.

'Shall I explore some more?'

Once more she nodded.

He held her eyes with his passionate gaze. This time when his fingers brushed the inside of her thigh, he stopped inches away from the area that needed to feel him the most. 'I want to touch you, Charlotte, but only if you'll allow it,' he said, studying her eyes.

Her body was aching for his touch. She needed it desperately.

'Tell me you want me to touch you,' he whispered, caressing the shell of her ear with his lips.

She had never talked during moments like this. Oh, lud, she'd never had moments quite like this. The overwhelming need for him was stronger than anything she had ever felt before in her life. Ladies didn't speak when they made love. They weren't even to utter a sound when a man entered them and, if they did reach fulfilment, they did everything in their power to hold back a moan or a groan.

It wasn't done.

It wasn't proper.

'I need you to touch me.' It was out of her mouth before she could hold it back.

As he finally stroked her ever so slowly between her thighs, he licked the shell of her ear. When she moaned loudly, she didn't even care. He trailed his tongue down her neck, while his fingers continued to slide back and forth with long slow strokes. The feeling was growing too intense.

When her body stopped trembling he removed his hand and, with passion in his eyes, he studied her. A cool breeze blew across her thighs as he made a point of looking down. She followed his gaze and watched as he unbuttoned the fall of his trousers, slipped his hand under the buckskin and rhythmically slid his hand up and down. 'Now we're both wet.'

The ease with which he was comporting himself, as if this was the most natural thing in the world, was pushing any sense of self-consciousness from her mind. She wanted to give him as much pleasure as he had been giving her and moved his hand away so she could take up the task.

Andrew dropped back on to his coat. 'Bloody hell,' he groaned.

He was so hard in her palm. Was there any part of his body that was soft? If so, she hadn't found it yet. Unless it was his lips.

Leaning over, she placed her mouth above

his. 'Tell me you want me to kiss you.' The air from her breath blew into his mouth, past his parted lips.

'Kiss me,' he groaned.

The kiss was deep and filled with all the passion inside her. The buckskin of his trousers and the leather of his boots rubbed against her legs as he rolled them over so he was on top of her, propped on his elbows. When they finally broke apart, he looked into her eyes and her heart flipped over in response.

'I want you, Charlotte, but I will stop if you tell me.'

She could not lie to herself. She wanted him. She wanted to feel all the pleasure she knew he could give her and she wanted to feel, one last time, that close to a man. Instead of voicing her reply, she wrapped her legs around his.

He brushed the tip of his nose gently against hers. 'I will pull out before I come, but in order to do that, I need to set the pace.' There wouldn't be a child. He was telling her he would make certain of it, but he needn't worry.

This was the first and only time she would have to admit that out loud to a man whom she was beginning to care about. The words felt stuck in her throat. 'There is no need. I am unable to conceive.'

'You're certain?'

She nodded. 'I was married for years and I

never did. And my widowed sister didn't either. It must be something in my family.'

He brushed the hair away from her forehead and kissed it. 'You're perfect, whether you can conceive or not. Never let anyone make you feel that you are less than that.'

If she had any doubts about wanting this kind man inside her before, she had none now. This time their kiss was soft and gentle. There was no urgency. Fireworks continued to explode across the valley as he shifted his hips and slowly entered her.

That feeling of being filled by him was so amazing, she closed her eyes to focus on every bit of the friction pushing against her. As if he was giving her body time to adjust to him, he didn't move his hips, until she raked her nails gently across his lower back. It was then that he slid out of her and pushed himself into her again.

With fluttered lashes, she opened her eyes and caught a sweet smile on his lips. A slow but forceful rhythm was forming between the two of them and she held on to the curves of his shoulders to ground her. She felt secure and cherished in his arms and wished this moment could go on for ever.

Chapter Ten

Staring into Charlotte's eyes as he thrust inside her as deeply as he could was having an odd effect on Andrew. From the moment he first saw her, he had wanted her. But after spending today with her, his need for her was more than physical.

He would be leaving soon. In all likelihood, he would never see Charlotte again.

Lowering his body, he carefully rested his weight on his elbows so as not to crush her. If only they could have done this the proper way—in a proper bed—able to completely undress. How he wanted to see her—all of her. But no matter how secluded they were up on this hill, it was still better to be somewhat clothed.

Charlotte's eyes held a fire and a passion, and she was so snug around him it was driving him mad. He wanted this to go on for ever, but just the feel of being inside her told him he would be lucky if this went on five more minutes. A bead of sweat slipped down his chest as he rocked his hips faster. Digging her nails into his shoulders, she let out a small cry. He wanted to give her so much pleasure. Knowing he would never get the chance to again was making his chest ache.

'Andrew...'

It was the first time Charlotte had referred to him in such an intimate way. She called out to him in a whispered plea. He had never liked the sound of his name more. Gently, he kissed her, as she met him thrust for thrust. He was about to explode, but he would not come until she did— and he was determined to make her scream.

Within a few more moments, he got his wish. A sensual guttural groan passed her clenched teeth. It was beautiful and raw—something he would not easily forget.

She grabbed the back of his head, pulling him down for a heady kiss. It was too much. She was too much. His head fell back as a sound tore through him that was close to her own, only much deeper.

They were both breathing hard as he snuggled his forehead into her neck. He inhaled deeply, taking in the fragrance she wore. The warmth of her fingertips felt wonderful as she stroked his lower back under his shirt. Andrew had never come inside a woman before—not without French letters. Now a part of each of them was mingled together, scenting the air. This entire experience with Charlotte had been a revelation.

He lifted himself up on his elbows and looked down at her. A sad, bittersweet smile was curving those full lips that he found so tempting. He kissed them softly, trying to memorise her taste.

She traced her finger down the slope of his nose, over the bump where it had been broken, and outlined his lips, as if she, too, were trying to memorise him for some time in the future when she might recall this night. 'Thank you for not embarrassing me when I became rather... rather...vocal.'

It was distinctly possible he had smiled more in the short time he had been with her than he had in the past year of his life. He hoped she wasn't regretting what they had done. He certainly wasn't. 'Charlotte, ever since we met I think you have been vocal...in one way or another.' It felt as if he would remember her when he was old, sitting by a fire, sipping what he hoped to be rather exceptional brandy. He knew he had to leave her, but he wished they had more time. The thought of saying goodbye to her was making his chest hurt. Was it possible to miss someone even before they were gone?

This was not good—not good at all. He was leaving in seven days. If he felt this way now, how hard would it be to leave her five days from now—or six? He was a man who didn't form attachments. He was a man who had secrets in his life and couldn't afford distractions. Distractions could be deadly. And Charlotte deserved a much better man than he was.

Suddenly, he pushed himself up, startling her.

'I should escort you home. I fear Mrs Knightly will be waiting up for me to make certain no harm has come to you. If I arrive back there at sunrise, we will have much to answer for.'

He couldn't bear to see the sadness in her eyes—the sadness he'd put there by getting too close, knowing they had no future together. She lived in the country. He lived in London. She was a respectable widow and he was an agent of the Crown. Considering all of it was making his chest hurt more.

He held his hand out and helped her up. Items from their once-proper attire were scattered around them in the grass.

'I'm missing a bonnet and gloves,' Charlotte stated, flattening her skirts.

'Your bonnet is over there and I have found one glove.'

'I have your gloves here and—' she reached over and picked his waistcoat off the grass '— here is your waistcoat.' She brushed it off and held it out to him.

'There, that's my cravat and your other glove. Is that all of it?'

'Aside from pins from my hair which we will

never find, I believe we have all the ingredients to make ourselves respectable. I'll just stuff my hair into my bonnet. Thankfully, it's dark.'

She was becoming very practical about their passionate encounter, which made him smile. He really would miss her.

They managed to find her prize arrow after she stated quite firmly she would not be leaving that hill without it and made their way slowly through the woods hand in hand towards her home. Eventually, they reached a clearing. Ahead of them was a large field of grass and wildflowers, probably used for grazing. Without the cover of the tree branches above to block some of the moonlight, the field appeared inordinately bright, making it easy to see the lines in the bark of a fallen nearby tree. They both stood at the edge of the wood as if neither wanted to take their first step into the light.

Charlotte pointed to a clump of trees across the field. 'My home is just on the other side of those trees.'

This was it. This was the end. For both their sakes he couldn't see her any more. He would leave tomorrow.

He tugged her hand to stop her progress. 'I want to kiss you one last time in the woods. In these woods.'

She took a step closer and, without a word, pulled his head down for a long drawn-out kiss before slowly pulling away. On their way across the field neither of them spoke, as if the enormity of what they had done together was now settling in. He tried to steal a glimpse at her face to try to gauge what was going through her mind now that they were reaching her home, but he couldn't see past the brim of her bonnet.

As they crossed the road to her house, she broke the silence stretching between them. 'You may borrow one of my horses to return to Knightly Hall. I will have my groom fetch it tomorrow. Turn left out of my drive and follow the road until you reach the church. At the church, turn a left on to that road. It will eventually take you to the Knightlys' estate. You will have to ride for a number of miles, but it is very direct so you should have no trouble finding your way.'

She lived in a pale stone house of a respectable size, with a walled garden off to the side. Rose bushes and neatly trimmed privet hedges adorned the front garden. The stable was behind the house and she took him directly there so he could saddle up one of her four horses.

The dirt from her drive drifted on to his boots as they left the stable, and he led the horse to the edge of the road. It was time to return to Knightly Hall, but all he wanted to do was to carry her inside and take her again. But her intent was clear when she took a step back, giving him room to mount the chestnut stallion. This was the horse of a soldier and he assumed it had once belonged to her husband.

He hadn't asked her about him. He knew she had worn mourning clothes for him for four years. That was all he had needed to know about the man. But now, as he was getting ready to leave for ever, he wondered what kind of man had stirred that kind of love and loyalty in her.

'Would you like me to walk you to your door?' He was having the hardest time riding away.

'No, thank you. You should go before sunrise.' She opened her mouth as if she wanted to say something more, but then closed it and gave him a bittersweet smile. It was apparent she was trying to remain composed and pleasant with their parting, but he sensed she was feeling melancholy as acutely as he was. And she didn't even know he had decided to leave tomorrow. She was stirring feelings inside him that needed to be locked away. She was no good for him or for the life he led. And he certainly was no good for her.

Placing his foot in the stirrup, he mounted the horse and rubbed his hand on the shiny coat of its neck. 'Goodnight, Charlotte.'

She looked down at the arrow clutched in her hand and back up at him. 'Goodnight, Andrew.'

With a tip of his hat, he kicked the horse into a gallop and didn't look back.

* * *

Charlotte entered her house on shaky legs. By the time she closed the door behind her and made it up to her bedchamber, she was a sobbing mess. She couldn't see him again. Even if he was only going to stay for another week, she needed to avoid him. In her head, she knew she should have never done what she did with him. She tried to tell herself it was all about passion. That his touch had left her unable to think clearly. But that wasn't entirely true and she hated admitting that to herself.

She liked him. She genuinely liked him and the thought that he'd soon be back in London and she would never see him again made her miserable. There was this driving need to feel close to him and to hold on to the feeling that he might care for her. His adventurous nature called to something inside her. It reminded her of a time long ago when she would take pleasure in climbing trees with her sisters, racing across the meadows and sneaking upstairs to the servants' floor just to say they could without getting caught.

That side of her had been buried when she'd become a wife. Domestic responsibilities demanded it. One couldn't be the respectable wife of an Army officer and behave like a hoyden. The arrow was still clutched tight in her hands.

It didn't feel as though she was a hoyden today. Today she'd felt alive for the first time in ages.

And that was wrong.

Andrew had her thinking about things that weren't possible. He deserved a woman who loved him and one who could give him a house full of children. Her heart belonged to Jonathan. There was no room for anyone else. Not that Andrew wanted more from her than what she gave him tonight.

Jonathan's signet ring thumped at her chest when she moved. How could she have betrayed her husband like that? She loved him. She always had. Never could she have imagined she would have given herself to anyone else. And yet, with Andrew, it had felt so right.

Another sob escaped her lips. Her emotions were in a jumble. What happened with Andrew tonight was over and she would make certain it never happened again. A crushing sadness filled her and she slid down the wall to sit on the floor of her darkened chamber. Her legs were too weak. She mustn't allow herself to fall for him. She had a respectable life to lead and one that would honour the memory of her husband who had sacrificed his life for her and their country.

Some day, Andrew would be a vague memory. She would not be able to recall his face or the sound of his voice. Or how his smile made her insides flip. And she prayed there would come a day when she didn't recall everything they had done together on the hill as fireworks lit the night sky.

Chapter Eleven

Charlotte had successfully avoided Ann's house for four days. Each day she made a mark in her daily ledger indicating she had managed to find a way to stay apart from Andrew when all the while she was fighting the urge to go there to see him.

Did he miss her? Had he thought about her? And had he enquired after her from their friends?

When the slowest four days of her life had finally passed, she thought it safe to visit Ann and Toby. Now she should be able to face him without everyone in Ann's household realising they had had a tryst. But when she arrived at Ann's, she was told Andrew had left for London the day after the fair. According to Ann, he needed to return to London on business, but Charlotte suspected he had thought it best not to see her again and had ended his visit with Toby earlier than he intended. And he hadn't even bothered to say goodbye.

'I hope it was nothing dire,' she said. Which was a lie, since she wished it was an outside circumstance that had pulled him away so suddenly. It was taking all of her strength to remain composed as her stomach fell with the finality of it all. Thinking she didn't want to see him again was proving to be very different from surmising he hadn't wanted to see her again.

'All Toby said was Lord Andrew had urgent business and needed to be back in London. It all seemed rather sudden.'

'He didn't say what kind of business?'

Ann shook her head. 'No, and I didn't think it was my place to enquire. Lord Andrew was a rather private guest. He didn't appear comfortable conversing about himself or his family. Our discussions tended towards general polite topics. The most animated I had seen him was when he was talking with you at the fair. Until then, I had the impression he was a rather reserved man.'

He hadn't appeared the least bit reserved when he was speaking with Charlotte. In fact, Lord Andrew was anything but reserved with her. Although, now that she thought about it, he hadn't really discussed his personal life with her either. She didn't even know how he spent his time. After she'd practically accused him of being a good-for-nothing wastrel, who could blame him for guarding his privacy. He was gone now…for ever. The less she knew about Andrew, the easier it should be to forget him. At least that was what she hoped.

'I thought you were going to give him a reason to prolong his visit with us,' Ann said.

'We were simply congenial with one another.'

'Congenial? You liked him, Charlotte. A great deal from what I could see.'

'What you saw was merely polite behaviour.'

'You hugged him.'

'I hit the centre of the target.'

'I haven't witnessed you do something so inappropriate or express such an unguarded feeling of excitement since we were young. There was something palpable between the two of you. Even Toby remarked on it and he tends to be oblivious to matters such as this.'

Oh, heavens, could Ann tell what she'd done? Would everyone know her shame? 'What are you insinuating?'

'I'm insinuating that there was something between the two of you. Some connection that, as much as you want to deny it, was there. You know I believe you should give yourself a second chance to find happiness with a man, but you believe that isn't possible. Well, I witnessed that connection that day between you and Lord Andrew and was hesitant to leave the two of you alone at the fair because of it.'

'Did you not trust me? Do you think so little of me that I would do something scandalous? You of all people know how much I loved Jonathan.' The lies were rolling off her tongue so easily.

'Your love for Jonathan has nothing to do with this. There was just something between you and Lord Andrew. I can't describe it, but I could feel it in the air.'

'Do not romanticise this, Ann. There was nothing between us.'

He was gone. It was over. She needed to forget it even happened.

But knowing he had returned to London without saying goodbye left her with a hollowness in her chest. For all his lovely words and actions, their time together meant nothing to him. He had already forgotten about her.

Andrew stared into his glass at the dining-room table of Gabriel's home, not even pretending to listen to his brothers as they sat together drinking port after dinner. He had recently returned from his trip and been out earlier in the day walking along Bond St when he thought he had spotted Charlotte from behind, dressed in grey, and entering a perfumer. He waited a full twenty minutes for the lady to emerge with his heart pounding just to get a glimpse of her, only to discover it was the Duchess of Skeffington. He knew his brain had been muddled since his visit to Toby's. He hadn't realised how much until today.

It had been easier not to say goodbye to her before he left. He preferred his final memory of her to be of their evening under the stars. His goodbye wouldn't have changed anything. He still would have had to leave. So why did his gut burn with guilt about the way he'd left every time he thought of her?

He took a deep breath and picked up his glass and finished off the remaining contents in one gulp. He caught Gabriel's eye as he reached for the crystal bottle to refill his glass.

'You've been particularly quiet this evening,' Gabriel offered, eyeing him from his chair.

'Have I?'

Monty held his hand out to Andrew for the bottle. 'Let him be, Gabriel. I much prefer a quiet Andrew to the cross one I've been facing.'

'I've not been cross. Why would you tell him I've been cross?'

'Perhaps because you have been. I cannot recall the last time that scowl was not permanently affixed to your face.'

'What is there to smile about?'

'What is there to prevent you from smiling?' Monty asked, pouring himself more port.

'I'm dealing with you. That is enough to make one cross.'

'I've been very patient with you, Andrew. But my patience is wearing thin. Whatever has caused this foul mood you are in, do not think it gives you permission to discharge your anger at me. And the next time you find yourself at White's ready to come to blows with another gentleman, you can find yourself another brother to step in to smooth it over. Oh, forgive me, you don't have another brother who would do that. Gabriel would have let you brawl it out and then have yourself barred from the club.'

Andrew directed a glance at Gabriel to determine if this was the first his brother was hearing about his altercation with Lord Aldrich.

From the look in Gabriel's eyes, it was. 'What was the argument about?' Gabriel asked, shifting his attention to the contents of his glass.

'Boreham accidentally bumped into Aldrich on the stairs going up to the card room,' Andrew explained. 'Aldrich made much ado about nothing and would not accept Boreham's apology. It was unnecessary and prevented the rest of us from reaching the tables. I told him he was being an ass and should accept Boreham's apology and move on. He took umbrage at my interference and we began to argue until Monty stepped in.'

'It was more than an argument. I've never witnessed anger like that from you over something so trivial and that had no impact on you.'

'It did impact me. I wanted to play cards.'

'You should have hit him,' Gabriel said off-handedly, observing the back and forth between his younger brothers. 'Aldrich is an ass. He would have deserved it.'

'Would you have Andrew barred from White's? I think it would be safe to say you will find him dining here more frequently should that occur.'

'I assure you I would make certain it was temporary and I believe Olivia would welcome it. She does appear to like the both of you more than necessary considering you are both rather vexing most of the time.'

'I'm trying to be responsible,' Monty replied. 'As the youngest I should be taking on the role of wastrel—instead I've been forced to play nurse-maid to him with his bad humour.'

'I haven't asked you to.'

'Someone needs to.'

'I am fully capable of handling my affairs and my mood. Go find some tavern wench to occupy yourself with and leave me alone.'

Before Monty could reply, Gabriel raised his hand to stop him. 'Finish your port, Monty, and let the ladies know Andrew and I will be joining you in the drawing room shortly.'

'But—'

'Let me speak to him, Montague.'

His younger brother downed his port, glared at Andrew out of the corner of his eye and walked out, leaving Andrew to face Gabriel alone. Why couldn't Monty keep his mouth shut?

With a lift of his hand, Gabriel dismissed the two footmen who had been on either side of the doorway and the sound of the door closing behind them echoed around the ornate red and gold room.

Andrew dropped his head back on his chair and stared up at the ceiling. 'I am in no humour to listen to you lecture me.'

'I wasn't aware I had been lecturing you.' Gabriel's brow was knotted when Andrew met him in the eye.

'Maybe not yet, but you know you want to.'

'What I want to do is find out what happened when you went to visit Knightly.'

'I don't know what you mean.'

'You were instructed to take leave for a fortnight. You agreed to remain disengaged from all operations. And yet you were only there for one week.'

'How do you know that?'

'Spence mentioned he saw you the next week in Windsor.'

'I spent most of my time in a tavern. I was nowhere near the castle or His Majesty.'

'But you told me you spent all two weeks with Knightly.'

Damn Spence. After years of working side by side in the field with the man and considering him a friend, one would think he would know when to keep quiet. 'I never said that I was at Toby's the entire time. You just assumed I was when I walked in this study exactly fourteen days after I left.'

'What did you find in Windsor that you are not telling me about?'

'Nothing. I am just partial to a tavern there.' There was no need to tell his brother he needed to be in Windsor, where he last served the Crown by foiling a plot against King George. It helped to remind him that what he did mattered. That the safety of his country, at times, would rest in his hands and that was why it was so important for him to leave Charlotte. That was why duty came before all else.

'You promised me you would disengage yourself from your responsibilities while you were away, yet you returned with information on the status of unrest in the area. I said nothing when you handed over that information. You're a grown man. Your instincts are what make you effective. But, since you've returned you are more on edge than before you left. Something has changed. Something has happened.'

Andrew let out a deep breath and pushed his chair back from the table. 'I haven't been any different from how I was before I left.' He had been telling himself this very thing over and over again. Part of him might have believed it.

'You and I both know that isn't true.'

He was not about to explain his feelings to Gabriel. He could barely explain them to himself. Charlotte had touched something inside him, and he had been unable to let her go.

'I am simply tired.'

'You didn't leave Cheshire because you were tired. Did you hear Mr Hunt speak? They say he can be very persuasive and impassioned in his views.' There was concern in Gabriel's voice, as if he, too, was thinking about how their uncle had his views turned all those years ago—and the fatal consequences of his actions.

'There were no speeches to be heard.'

'Then what?'

Andrew tilted his head back and squeezed his eyes shut, pressing the image of Charlotte out of his head. When would he forget what she looked like?

He hated when Gabriel pushed him on things he'd rather not discuss.

'I met a woman at Toby's.'

Gabriel grew still as he gave Andrew his undivided attention.

'I can't get her out of my mind. I liked her. I just liked her.' He pushed his palms into his eyelids as if he could prevent himself from seeing her face in his mind. 'I've always been able to separate my work from my emotions. I've always believed I could stop anyone who was plotting against the Crown or this organisation with any means possible. That having killed one person to protect you and the Crown, I could do it again. What's one more body to the list? But with her… I think I might have found the one person that if I was forced to harm, I wouldn't be able to, which is mad since I barely know the woman.'

'You had sex with her.'

'What? No. How would you…? Why would you—?'

'Deny it all you want, but you will not convince me you did not have sex with her. That is the only reason neutralising her would be impossible for you.'

Andrew was not about to tell Gabriel what he did or did not do with Charlotte. 'I've become compromised. I'm a danger to this organisation. She has me at sixes and sevens, and I don't know what my instincts are where she is concerned.' If he was to be completely honest with Gabriel he would tell him his instincts were screaming at him to head back to Charlotte.

'What is her name?'

'Lady Charlotte Gregory.'

'Did you include her name in your report?'

'No. I don't believe she poses any threat.'

'I've just received a letter from Spence today. He is following up on those leads you gave me in Cheshire. Would you like me to confirm that he also did not find reason to concern ourselves with her?'

'I have already put her out of my mind.' It was a lie and thinking that he saw her today had not helped his mood.

From Gabriel's sceptical expression it came as no surprise when he took Andrew into his study, removed the paper from a locked box and looked it over. Andrew held his breath as Gabriel worked on the cypher of each name on the list.

Finally, he looked up at Andrew. 'Her name isn't mentioned, which means she has done nothing to warrant suspicion.'

Andrew dropped into one of the upholstered chairs by the unlit hearth, his muscles weak with the news. 'Thank you, but you did not have to look for me. It no longer matters.'

'You mean she no longer matters.'

'It's all the same.'

Gabriel flicked his tailcoat and sat down across from Andrew. 'You did the right thing by leaving. It was better to err on the side of caution. Knowing your limits is the sign of a good agent.'

'Not having limits is the sign of a good agent.'

'Is that what has been bothering you all this time? You are one of the finest agents I have. Do not concern yourself with leaving her. You provided us with useful information.' He leaned forward on his elbows and grinned. 'Even when you weren't supposed to.'

Chapter Twelve

Andrew spent most of the morning in the ring with his partner Jackson. The physical exertion felt good and exhausting. His plan was to return home and try to sleep. Most nights he didn't sleep well. If he could work his body hard enough in the morning, he could immediately go home and sleep for five hours. That was more than he would get when he went to bed at night. Now his muscles were soft and pliable from the long sparring match and he was grateful another morning had gone by where he could find some sense of peace in the ring.

The hair on the back of his neck was still damp with sweat as he stepped from the brick building on to Bond Street. A pair of gentlemen was heading inside and they tipped their hats to him before he turned and made his way towards Piccadilly.

He held in a yawn as he adjusted the brim

of his hat to block out the sun on this unusually sunny day. Walking at a leisurely pace, he made his way past the iceman's cart before almost walking into the gentleman in front of him because of the sight ahead. A woman dressed in lavender with a fashionable bonnet that obstructed the view of her face was peering into a shop window. She clutched an embroidered reticule in front of her. He recognised that reticule. Charlotte had carried one just like that during the fair. He had mistaken the Duchess of Skeffington for her once before. But now, studying the way this woman moved, he was almost certain this was Charlotte.

He approached her, wanting to know for sure. His stomach was jumping around so much, it felt as if he were still boxing. The lady was standing in front of a milliner's shop. Various hats were visible through the clean glass windowpanes. The brim of her bonnet continued to obscure his view. His uncertainty lifted the moment a soft breeze blew along Bond Street and he caught a whiff of that light floral scent of Charlotte's.

She appeared intent on the contents of the window display and didn't even bother glancing his way when he had stepped up to her side on the pretext of admiring the hats as well. What should he say to her? What did one say to a woman you had had sex with and then never bothered to say goodbye to?

Approaching her was a mistake. He should have pretended he hadn't seen her and moved on. In all likelihood, they never would cross paths again. But while he was free to walk away now before she realised he was there, he couldn't.

What could have brought Charlotte to London? According to Mrs Knightly, she very rarely ventured outside the county. Six weeks and three days had passed since he had last seen her, yet standing beside her now it felt like yesterday.

'Charlotte, I do hope you're feeling better and—'

The sound of the Duchess of Skeffington's voice made the hair on his arms stand up. He was very close to telling her to leave him alone and stop following him, when he realised she hadn't been speaking to him. She had been addressing Charlotte.

'Lord Andrew?' the Duchess exclaimed, evidently just as surprised to see him as he was to see her.

He peered around the back of the woman beside him to the Duchess's eager expression. How in the world were the two women acquainted? At the mention of his name, Charlotte looked his way. The colour drained from her face and her eyes widened. If he was at a loss as to what to say to her before, having the Duchess standing with them had turned him mute.

The Duchess, on the other hand, had no problem speaking. 'Lord Andrew, what a pleasant surprise to see you here. One never knows who one will run into on Bond Street. Lady Charlotte Gregory, may I introduce you to Lord Andrew Pearce. Lord Andrew, may I present my sister Lady Charlotte.'

Sister? Sister! How was it possible someone as lovely and discreet as Charlotte could have the Duchess of Skeffington for a sister?

Charlotte was still staring at him as if she had seen a ghost. There was a distinct possibility she had grown even paler than when she had first turned and laid eyes on him.

He gave a polite bow to both of them and caught Charlotte's eye as he straightened up. Her discomfort in the situation was evident in her expression and the way she was fiddling with the handle of her reticule. Apparently, she hadn't told her sister about him. And by the way he left without saying goodbye, he probably should be grateful. If she had said anything, it probably wouldn't have been complimentary.

'We've been introduced,' he replied in the most even tone he could muster.

The proper thing to do would have been to allow Charlotte the prerogative of revealing that they had met before. However, seeing her here and knowing their time together hadn't even warranted a mere mention to her sister was picking at his pride and he wasn't in the mood to be proper about anything at the moment.

The Duchess appeared startled by his admission that they were acquainted. 'You've met? But how? My sister has just arrived in London.' She turned to Charlotte. 'How could you not tell me?' It almost sounded like an accusation.

'I didn't know that you and Lord Andrew were acquainted.' Charlotte's forehead wrinkled. 'Had I been aware when I met him, I would have taken that into account and included the detail in one of my letters.'

'How is it possible that you did not know Lord Andrew—?' The Duchess bit her lip and looked away. Whatever she intended to say about him, she clearly didn't want him to hear.

Charlotte appeared just as confused by the Duchess's odd reaction as he was. Looking at the two women standing side by side, he noticed a resemblance. It was easy to see how he could have mistaken the Duchess for Charlotte. They both were rather tall with long curves and they both had black hair and similar facial features. But while the Duchess's eyes were brown, Charlotte's were a mossy green.

Those eyes were still narrowed on her sister. 'Lord Andrew is a friend of Toby's and had been staying with the Knightlys. We met when Ann invited me for dinner.' If she was hurt by his leaving abruptly without a word, he could not tell.

She looked down and adjusted her gloves. 'I hope your travels back to London were safe and uneventful, Lord Andrew.' They were the first words she had spoken to him since she bade him goodnight under the stars outside her home. And they were said with the bland politeness of one who was barely acquainted with him. He could almost believe that he had imagined being inside her on the grassy hill, with fireworks exploding in the distance.

Almost.

His trousers tightened, reminding him how incredible she had felt. He cleared his throat and waited for her to look up at him. 'My travels were uneventful, thank you. I'd planned to stay another week in Cheshire, but needed to return to London urgently.' It offered no real excuse as to why he hadn't said goodbye, but it was all he could think of to say at that moment.

She seemed to search his eyes. Could she tell that she was the reason he left?

'I do hope your family are well, Lord Andrew,' the Duchess broke in, pulling both he and Charlotte out of their own thoughts as they both suddenly recalled she was standing with them.

'They are, thank you.' For once he was grateful for the Duchess's presence so that he didn't make a fool out of himself by continuing to offer

Charlotte some convoluted explanation as to why he had suddenly left without a word to her. There was no reasonable explanation.

'Then it wasn't an illness in your family that called you home so urgently,' Charlotte asked with an arched brow.

'No. There was an urgent business matter that needed my attention,' he replied, falling back on the vague excuse he used whenever he needed to leave somewhere because he was called away on some mission to protect the Crown.

'It must have been very urgent,' Charlotte said, 'for you to leave so quickly.'

'It was.'

'And what kind of business are you involved in, Lord Andrew?' she asked. 'Younger sons are typically military men or clergymen. But you are neither. To my knowledge, you never served our country. Pray tell, how does a man who has not chosen to sacrifice himself for his country spend his time, my lord?'

Oh, she wasn't pleased with him. That sharp comment served a direct hit.

The Duchess of Skeffington came to his defence before he had the chance to respond. 'Lord Andrew is involved in a number of establishments here in London. His investments have made it possible for men to open businesses here and provide for their families. Not everyone needs to sacrifice themselves on the battle-field to improve society.'

The Duchess made his ability to throw capital at a number of men sound almost heroic. From the expression on Charlotte's face, she did not believe the actions were comparable. What would she think if she knew he frequently put his life in danger?

'Well, we would hate to think we were keeping you from your business now,' Charlotte said.

In her eyes, he could read what she probably wanted to say. *Scuttle along. My sister may find you an honourable man, but I do not.*

Acid burned in his gut.

He adjusted the brim of his hat, still astonished that he was standing beside Charlotte. The noise of the carriages and carts along the cobblestoned street was mixed with the voices of the people moving past them. Most everyone seemed to be in a hurry. And his head was telling him to flee as well—just leave and forget he had ever spoken to her.

But his legs wouldn't move.

The Duchess placed her gloved hand on Charlotte's sleeve, preventing her sister from turning away. 'I assume you are coming from Jackson's, Lord Andrew. I have heard how much you enjoy boxing. May we give you a ride to your destination? My carriage is just over there.' She gestured to the highly polished black barouche with the Skeffington crest on the door that had pulled up a few feet away.

Being in the closed confines of a carriage with Charlotte was the last thing he needed at the moment. 'Thank you, but my home is a short walk from here.'

The bright smile on her face slipped before it was back again, giving her an almost childlike enthusiasm. 'Do give my best to your family.'

He glanced at Charlotte, who it appeared was finding the hats in the shop window much more interesting than their current conversation. It was just as well he would be home soon. All that time in the ring this morning was for nothing. The muscles in his neck and shoulders were stiff. A good hot bath would help ease the pain.

Pasting on a polite smile, he addressed the Duchess, since she was the only one who appeared interested in anything he had to say. 'I will give them your best, Your Grace,' he replied with a tip of his hat. 'Ladies, I bid you a good day.'

'Good day, Lord Andrew,' the Duchess said, lowering her chin in a coy manner.

Charlotte continued to study the shop window, but managed to grace him with the lift of her hand over her shoulder in a parting gesture. He would hate for her to strain herself by turning around to face him and say a proper goodbye.

With a clipped motion, he stormed around

them and down Bond Street. The sound of his boots hitting the pavement mixed with the sounds of the street around him.

Charlotte waited until she could no longer see Andrew's reflection in the shop window before she turned around. Summoning up all her determination, she refused to watch him make his way through the crowd of people.

'Well, that was unexpected,' Lizzy said from beside her as she adjusted her bonnet with a smile so wide it would be a miracle if her face didn't hurt for a week.

Unexpected was an understatement. Seeing Andrew was so unexpected, it had practically brought Charlotte to her knees. She was aware he lived in London, but London was a very big city—surely big enough that she would never run into him. She should never have agreed to come to Town to visit Lizzy. Her sister would not have been surprised if she had declined the invitation.

Lizzy had written to her and asked her to come to Town because Skeffington's heir had been found. It might be weeks before he finally reached London, but she wanted Charlotte with her when she met him for the first time. Lizzy appeared to the world to be self-assured, but Charlotte knew her sister was afraid the new Duke would be as horrid as the old and she knew he could make her life difficult if he so chose. Lizzy needed her. She could not say no. Their father had signed away Lizzy to a decrepit duke for his own gains. Lizzy had no protector. She never had. Charlotte felt she should be there to look out for her now.

'Why did you not tell me you had met Winterbourne's brother?'

'Because I have not.'

'Yes, you have. Lord Andrew is the Duke of Winterbourne's brother.'

Oh, dear God, no! Andrew was the man Lizzy had been pining for since she was seventeen? Suddenly the ground did not feel as solid as it had a few moments before.

'Charlotte, what is wrong?' Lizzy asked with concern in her voice. 'When you said you needed to step outside for some air, I thought you were weary of waiting for me and were offering an excuse. But you truly are unwell. Come, let's get you into the carriage and you can sit. It was unfair of me to prolong our conversation with Lord Andrew, but I've never witnessed him so agreeable.' She took Charlotte by the elbow and walked slowly with her to the carriage. 'Do take care assisting her ladyship,' she instructed her footman as he lowered the carriage step for them.

As they settled on to the velvet cushions, Lizzy opened one of the windows. 'Perhaps some air from the moving carriage might help.'

Nothing was going to help. Her stomach rolled and she moved her body closer to the open window. In the event she would be sick, at least she could lean out of her sister's expensive carriage.

'You truly look green, Charlotte. If I knew you were feeling this poorly, we would have left right away. Instead you let me continue with my fitting while you silently suffered outside.'

Silently suffering was exactly what Charlotte was doing at the moment and it had little to do with her unsettled stomach. She rubbed her fingers against her eyelids. Dear God, not only had she let herself get carried away by her passions with a man she barely knew—she'd had sex with the only man her sister had ever wanted! She was the most horrid person in England!

Lizzy reached across the carriage and took one of Charlotte's hands. 'I assure you my house is not far, but should you think it best to stop the carriage, I can have my driver stop and we could just sit in here until you are feeling better.'

Better? Better? She was never going to feel better. From this day forward she would feel like the wretch she was. She couldn't look at her sister. She would never be able to look Lizzy in the eyes again. 'I think it best if we continue on to your home without stopping.' The sooner they arrived at Lizzy's house, the sooner she could hide in her room. Then she would make arrangements to return to her home immediately without having to look at Lizzy again.

'You are certain?'

Charlotte nodded, pressing her fingers harder into her eyelids. 'I will be fine.' Not even if she scrubbed herself with soap fifty times would she feel the slightest bit better.

She heard, rather that saw, the impatient rat-tat-tat tapping of Lizzy's boots as she sat across from Charlotte. Her sister was never one for patience and it wasn't long before she broached the topic Charlotte was praying she had somehow forgotten.

'Winterbourne's brother is acquainted with Toby and Ann, how extraordinary.'

Sickening was a more appropriate term. 'He went to Cambridge with Toby.'

'How did that never occur to me knowing they were the same age? But to think they were good enough friends that Lord Andrew would spend time at Knightly Hall all these years later. When did he arrive? How long did he stay?'

The rocking of the carriage was not helping her stomach. 'He visited with Toby at Knightly Hall not long after you left and stayed for about a week.'

'Just think, if only I had stayed...'

Oh, if only she had, none of this would have happened! Charlotte would possibly have met Andrew, but she would have known he was Winterbourne's brother and she would have never spent any significant time with him. She most certainly would not have had sex with him... under the stars, atop his soft brown coat, feeling as if she had been the centre of his world for just a little while.

'Stop the carriage.' If the carriage continued moving she was bound to lose the contents of her stomach.

Her sudden command startled Lizzy. 'What? Oh, of course.' Her sister rapped on the roof and instructed her driver to find somewhere to pull the carriage to a stop.

Luckily for Charlotte, they were near a London square and within a few minutes the carriage was parked under the shade of some trees. Lizzy opened the other window to get a cross-breeze through the confining space while Charlotte rested the back of her head on the well-cushioned velvet seat, taking in deep breaths.

'Is there anything I can do to help you feel better?' Lizzy asked.

Find another man to set your sights on.

It wasn't as if Lord Andrew was all that wonderful. He wasn't. Not really. He was especially lacking in consideration, as evident by the way he left prematurely without informing her of his hasty departure or having the decency to say goodbye. She had no experience with brief liaisons, but she was certain words of 'goodbye' and 'it's been lovely' where normally uttered.

She eyed Lizzy through half-opened eyes. 'I know that you are partial to Lord Andrew—'

'I adore the man.'

Charlotte lifted her head. 'Yes, yes, well, you think you do, but how well do you really know him? What do you know of his sense of honour? It's possible he is one of those men who think only of themselves and gives little consideration to those around them. You yourself have told me on more than one occasion that the man is typically in ill humour and uncommunicative. That there is a coldness about him. How would that make for a pleasant marriage?'

'I said he keeps himself at a distance from the world and with the proper woman by his side he would not appear to be so cold and brooding.'

'Men do not change who they are for the women they are with. That is a false romantic notion. From the first moment you meet them, men exhibit exactly who they are. There is no hidden depth to them. You cannot change a person's nature.'

'I have no wish to change him.'

Lizzy had once told her that she wondered if the Duke of Winterbourne's brother had remained a bachelor because he was partial to her and knew Skeffington was old and was waiting for him to die. Could that be true? She should have thought to ask him why he had never married. While it was a deeply personal question, they had done deeply personal things together.

'What do you think of him, Charlotte?'

'Who?'

'Winterbourne's brother?'

'Why do you do that?' she shot back unexpectedly. 'Why do you always refer to people by their status in society? Why couldn't you have just called him Lord Andrew Pearce? Even now, you can't use his name!'

Her outburst startled Lizzy who, for the first time in ages, appeared to be struck mute.

'If only you had told me his name… If only you had referred to him as Lord Andrew Pearce when you discussed him with me, I would have known he was the man you were attached to when I met him. I would not have treated him as some unimportant bachelor from London who went to visit his friend in the countryside!'

'If you were short with him or not overly agreeable, I'm sure it can be rectified should he express romantic intentions towards me in the future. You needn't worry that you will have ruined any chance I have with him.'

Charlotte leaned her forehead on the window frame and sucked in air, needing to hold in the bile that was threatening to escape. After a few deep breaths, her stomach settled. 'You said he barely speaks. How do you know he is not like

Skeffington? It is distinctly possible you would be just as miserable with him as you were with the Duke.'

'Toby would not be friends with him if he was anything like Skeffington. And why are you in such a foul mood with me? I understand you are feeling poorly, but you are being rather waspish.'

Feeling poorly was a vast understatement to how Charlotte was feeling at that moment. Dropping her head back, she closed her eyes. She could not go back in time. She could not undo what had been done, as much as she wished she could. Lizzy's future happiness was paramount. Charlotte had had a happy marriage. Her sister deserved one as well.

She needed to find a way to make certain that what happened between her and Andrew did not interfere with Lizzy's chances with the man. He had appeared rather shocked to find out they were sisters. The idea of having sex with two sisters must have been unsettling to say the least. It was appalling to her. However, he hadn't made any attempt to contact her and he had left the Knightlys so quickly after their liaison that it was apparent their time together was something that meant nothing to him. He might not even remember it.

Lizzy must never find out what happened between them. The only way was if Charlotte left London and never returned. When Skeffington was alive, she barely saw her sister. If, by chance, Lizzy did marry Andrew, she would find a way to avoid seeing both of them for the rest of her life. They could live together happily and she would live out her years in her cottage—alone.

Her stomach rolled again. She certainly didn't want Andrew. Her heart belonged to Jonathan. But if she was being honest with herself, she didn't want Lizzy to have Andrew either.

She was a horrible, horrible person.

If Lizzy had any chance at finding happiness with the man, Charlotte needed to leave London as quickly as possible. It might also help her put this entire mess out of her mind. It wouldn't be easy. She had been thinking about Andrew a lot since she'd returned to London. While home, she purposely avoided walking through the woods at Oakwood Hall for fear she would find herself up on the hill that held so many memories—memories that she would like to forget, but knew no matter how hard she tried, she never would.

'Let's get you home,' Lizzy said, patting her hand. 'A cup of mint tea may settle your stomach.'

All the mint tea in the world wouldn't fix what Charlotte was feeling. As they rode back to Lizzy's house, she tried to think of a reasonable explanation as to why she needed to return home. Their sister Juliet was supposed to arrive in London today with their Aunt Clara. Lizzy

wouldn't have to be alone when she met Skeffington's heir. If all went well, Charlotte could
leave London by nightfall. Then she could try to
put this horrid mistake behind her and her sister
would be free to pursue Lord Andrew.

Chapter Thirteen

The knock on her bedchamber door was so soft, Charlotte almost didn't hear it. She had informed Lizzy she thought it best if she were to return to Cheshire because of how poorly she was feeling. Juliet or Aunt Clara could accompany her to meet the new Duke. But Lizzy insisted that all Charlotte needed was rest. How would she ever fall sleep again with the weight of her actions hanging over her? Lizzy said they would revisit her leaving in the morning. Charlotte didn't want to revisit it. She just wanted to leave. The morning light would not change what she had done to her beloved sister.

Another soft knock followed the first and she threw aside her covers and sat up in bed. There was no sense in prolonging the inevitable and she called for Lizzy to enter her room.

The heavy wooden door opened slowly, but instead of Lizzy, her sister Juliet walked into her room, carrying a cup and saucer. The surprising sight was enough of a relief that it almost brought Charlotte to tears.

'Lizzy told me you were feeling poorly and I offered to bring this tea up to you. I hope you do not mind.'

Once Juliet placed the tea on the table by her bed, Charlotte threw her arms around her for a tight hug. A small bit of comfort washed over her. They settled together, side by side on the bed, like they usually did when Juliet visited Charlotte's house before she retired to her bed-chamber and turned in for the night. Juliet was ten years younger than Charlotte and they had spent a lot of time together over the years, even before both their parents passed away in rapid succession of consumption eleven years ago. Just sitting next to Juliet in their usual fashion was making Charlotte feel a bit better, as if somehow things could go back to the way they had been before she met Andrew.

'When did you arrive in Town?' Charlotte asked, reaching for the teacup.

'Aunt Clara and I arrived this morning. Luckily no one is leasing her town house at the moment. It was a long journey from France and it's lovely being able to stop in London on our way home. We were both eager to see Lizzy and were thrilled when she left word that you were in Town as well. Our aunt suggested we settle in before we sent our cards around, but I was so eager to see you both, I could not wait for Aunt Clara to finish writing her letters and left as soon as I could.'

'How is she?'

'From the moment I began living with her I came to realise she has more tolerance for constant activity than I ever will. You should have seen her in Paris. There were many nights I wished to leave a ball or rout and she insisted we stay just one more hour.' Juliet took Charlotte's hand in hers. 'I wish we could have been here for Lizzy when Skeffington died, but knowing you were here to support her through it all was a comfort to the both of us. You always have been the best of sisters.'

She might have been months ago, but now she was the worst. If only she hadn't decided to watch the fireworks that night. If only she had left when Ann and Toby did.

Juliet broke into her thoughts. 'Lizzy informed us that Skeffington's will stipulates all parties mentioned need to be present before it can be read and they have finally located his heir.'

'They are just waiting for him to make his way to Town from the Continent.'

'Why do you think Skeffington made that stipulation?'

'I suppose he wanted to exert his control over the proceedings even from the grave.'

'He was a horrid man, was he not? I had two Seasons in London...two, because I could not bear having him dictate who I was allowed to dance with and speak to.' A faraway look crossed her face before it was replaced with obvious disdain. 'Lizzy tried to intercede on my behalf regarding a few of the gentlemen who I thought appealing, but he insisted I was not to associate with anyone who was less than an earl and they had to be from only a certain set of families. He really had little use for those below him.'

'I gathered as much over the years. Why did you not ask me to chaperon you?'

'The grief of losing Jonathan was too fresh. You were not in the ideal humour to be a chaperon to me in a city you are not fond of. And I did have Aunt Clara to help with my second Season. Please do not tell Lizzy, but I was so relieved when Aunt Clara told Skeffington she'd like me to live with her as her companion. Living with him was so oppressing, especially during my first Season.'

'I wish Father would have made Jonathan your guardian, but I suppose an army officer who is away for months at a time is not an ideal guardian.'

'I enjoyed my time with Lizzy. It was only when Skeffington was around that I wanted to spend most of my time in my room. He was the surliest man I know.'

'I can't imagine Aunt Clara being easily swayed by Skeffington's wishes during your second Season,' Charlotte mused with a smile.

'She wasn't. However, it appeared most of the gentlemen of the *ton* had been advised to give me a wide berth at most of the entertainments I attended. I do believe I was not a sufficient enough temptation to risk Skeffington's displeasure,' she spat with obvious disgust at these men from the past.

'Why do I not remember any of this?'

'Because you were dealing with your own grief.'

'I'm sorry, Juliet. Every girl should have a glorious Season. It's not too late. You are only two and twenty.'

'But now I find I much prefer life in Bath with our aunt. There is enough to keep me entertained there with a well-stocked rotation of young men into the area to keep it interesting.'

'I always thought Aunt Clara would be a terrible influence on you,' Charlotte said through a teasing smile. 'Do not allow any of those young men to lead you astray. I trust you to use good judgement in your actions.' The hypocrisy of her words burned in Charlotte's stomach. She should not be lecturing anyone about moral fortitude. Not now.

'You have nothing to fear. I will not be falling for the pretty words of a gentleman and going off behind closed doors with one. Our Aunt Clara might be adventurous, but she has reinforced certain rules of decorum with me far too many times to count.'

If only Charlotte had paid attention to those words, she would be better off right now. But it wasn't a closed door that was her undoing— it was being with Andrew...on a hill...in the grounds of a neighbour's park. She needed to stop thinking about it and try to forget it ever happened. She needed to stop thinking about *him*.

'You looked flushed. Are you still feeling poorly?'

Charlotte stood and walked towards the window. Looking through the branches of the trees, she watched men walking in pairs and by themselves on the gravel pathways of Green Park. As she toyed with the handle of the cup in her hand, the open green space reminded her how much she missed her home.

'Drink some tea, Charlotte. It should help to settle your stomach. I know it helps when I have pains during my monthly courses.'

The teacup slipped from Charlotte's hand and broke into pieces on the wooden floor. Juliet jumped off the bed and rushed to her sister, who was now shaking uncontrollably.

'What is it? What is wrong?' She pried the saucer out of Charlotte's left hand and placed it on the writing table beside them. 'Sit back on the bed. We can ring for the maid later. It was insensitive of me to go on so and force conversation when you aren't well.' Gently, she guided Charlotte by the elbow to the edge of the tester bed and pulled her so that once again they were sitting side by side.

This could not be happening. Her courses had always been very regular. Every thirty days they would begin. She always knew the exact date. But she hadn't bled since before she met Andrew. How had it escaped her notice?

Ten years she had been married to Jonathan. Ten. And even though he had been away on a number of military campaigns during those ten years, when he had been home she had never conceived a child. When Lizzy married and also bore no children, they assumed it was because of some physical condition in their family that prevented both of them from conceiving. Could she have been wrong? Oh, heavens, he had told her he could prevent this very thing. And she had told him there was no need. This was all her fault.

'Charlotte, you are frightening me. You are shaking and I've never seen you this pale. I'm going to have Lizzy summon a physician.'

As she stood, Charlotte pulled her down by her arm.

'No. I'll be fine. Give me a moment. There is no need to alert Lizzy.'

It was impossible to swallow. There was a lump in her throat the size of an apple.

'Shall I fetch you more tea?' Juliet looked almost as panicked as Charlotte felt.

Blocking everything out as best she could, Charlotte closed her eyes and tried to recall the last time she had bled…and came back with the same date, which was two weeks before she met Andrew. Her hand instinctively went to her stomach. Could she have been walking around all this time with his child inside her? How was it possible she hadn't realised it until now?

'I'm going to fetch you a glass of sherry. It might not help your stomach, but it should help with your tremors.'

Charlotte grabbed her wrist. 'Don't leave me.'

Juliet's eyes widened. Charlotte had always been emotionally strong and stoic. She was the oldest Sommersby. It was her responsibility to care for her younger sisters. Even immediately after Jonathan's loss, she shut herself away from the world rather than allow herself to be comforted by others. In solitude, she found her strength.

Except this time. This time the thought of being alone was terrifying.

The pressure of Juliet's hand on hers was her anchor. She would concentrate on her sister's warmth. If only she could absorb the calmness of her sister at this moment, she could stop shaking. When Juliet slipped her arm around Charlotte's shoulders, the comfort became too much and Charlotte broke down in sobs.

'Please tell me what is troubling you, Charlotte. I need to know how I can help you.'

How could she tell Juliet what had happened? How could she admit to being a wanton? Juliet would never understand how she could have given in so easily to her passion with a man she barely knew. Her sister would never look at her the same way again.

And yet, she could not go through this alone.

'I've done something so foolish, Juliet, and now I am to pay the price for it.'

'I'm certain whatever it is you said to Lizzy, she will forget it in a day or two. She told me how uncharacteristically sharp you were with her in her carriage today.'

'It is not that simple. I don't think Lizzy will ever forgive me.'

'Whatever did you say?'

Charlotte leaned forward and dropped her head in her hands. The thought of Juliet pulling away from her once she heard what Charlotte had done was giving her chills. 'Juliet, I think I'm with child.'

After receiving no response from her sister for what felt like hours, Charlotte glanced to see Juliet staring at her as if she had confessed everything to her sister in Italian.

'I don't understand. How is that possible? You always said you could never diminish your love for Jonathan by marrying again. You always said that no man could ever compare to him or turn your head. How can you be carrying a child?'

'I don't know what happened!' she replied with a choked sob. 'I met a man at home while he was visiting a friend. We spent a wonderful day together and that night he kissed me. And I didn't think about Jonathan. I didn't think about how it wasn't proper. I just knew that at that moment, I wanted him to kiss me.'

Juliet put her hand on Charlotte's back and began to softly rub her hand in circles. It was just what Charlotte would do to soothe Juliet when they were younger.

'You cannot be carrying his child from a kiss. Even I know that. You're certain you're with child? Is there a chance you are mistaken?'

'It hadn't occurred to me until you mentioned the tea helping with your monthly courses. I have not bled in six weeks.'

'Perhaps you are late.'

'I am never late.'

'This could be an anomaly.'

'It isn't.'

'Will you tell me his name?'

She closed her eyes and took a breath. 'Lord Andrew Pearce.'

'Lord Andrew Pearce?' Juliet's voice rose an octave before she was struck mute once more. Did she know Andrew was the only man Lizzy had wanted?

'Say something, Juliet.'

'Did he force himself on you? Is that what happened?'

'No. No. It was a kiss that, before either of us knew what was happening, turned into so much more. He asked if he should stop. He gave me time to say it wasn't what I wanted. He is not to blame.'

'The look in your eyes leads me to believe you liked being with him.'

'I did. Very much.' And even though he had left abruptly, she hadn't truly regretted what happened between them until today—until she brought scandal and pain to her family, and discovered she could not place those memories in a box and forget about them. Lying under the stars with Andrew that night had changed her life for ever. At the time, she had no idea how much her life would change—how much her actions would change all their lives.

Juliet rubbed her lower lip as she appeared to be pondering the ramifications of what it all meant. 'What will you do?' Her voice was slow and quiet, as one would talk to a skittish horse.

'I need to tell him.' There was no hesitation—no other option. 'He cares nothing for me and I am terrified of his reaction, but he needs to know. He needs to have the opportunity to give this child a name. Once he decides how he will proceed, then I will determine what I need to do next.' She was forming a list in her head. It was helping her feel as if she had a bit of control over this situation.

Considering that he might not ask her to marry him was making her body run cold. She would not beg him. She was too proud for that. However, the life of an unwed mother was not an easy one. She knew of one woman in her village who had moved away not long after the child was born. People could be cruel and children were an extra expense.

'You said you met when he was visiting a friend,' Juliet said, interrupting her depressing thoughts. 'Do you know where he lives? How will you send word to him?'

'He lives here in London. I saw him today when I was with Lizzy.'

'She may know how to get word to him. It seems, at times, she knows every member of the *ton* and she has been known to be rather resourceful.'

'Juliet, we can't tell her.'

'Why not? She loves you. This burden will be lessened if you share it with the both of us.'

'If he doesn't ask me to marry him, this burden will be our family's downfall. No man will want to marry you or Lizzy because of me—because of what I've done. Why are you calmly offering your help and not railing at me and calling me a trollop? How can I say that I hold my marriage to Jonathan so dear and then do what I have done? I've tarnished the memory of my life with him. What does that make me?'

'A woman who does not have one foot in the grave because she is living out her life counting the days until she can be reunited with her dead husband. Ever since Jonathan was killed, you've retreated to the past where you like to recount stories about your life with him. But that part of your life is over and you have many years yet to live…to really live. And if you have found a man who kissed you and made you feel that you wanted more, then I am happy to hear you might have more of life to enjoy. I will not desert you. I am here for you always.'

'When did you become so knowledgeable about human nature?'

'When you were busy telling yourself your life was over. What do you think he will do?'

'I do not know. He was truly lovely. But then he suddenly left the next day without informing me he was going. Perhaps he believed I would expect some declaration from him. That is not the action of a man who will want to have any kind of future with me.'

'He is a Pearce,' Juliet mumbled and looked down at her lap with a sigh. 'If he has an honourable bone in his body, he will ask you to marry him. It is possible something took him away from you that was out of his control. You are a caring, beautiful woman. Any man would be a fool not to want you for a wife.'

But what if he was meant for Lizzy? She had just destroyed her sister's chance at happiness. All of it was making Charlotte's head hurt.

'You need to tell Lizzy,' Juliet continued.

'I can't.'

'She will find out eventually. I don't think a baby is something that is easy to hide. Especially when they become fussy.'

'I can't tell her.'

'You're being unreasonable.'

'How much has she told you about her plans for marriage now that Skeffington is gone? About the man she has set her sights on?'

'She hasn't told me a thing. What man? Skeffington just died a few months ago.'

Burning heat crept up Charlotte's neck to her cheeks.

'Please don't say—'

'Since Skeffington's death, Lizzy has been telling me how she has wanted the Duke of

Winterbourne's brother since her debut. Lord Andrew Pearce is the Duke of Winterbourne's brother, which I would have known when I met him if she didn't have this fascination with titles and Society and she had simply told me his name.' It came out more forceful than she intended and her nails were digging into her palms, but she was starting to think Lizzy was almost as much at fault in this as she was.

Juliet rubbed her brow, as if she wanted to scrub away everything she had learned. Now she would understand why Lizzy must not find out. When Juliet's hand finally stilled, she looked at Charlotte. 'You still need to tell her.'

'What? Why? Can't I go back home without letting her know? I barely saw her these last few years. There is a good chance I will barely see her now. Perhaps there is a way I can hide this from her.'

'And should the Duke of Winterbourne's brother ask for your hand? What will you do then? Would you rather she read about your nuptials in the papers or hear it from your lips, where you can offer her some explanation, no matter how flimsy it might be to her? You cannot hide in your home for the rest of your life and lock yourself away from her. I think she will grow suspicious.'

'She will hate me. She will refuse to speak to me ever again.'

'You do not know that. I will not lie and tell you she will smile and wish you well. She won't. But she needs to hear about this from you and she needs to hear the truth. Above all else, you are her sister and she loves you. Give her a chance to be by your side should you suffer in scandal if Lord Andrew proves he is not an honourable man.'

'Should he not ask for my hand, we will all suffer in scandal because of me.' It came out a faint whisper. The sound of her voice was barely audible with the sound of her heart pounding in her ears. 'I will leave. I'll travel far away. Perhaps I shall go to America. In truth, I had no idea he was the Duke of Winterbourne's brother. I had no idea this was the man Lizzy wanted. If I had known, I would not have spent any time with him and would have been sure to have maintained a polite distance. I did not intend for any of this to happen.'

'Then that is what you will tell her.'

The tears started to fall again. This time without the breath-hitching sobs. 'I am afraid. I'm afraid of having this child. I'm afraid of what will happen to this family because of it. I'm afraid of losing the affection of our sister. And of what will happen when I tell Lord Andrew that I am carrying his child.'

'Your fears are justified, but the longer you wait, the stronger your fears will become. Do not allow them to take hold for very long. They may stop you from action.'

Wise words from someone Charlotte still thought of as being so young.

'Will you stay with me when I tell Lizzy? Your presence may help soften her pain.' Pain that she was going to inflict on her dearly loved sister.

'If you'd like. Let's put some water on your face and call for the maid to clean up the tea. Then we will go downstairs and face our sister together.'

Chapter Fourteen

Andrew had been soaking in his tub until the water had turned cold and his fingers were wrinkled. The coolness of the water was doing nothing for the stiffness in his muscles, but it was doing wonders to help with his body's reaction to seeing Charlotte again.

Since he'd returned to London, he had tried to push all thoughts of her out of his mind. But there were times on especially clear nights that as he walked home from White's or rode home from other various entertainments, he would glance up at the sky and memories of their time together on the hill would push their way into his head.

The feeling of being inside her was still fresh in his mind after all this time. It had been six weeks and he could still recall that delicious friction. If only they had found a bed, he could have explored every delicious inch of her slowly—

maybe more than once. After all this time, he still had a desire to.

Maybe that was why he had needed to find out if it was indeed her today looking in the window of that shop and why he had almost stopped breathing when he was standing next to her. She looked beautiful in her very proper bonnet. It might have been the same one she was wearing the day they spent together at the fair.

Andrew imagined her here in his set of rooms. He would remove that bonnet and her garments and feast upon her till they were both spent. How he wished he could hear her cry his name once more and touch her soft skin.

How long would she be in London? Was she staying at Skeffington House? That wasn't far from here. In fact, it wasn't far from White's, where he frequently dined and played cards. Had he passed her in the street at other times and not realised it? He wondered how she was and if she had thought about him at all.

During their short time together in Cheshire, she stirred feelings inside him that needed to be locked away for him to do his job effectively. A man who regularly placed himself in mortal danger was not a man who should form emotional attachments to any woman.

This was why it was dangerous for him to stop working. Gabriel was wrong. He didn't need time away. He needed to be constantly reminded that the world was comprised of ghastly people who wanted anarchy at any cost.

Just the notion that he needed to remind himself why he needed to live his life away from a woman who he had started to really care for told him that if he saw Charlotte in the future, he should just walk away. Lady Charlotte Gregory was a complication he did not need.

Charlotte held Juliet's hand as they stood just outside the doorway to the gold-and-white drawing room in Lizzy's home, as she gathered the courage to face her sister. Their conversation would probably be over quickly and, by this evening, Charlotte would know if her sister could forgive her. She let go of Juliet's hand, afraid she was crushing her sister's fingers.

'Are you ready?' Juliet whispered.

Squeezing her eyes shut, Charlotte took a breath. 'No, but I don't think I ever will be ready to do this.' As she placed her hand on her stomach, she drew up every ounce of courage she could muster and walked into the room.

The needlework Lizzy had been working on as she sat by the window fell to the floor as she hurried across the room and grabbed both of Charlotte's hands. 'You still look unwell. Will you let me summon a physician? It appears the tea did little to help. I have been so worried. I wanted to see if you were feeling better earlier today, but you were asleep. I hope you do not mind that I told Juliet you were unwell.'

'No, I don't mind.'

'Do you feel any better? Even a little bit?' Lizzy raised her brows hopefully.

'I believe I'm feeling worse.'

'Oh, heavens, do come and sit. Perhaps by the window where the breeze will reach you.'

But as Lizzy went to guide her towards her vacant seat, Charlotte held her ground. 'I'm with child.'

Juliet dropped her head down. 'I thought we agreed to broach this gently.'

'There is no gentle way to do this,' Charlotte replied.

Lizzy was staring at her with wide eyes. Her breathing was becoming more pronounced. 'Oh. Oh. I see. Oh.' She licked her lips and scrunched up her forehead before she continued. 'How is that possible?'

Charlotte swallowed the lump in her throat. 'I met someone. We let our passions overrule our judgement. It only happened once.'

'But you and I have discussed this. We cannot bear children.'

'Apparently, we can. I would have never been so careless if I thought this were possible.'

By the look on Lizzy's face she was trying hard to accept what she was hearing. 'It only happened once?' she mumbled, almost to herself.

'Just once.'

She met Charlotte's gaze with hope in her eyes. 'Then I might be able to bear children as well?'

'There is a distinct possibility.'

'Why did you not tell me sooner?'

'I just realised it when Juliet came to bring me tea.'

'Tea. Yes, that's what we need. We need tea. Aunt Clara always says important things should be discussed over tea.'

'Or sherry.' Juliet shrugged at the glare Charlotte gave her.

'I will go and ring for tea,' Lizzy said with excitement shining in her eyes. 'Why don't we sit by the hearth?'

Before Charlotte could confess that Andrew was the father of her child, Juliet gave her a gentle shove towards the two sofas that were facing one another. Charlotte perched herself on the very edge of one as Juliet sat down next to her and settled herself on the cushion.

When Lizzy sat across from her she appeared calm, like a woman who was ready to face a problem. 'Well, I assume you intend to inform the baby's father of this.'

The lump was back in Charlotte's throat. She would have to tell her. 'That is my intention.'

'Good. Do you believe him to be an honourable man?'

'Yes, I believe so.'

'Is he a bachelor?'

'Of course he is!'

'Well, under the circumstances, that is an important detail.' She reached across and grabbed Charlotte's hand. 'You will not go through this alone. Juliet and I will be by your side. Should this gentleman...he is a gentleman, is he not?'

'He is.'

Lizzy seemed to breathe a bit deeper. Who did she imagine the father was, one of Charlotte's footmen?

'Well, should this gentleman decide that he is not inclined to offer marriage, I'm sure there is something in his past we can uncover to entice him into making an offer.'

'Lizzy, I will not blackmail him into marriage!'

'That is such a harsh word. I prefer coax.'

Juliet slapped her hands on her knees. 'Oh, lud, just tell her, Charlotte.'

Lizzy eyed them both. 'Tell me what?'

'Who the father is,' Juliet replied on a rush of breath.

'I assume the man is from Cheshire.' She turned to Charlotte. 'Do I know him?'

Charlotte closed her eyes and rubbed her brow. 'Lizzy, why did you always refer to Lord Andrew only as Winterbourne's brother? Why did you never mention him by name?'

'Why ask me such a thing now? We should be discussing…' Her entire body stiffened.

Charlotte and Juliet sat perfectly still as they both anticipated the approaching storm.

'Tell me it is not so.'

'Lizzy—'

'Tell me you did not seduce Lord Andrew.'

The nerve of her sister! 'I did not seduce him. There was a mutual attraction. He was just as eager for it as I was.'

The storm clouds were settling in Lizzy's eyes.

'Might not be helping,' Juliet whispered from the side of her mouth.

'Had I known he was the man that you had set your sights on, I never would have spent any time alone with him.'

'You should not be spending time alone with any man.'

'You think I don't know that! We were at a fair, with friends and neighbours around us.'

'And yet you managed to somehow conceive a child. You said he had stayed with Toby and Ann for only a very short while.'

'He did. We barely spent time together.'

'Apparently you did spend enough time together.' Her hands balled into fists. 'How could you do this to me?' she cried. 'How could you betray me like this? You have had everything you've ever wanted. You got to marry the man you loved. You had a happy marriage with a man who loved and respected you. I was forced to marry a man older than our father who was a wretch and cared nothing for me. You got to try to have a child with a young man. I had to endure the grunts and groans of a disgusting old one.'

Juliet visibly shuddered, and Lizzy stood up, pointing her finger at Charlotte.

'You had every bit of happiness God could bestow on a person. I had none of it. And now, now when I am finally rid of that beast and there is one man in all of England—one man—that I want and think will make me happy, you find a way to get that bit of happiness, too?'

What did Lizzy know about Charlotte's happiness? 'You think I'm happy about this?' she bit back. 'You speak of the happiness I had, but you forget, Sister, of the loss. I was happy with Jonathan. I did love him and he loved me. But God took him from me that day on the battlefield. He never came home. I never saw his body. He is buried in some grave, they tell me, with others he served with. Even in death we will not be together. And I never got to say goodbye to him!' She covered her mouth with her hand to hold back her cries. 'You think I want this? You think I want any of it? This baby is not his. It belongs to a man I do not love—that I barely know. I do not want to marry Lord Andrew, but I know that is what this world demands I do. I have no choice in this. I had one perfect marriage and destroyed the memory of it on one foolish night.' It was hard to catch her breath, it all came out so suddenly.

'Get out.'

Charlotte's heart crashed to the floor. 'What?'

'Lizzy, you don't mean that,' Juliet said, standing up at her oldest sister's side and threading her fingers through Charlotte's icy hand.

'I do mean it. I want you out of my house, Charlotte. I don't need you here. I will meet Skeffington's heir without you. I can do that on my own. I don't want to see you any more.'

There was a finality to her words that sounded as if she meant for ever. 'Lizzy, I never meant for any of this to happen. Had I known Lord Andrew was Winterbourne's brother—'

'But it no longer matters now. You will have him and I will not. You will make a lovely family together. I just never want to witness it. I'm going out into the garden. By the time I come back inside, I expect you to be gone from my home.'

Charlotte's heart was still down by her feet, but now it felt hollow inside. She loved Lizzy and the thought of losing her sister was breaking her heart.

'Lizzy, Charlotte needs us. Can you not see that? Can you not see that we are all she has?'

'She has Lord Andrew. That is what I see.' And with that she stormed out of the room.

Charlotte's knees gave way as she sank to the sofa, covering her mouth to muffle her sobs. How had her life fallen apart like this in just a few short hours?

Juliet sat beside her and put her arm around her shoulders. 'She will not feel this way for ever.'

Charlotte wasn't convinced of that. 'I cannot go back home. Not now, not until I have spoken to Andrew. Where will I go?'

'You will come with me to Aunt Clara's house. You can stay with us.'

'I don't want to have to tell Aunt Clara. This is all so humiliating.'

'Aunt Clara has seen so much in her lifetime. I'm sure, while she will be surprised, she will also have advice on what to do and how you can contact Lord Andrew. Come, we will go up to your bedchamber and you can call for Violet to help you pack. Then you will go with me back to our aunt's.'

They arrived on the stone steps of Aunt Clara's Mayfair town house an hour later. The terraced brick building looked very much like all the other homes on the street and exactly the way Charlotte remembered it from her childhood when she would visit her aunt and her uncle Robert, who was her father's younger brother. As they walked into the entrance hall, they were met with the scent of roses coming from a large vase on the highly polished table by the staircase. Ever since she was little, Charlotte equated the smell of roses with her aunt—either she or her homes always smelled of them.

'It appears Aunt Clara has been out in the garden trimming the rose bushes while I've been gone.'

'I grew bored of waiting for you to return.' Their aunt's voice carried from the top of the staircase. 'I had to occupy myself somehow after I finished all my correspondence.' Aunt Clara walked slowly down the stairs, holding the skirt of her emerald-green silk gown in her hands. 'It's so lovely to see you again, Charlotte.' There was nothing quite like an Aunt Clara hug. She enveloped you in her soft arms and you were magically transported back to being a ten-year-old. You almost expected her to slip you a sweet when she let you go. Except now the top of her petite aunt's head rested under Charlotte's chin and her brown hair was tucked into a fashionable lace cap. If only she could spend the next nine months being held by her aunt...

'I have invited Charlotte to stay with us here,' Juliet said through a rigid smile. Watching her older sisters argue hadn't been easy for her.

Aunt Clara's brow wrinkled a bit before she

acted as if it was commonplace for Charlotte to leave Lizzy's home to stay with them. 'That means that I get to spend even more time with the both of you in London. How delightful! And how lucky for us that Lord Henry had to break his lease on this house and flee to America over shooting Lord Overton in that duel. Has Skeffington's heir arrived already and taken possession on the house?'

'No, not yet,' Charlotte replied, taking off her spencer with unsteady hands.

'Why don't you girls come into the drawing room and we can have some tea. Then you can tell me what has brought Charlotte to my door for this happy occasion.'

They sat down in the well-appointed celery-green sunlit room and within fifteen minutes Charlotte had told their aunt all about the child and her argument with Lizzy. Aunt Clara listened without interrupting, sipping her tea and occasionally nodding. In one instance, she handed over her napkin so Charlotte could blow her nose and dry her eyes.

Like a general preparing for battle, Aunt Clara put together a strategy for how Charlotte could reach Andrew. 'No women are allowed into the building where he resides,' she explained. 'You would never be able to visit him there, not that propriety is all that crucial at this moment.'

'I thought I'd send him a note to request we

meet somewhere of his choosing. I don't know London, but I'm sure we could find somewhere to meet and talk. A park or a church might do.'

'And if he does not respond?' Aunt Clara shook her head. 'This matter needs to be settled quickly so no one is the wiser. We will not have you standing in a church marrying the man when it is obvious to all that you are carrying his child.'

'You speak as if he will ask for my hand, but I'm not convinced he will. We barely know one another.' She covered her face with her hands to hide her embarrassment.

'That is not a requirement for marriage, my dear. If it were, half the marriages of the *ton* would not have happened. A marriage of convenience is nothing to be ashamed of. I know you married for love once, but now it will be different. If you are fortunate, you and Lord Andrew will lead separate lives and only see one another when it's time to conceive another child.'

It sounded so cold and impersonal. What was to become of her and this child? The events of the day had unfolded so quickly she hadn't had time to think about the baby as more than an enormous hindrance to her quiet life.

She was going to have a child and be a mother. It had been years since she had thought that would be possible. Resting her hand on her stomach, she tried to feel something, anything that let her know it was in there. Aside from a slight gurgle of her stomach, she didn't feel a thing. She had wanted a child with Jonathan. She had prayed for a child with him. But it never happened. Why was she going to have one now? And why with Andrew?

Chapter Fifteen

It was mid-morning and Andrew could have gone another round in the ring, but Jackson had convinced him that after three hours of exerting himself in some form or another, his body needed rest. Although Andrew would admit to being physically exhausted, his mind would not stop working as his thoughts continued to turn to Charlotte. It was only during the last few hours that he had found some peace in the concentration that was required to avoid getting knocked out by his opponent. Perhaps now he could get some rest.

Exiting Jackson's saloon, he looked up at the thick grey clouds above Bond Street and adjusted the collar on his brown-linen coat. He was just about to turn down the street towards Piccadilly when a woman's soft voice called out his name.

Standing in front of an unmarked black carriage parked at the curb was a well-dressed petite woman around his mother's age. Past the brim of her red bonnet was a pair of keen assessing dark eyes. She obviously knew who he was—however, he could not recall ever having seen her before. Her right hand rested on a gold-tipped walking stick and he wondered if, like his, it served more than one purpose. She seemed harmless enough, but he knew from experience that one could never be too careful.

The footman that stood beside her in pale blue livery remained by the carriage as she took a few slow steps closer to Andrew. 'You are Lord Andrew Pearce, are you not?'

He tipped the brim of his hat in a cautious greeting. 'I am. However, you have the advantage, madam. I do not know who you are.'

'I am Mrs Robert Sommersby. You and I have a mutual acquaintance.'

'We do?'

Without elaborating, she nodded and looked up. 'I notice the sky is rather grey. There is a strong possibility a storm is on the way.'

'So it would seem.'

People walked between them, too busy with their own business to pay attention to their conversation.

'May I interest you in a ride to your destination to save you the inconvenience?' She was speaking in a pleasant enough manner, but threats could be hidden in sweet voices.

He eyed her walking stick again and his muscles tightened, preparing for the unexpected. 'And if I decline your kind invitation?'

'Then you risk getting caught in a downpour,' she replied as if that would be an obvious conclusion. 'My driver is quite adept at handling Town roads and I assure you my carriage is quite comfortable.'

Not one to shy away from intrigue, Andrew stepped closer. When he was about two feet from her, she glanced at her footman and lowered her head. He opened the carriage door.

The curtains inside were closed, so it was nearly impossible to see into the darkened interior. He sensed movement as one of the curtains was pushed aside. Through the now-dim light he spied Charlotte, looking a bit uncertain.

Who was Mrs Sommersby and how did she know that he knew Charlotte? He glanced down at Charlotte's gloved hands and released a breath when he saw they were not bound.

'What is this about?' he demanded of Mrs Sommersby in a low voice.

If anyone was planning on harming Charlotte, they would have to get through him.

'Now, my lord,' the woman said in a sweet tone, 'the storm seems to be approaching and I have some shopping to do. Won't you take my carriage?'

It appeared she was giving him a choice. He

didn't know what she would do if he declined. Eyeing Charlotte, he rubbed the handle of his walking stick. If he didn't get into the carriage, he would be cursing himself for it tonight. He gave a nod to the footman, indicating the man should lower the step.

'That's better,' the mysterious woman said. 'I believe you will have an extraordinary ride. Good day, Lord Andrew.'

He tipped his hat to her, but his attention was now firmly fixed on Charlotte.

Placing his boot on the bottom step to the carriage, he leaned inside. Charlotte's attention was fixed on the ring she wore around her neck. Once he was settled across from her, the footman closed the door with a click. The carriage smelled faintly of roses, and the light streaming in from the small gap in the curtain gave a little illumination with which to see each other. It felt intimate. In order to think of a way to get Charlotte out, he needed to change that.

'Have they harmed you?' he asked, scanning her form for any indication of restraint or injury.

'Who?'

'Mrs Sommersby and anyone else she is working with who coaxed you inside this carriage.'

She finally looked up at him and wrinkled her brow. 'Of course not, she is my aunt. Coming here today was my idea.'

'Your idea?'

'Yes.'

His suspicions were stirred. 'Am I being kidnapped?'

Her head snapped back. 'Of course not, you are free to leave this carriage at any time.'

'And where are you taking me?'

'Wherever you wish. Shall we drive you home? Yes, let's drive you home, straight away. I will have the driver go directly to your residence. It's Albany on Piccadilly, is it not? Unless you were going somewhere else. Then we could take you there. The distance is of no concern. We could even take you outside London, but you wouldn't have been going outside London if you were walking, would you? Even though you are a man that enjoys physical exertion, I think even you would find a walk that long—'

He laid his hand over hers. When she wouldn't look at him as he entered the carriage, he assumed it was from fright. Now, he could tell it was from nerves.

'Charlotte, I can have the driver take me home, which should be a short ride. Or I can tell him to drive around Hyde Park until I give him further direction. Which would you prefer?'

She licked her lips and finally looked at him. 'The park.'

As he held her gaze, he rapped on the ceiling with his walking stick and gave the driver instructions.

With the removal of a possible threat, his body began to relax and he leaned back on the plush bench. She hadn't been very pleased with him the last time he saw her. She was probably looking for an explanation as to why he had disappeared on her. What lie could he possibly use that wouldn't hurt her? 'What is it you want, Charlotte?'

'We need to talk.'

'I commend you for your ingenuity. You could have sent me a note. You know where I live.' It was odd how just being around her made him want to smile. He should have insisted that the driver take him home. No good would come of spending any time with her.

'I thought this would be more efficient.'

'Efficient? Now I am truly intrigued. What shall we discuss that demands efficiency?'

'I'm carrying your child.'

The carriage could have crashed into Apsley House as it turned into the park and Andrew wouldn't have noticed.

'Pardon?'

She cleared her throat and said it again.

Being able to analyse things logically when faced with difficult situations was what he was trained to do. So even though his heart was pounding and every instinct was telling him to jump out of the carriage and run, he said the first thing that came into his mind. 'You told me you could not conceive.' It was an accusation and he was not going to soften the statement.

She licked her lips and let out a breath. 'I thought I couldn't. I hadn't in all the time I was married.'

'You told me I could finish inside you. You said there would be no child.' His voice was getting stronger and louder.

'If I ever thought there was a chance I could have one, I wouldn't have said it.'

He leaned forward and rested his elbows on his knees. Rubbing his eyelids with his fingers was a bit better than looking at her. However, it didn't change anything. It didn't change the fact that his child was inside her. 'You're certain?'

'If you are asking if this child is yours—'

'I'm asking if you are certain you are with child.' He hadn't missed the indignant tone of her voice.

She dropped her face in her hands so her voice was muffled. 'I have always bled every thirty days and I haven't yet and fifty days have passed.'

'That means...'

She raised her head and looked at him in exasperation. 'That means I am pregnant.' It was hard to tell in the dim light, but knowing Charlotte she was probably blushing.

Damn! Damn! Damn! He couldn't be a father.

He didn't lead the life of a man who should be a father. Every day he placed his life in danger. Every day he woke up prepared to die to protect his sovereign. He wasn't like Gabriel. He spent his days in the field and he didn't need an heir.

The confines of the carriage were closing in on him and the scent of roses was cloying, making it hard to breathe.

She had said she was not going to trap him into marriage that morning over breakfast. He should never had trusted her. He should have left the room the moment she walked in. Why hadn't he left the room?

Picking up his walking stick from where it rested next to him, Andrew rapped the ceiling, startling Charlotte. He ordered the driver to pull over. When the carriage rolled to a stop, he opened the door and jumped down into the dirt of the deserted bridle path.

'That's it? You're leaving?'

There was a tremble to her voice, but he pushed any sympathy he felt for her aside.

He needed air. 'I'm going for a walk.' Turning to the driver, Andrew ordered him to remain where he was and to wait for his return. Then he stalked across the grass towards the Serpentine. Dark clouds covered the sun and the air smelled of a coming storm. This wasn't his plan. A wife and child weren't part of his plan. He wanted his original plan back.

* * *

Charlotte reached over and closed the carriage door. Pushing aside the curtain, she watched Andrew march across the grass towards a thick clump of trees. Storm clouds were rolling in, making the tree branches sway and appear dark and ominous—like creatures that were going to swallow him up and never spit him out.

Could she do this without him? Could she have this child—raise this child—without a husband to provide for them?

Her body grew cold and she fought the tremors that were threatening to overtake her. Since Jonathan's death, she had economised in different ways to ensure she was not dependent on others. Her steward was knowledgeable in the latest farming techniques and she had made some prudent investments. The life she was leading was not as luxurious as Lizzy's, but it was respectable. Would it remain that way with an extra mouth to feed? Would her neighbours shun her for what she had done? And what of the child? What kind of life would a bastard have when its father refused to claim it? She placed her hand on her stomach and, for the first time, had a fierce urge to protect the child inside her.

Tears rimmed her eyes, blurring the image of Jonathan's ring that she held once more in her hand. To steady her nerves, she took deep breaths through her mouth.

Where had Andrew gone? It was apparent he blamed her. How could he not? It was all her fault. He might feel bound by honour to offer for her hand, but it wouldn't be what he truly wanted. Perhaps he was already attached to someone here in London. Perhaps he had been waiting for Skeffington to die to pursue her sister.

She banged her head softly against the cushion behind her and closed her eyes. The plunking of soft raindrops on the roof filled the carriage, giving her something to focus on.

Just listen to the raindrops. Don't think of anything but the raindrops.

But thoughts of raising a child alone pushed their way in.

Her gaze wandered to Andrew's expensive walking stick with the silver horsehead handle that he had carelessly tossed on the bench before he walked out. Was he this careless with most of his possessions? She barely knew him. How could she marry him?

Once more, she dropped her head back and closed her eyes. *I can do this. I can raise this child by myself. All will be well in the end.*

A boom of thunder shook the carriage and raindrops now hammered on the roof. She moved the curtain aside. Sheets of rain obstructed her view. If Andrew was walking back to the carriage, she wouldn't be able to tell.

Suddenly the door opened halfway and Aunt Clara's driver peered inside.

'Forgive me, my lady. Would you still like to wait? There are lightning strikes in the distance and they are getting closer. There are too many trees where we are to make it safe to remain here.'

She looked past him for any sign of Andrew, but couldn't see much beyond a few feet. 'Do you see him?' she practically yelled over the sound of the rain.

The poor man was soaked and, as he turned to have a look, raindrops splattered off the brim of his hat. 'It's hard to see with all this rain coming down,' he yelled back.

A bolt of bright white lightning illuminated sky and carriage, and the accompanying crack of thunder shook her body.

'We should move, my lady. The trees—'

'How far are we from a clearing? Will he be able to see us if we move?'

'This entire stretch of the bridle path has trees. We need to turn around and go back the way we came.' He paused as if considering if he should say something as rain pelted his face. 'If I may, he might not be coming back. He seemed most upset when he left.'

How long would she wait for him? How long would she stay in this carriage under the trees and wait? An hour? Two? Until tomorrow?

At what point do you realise you are utterly and completely alone?

'Damn it, man! Can you not see this is no place for a carriage in a storm?' Andrew's deep voice boomed over the rain as he threw open the door and climbed inside. One would think he had almost drowned in a lake. He took off his hat, which had done little to keep his head dry, and tossed it on the bench next to him. Water droplets dripped from the ends of his hair, down his temples. 'Go to Piccadilly,' he instructed the driver. 'Just before Burlington Arcade is a drive leading to Albany. Do you know where that is?'

'Aye, my lord.'

'Go there.'

The driver nodded with a relieved expression and quickly shut the door.

Rain continued to pound on the roof and the windows. As the carriage suddenly lurched forward, it made Charlotte gasp. He looked intense. Focused. Assessing.

She wanted to ask him if he wanted to marry her. She wanted to ask him how much he hated her. But instead, she sat there silently looking back at him for what felt like ages.

Droplets of water clung to his lashes, and she could no longer resist the urge to reach across the carriage to gently brush them away.

He grabbed her wrist. 'Don't.'

It was one word, but it said so much.

'I'm so sorry.' She didn't know what else to say. There wasn't anything else left to say. Her heart took over and tears filled her eyes.

He let go of her wrist.

'I'm sorry,' she continued. 'I'm sorry that I have disrupted your life and wasn't able to let you leave and never think of me again. I'm sorry I had to tell you about the baby. I'm sorry there is a baby. I never thought...'

'Charlotte—'

'I shouldn't have told you.' If she could have jumped out of the carriage and run away, she would have. 'I'll go back home and you can forget this happened...all of it.'

'This is not something I can forget.'

She looked up from her clasped hands and met his unreadable gaze. 'You must hate me,' she said softly.

He shook his head, sending water drops on to her open pelisse. 'I don't hate you.' His voice had softened for the first time since he entered the carriage.

'I hate me. I hate what I have done to us. I swear I never thought that I would be able to have a child and when you...when you offered...' Not knowing how to finish that sentence, she licked her lips. She still remembered what it felt like to have him inside her. She still remembered not wanting him to pull away from her.

He let out a sigh. 'I realise that it's logical for

you to have believed you could not bear a child. I will not lie, Charlotte. There is a part of me that wants to hate you and wants to blame you for this. But I can't. I don't. We share the blame for this. One is no more at fault than the other.'

A small sob slipped out, and she covered her mouth. 'I am not usually this emotional. I do not cry easily. I don't know why I am now.'

'When my brother's wife was carrying their second child, she cried quite a bit. Perhaps it's the child.'

'Perhaps,' she replied, wiping her eyes.

The carriage rocked to a halt. Rain continued to cascade down. Andrew rapped on the roof and told the driver to go inside and wait for him there, away from the rain.

'My life is here, Charlotte, in London. Your life is in Cheshire. I live in a building where women are not even allowed to enter. I'm frequently out at all hours dealing with one crisis or another, or gone for days. I have lived my life as a bachelor for so long, I have no notion how to be a husband or a father and have no desire to be either. That was why I left Toby's house. That was why I knew seeing you again would do neither of us any good. There was no future for us.'

He wasn't going to ask her. Ice ran through her veins.

You can do this alone. You can do this alone.

Andrew looked out the window at the deserted cobblestone courtyard and then back to Charlotte. 'You see. I don't even have a notion how to propose.'

She knotted her hands together to keep them from trembling at the idea of having this child without him and the scandal she had brought to her sisters. 'What are you saying?'

'I'm trying to say that if you will have me, I'd like to give that child my name.'

Charlotte's entire body felt like an unravelled ball of yarn. 'Are you asking me to marry you?'

'Yes, I would have thought that was fairly clear.'

A soft laugh broke from her lips. It might have been from his comment, or it might have been from the relief she felt at not having to raise this child alone.

'We will have much to settle between us in the coming days. That is, if you accept.'

While marrying her was the honourable thing to do, she knew it was still a sacrifice 'You're certain this is what you want? Perhaps there is someone else you had set your sights on.' Was he the type of man to take her under the stars if there was someone else in his life and would he even admit to her if he was partial to Lizzy?

'There is no one else, but I doubt this is truly what either of us wanted. You told me you did not plan to marry again. I know you do not want this either, but it is what is best for the child. And it is what we must do to preserve our reputations and that of our families.'

Her heart sank like a stone. She didn't love him. It would be absurd to think he loved her. They barely knew one another. And yet, having him state the only reason they would be wed was because she was carrying his child left her heart heavy. Jonathan's proposal in the drawing room of her parents' country house fourteen years ago was filled with declarations of love. This one was more like a business arrangement. She wanted to reach for Jonathan's ring, but stopped herself.

'If you are inclined,' he continued, 'I shall ask my brother, the Duke, to arrange for a special licence. We could be married in a week. Do you agree?'

It was moving much too fast. She wanted him to marry her to give their child a name, but it suddenly seemed so real. In one week, they would be wed and she would no longer be a widow. In one week, she would be his wife. And he was going to tell his brother they needed a special licence because she was with child. How could she possibly face the Duke and Duchess of Winterbourne and whoever else comprised his family? What would they think of her? Certainly, they would assume she had trapped him into marriage. She suddenly didn't feel very well.

Andrew took off his glove and held his right

hand out to her. Strangely, for the first time in a long while it felt as though she wouldn't be alone.

She took off her right glove and slipped her hand is his. 'You are so cold,' she said. 'Why did I not think to send you inside straight away? We can talk about this tomorrow. You need to get out of those wet clothes.'

'I expect my valet will be vexed when he sees how I've ruined this coat. It's a pity since he took great pains to remove the grass stains.' There was a wet leaf on his sleeve that he tried to pick off with his other hand, but his glove was still on and he was having difficulty. His determination was thwarted by a sneeze.

Using the tip of her nail through her glove, Charlotte was able to remove the offending leaf. 'Please go inside and take a warm bath. It should help with the chills.'

His body stilled and she found herself anxious for him to say something. Anything.

'I have a mother, Charlotte. I do not need another.'

There was gravity in his tone that had her swallowing the next thing she planned to say to him. How would she fit into his life? Suddenly she needed to know now, regardless of how wet his clothes were. 'Why do I think you already have an idea of how you would like us to proceed?'

His gaze dropped to the ring around her neck

and he let go of her hand. 'I think we should live apart. Not immediately,' he clarified. 'Just long enough for it to appear this marriage wasn't to stop a scandal. My life is here in Town and your life is in the country. You have no desire to be my wife. You still mourn your husband. Of course, I will support both you and the child, and visit. I do want to know my child, but there is no reason either of us has to alter our lives completely because of this.'

'How long would that be?'

He shrugged and let out another sneeze. 'I don't know. Not long—a month, maybe two at the latest. Just long enough for me to become acquainted with your staff and familiar with the property. We don't want your servants speculating on the nature of our sudden marriage or your neighbours gossiping. We can eventually say we each could not agree on where we wanted to live together. You enjoy the country too much and my life is centred around Town. It is not unheard of for husbands and wives of the *ton* to live apart.'

'It seems you've given this much consideration.'

'I had time to think of many things during my walk. Do you agree this is the best way to proceed?'

Charlotte looked down at her hands that were once again clasped tightly together on her lap and nodded. He was giving her everything she

could have wanted. She could resume her life
in the home she had lived in for the past nine
years, but now she would do so with a child at
her side—her child. So why did knowing they
would live apart make her feel so hollow inside?

Chapter Sixteen

Even though Gabriel had handed him his favourite brandy, Andrew wouldn't have known it since he couldn't taste a thing. He was still trying to accept that he was standing in his brother's drawing room awaiting the arrival of his fiancée and her family.

His fiancée. The mother of his child.

Even the warm smooth liquid sliding down his throat wasn't relaxing him the way it normally would. Nothing had relaxed him since Charlotte had told him about the baby two days ago—not even racing his stallion through the parkland of Richmond in the early morning hours. No matter how far he rode, he could not escape his fate. He was going to be a husband in less than a week and a father in a matter of months. How could he be there for them, when every mission he took could be his last? How could he marry her and promise her a stable life, when his life was the very definition of unstable?

There were people depending on his survival now. The thought of it made him want to get back on his horse and ride further than Richmond—further than England.

He went to down the remainder of his brandy, and discovered the glass was already empty. 'I need you to give me something to do,' he said, turning to face Gabriel.

His brother was seated in a wingback chair in front of the hearth, swirling the brandy in his glass.

'Would you care to assist Bennett polishing the silver? I'm sure he would appreciate the help.'

'You're amusing. I don't know why I've never mentioned it before.' Andrew ran his hand through his hair. 'All this time without being in the field is giving me too much time to think. I have too much time to tell myself this is all wrong. She doesn't need a husband like me and that baby certainly doesn't deserve me as a father.'

'You'll make a fine father. I see how you are with my boys.'

A nephew was not a son. What he wouldn't admit was that his own child deserved a father who would be alive to see him grow up. Andrew didn't know if he would be alive next month. Finding and subduing traitors and would-be assassins was in his blood. It wasn't what he did. It was who he was. He could never give it up. And yet for the first time in his life, his very existence determined the stability in the lives of two people. Now he wasn't just protecting the Crown. Now he was also protecting Charlotte and their child. What if he couldn't do that?

'I need more brandy.'

'It's over there,' Gabriel said, motioning to the crystal decanter on the table Andrew had just walked past. 'I'm sure every man feels as you do when they find out they are going to be a father.'

He couldn't relay his fears to Gabriel, no matter how close they were as brothers, as well as friends. If he did, Gabriel might relegate him to desk work and, if he had to decipher codes or track correspondence most days, he would go mad. 'My mind might be at ease if the papers were already filed and I was certain that, should anything happen to me, Charlotte would have the necessary funds to take care of herself and the child.'

'Warren is the epitome of efficiency. It will all be completed tomorrow. Your Will will be set.' Gabriel picked a speck of lint off his sleeve. 'Perhaps a different line of work would suit you better now. You do have a head for successful investments.'

'Don't do that,' Andrew practically shouted.

'Don't change my life for me. It's changing enough as it is.'

Gabriel held up his hands. 'I am merely stating it is something to consider.'

Andrew paused from placing the stopper back on the brandy decanter. 'Could you consider changing what you do?'

'Of course not,' Gabriel replied indignantly. 'But we are referring to you and your need for reassurance at this time.'

Andrew approached Gabriel's desk and rested his hip against it. 'I imagined you to be much more upset about this than you are. Why is that?'

'You're conducting yourself with honour. No scandal will mar our family and it's your life, not mine.' Gabriel tilted his head and his eyes narrowed. 'Will you be able to hide all of this from her? She cannot know what we do.'

'As we've already discussed, Charlotte and I will only be living together for a month or two. We won't be living together long enough for her to find out. You lived with Olivia for six years before she found out. Unlike you, my marriage is in name only and *I* can keep secrets.'

'I *can* keep secrets. The only reason Olivia found out was because she was inadvertently caught up with a duplicitous friend and stumbled upon what we do. My recommendation is to distance yourself from your bride as quickly as you can and pray she has no friends who are interested in harming Prinny or George. I am rather amazed you have found yourself tied to one of the Sommersby sisters. I know in the past you have felt rather hunted by the Duchess of Skeffington.' There was a look of amusement in his eyes. 'Now you will be able to spend Christmases with her.' He smiled into his glass of brandy. 'I imagine family gatherings would be awkward since the woman had her eye on you for ages.'

Andrew walked around the chair and dropped into the plush cushion. His family always spent Christmases together in Kent. Would he want to spend Christmas with his child? Would Charlotte want to spend them with their child and her family? He rubbed his brow, trying to wipe away the pain in his head. He wanted his old life back. 'I haven't given a thought to any of this until now.' Andrew was so focused on Charlotte and the baby that it hadn't occurred to him that the Duchess of Skeffington would be his sister. 'Skeffington's widow will be here today. That will be…'

'Awkward?' Gabriel arched a brow and had the nerve to smirk. 'You'll be happy to hear Her Grace will not be here tonight. Your fiancée sent word to Olivia. Lady Charlotte will be arriving with just her youngest sister and an aunt by the name of Mrs Robert Sommersby.'

'It wouldn't be awkward if she were here. I'm

sure there are numerous men who have caught her eye.'

'Not that I've noticed. I still have no idea what she finds attractive about you.'

'Well, I am marrying Charlotte, so I'm sure the attraction is over.'

'You don't understand women, do you? Is Lady Charlotte anything like her sister?'

'No. Where the Duchess is concerned with status and prestige, Charlotte is more concerned with character. Where the Duchess has been known to spend to an excessive degree, Charlotte appears content to live a quiet life in the country in a small but respectable home. She's…'

Gabriel sat patiently waiting, but Andrew couldn't finish the thought. Charlotte was many things—many good things—and it was for the best that he didn't dwell on them. No good would come from a strong attachment between them. She had lost one husband to violence prematurely and mourned him still. He couldn't let her grow attached to him and mourn him as well. It might destroy her.

When it was apparent he was not going to elaborate more on Charlotte, Gabriel stood up and placed his glass on the small oval table beside him. 'They will be arriving soon. We should join the others in the drawing room and greet them there.'

Andrew's stomach dropped and the urge to escape on his horse once again was overwhelming.

'Come now,' Gabriel said, motioning towards the doors. 'I bet you Monty says something inappropriate at least once this evening.'

A wager... Andrew could focus on a wager. It would give him something to concentrate on all night that didn't have to do with this mess he had got himself into.

'I wager five pounds he says two inappropriate things,' Andrew replied.

Gabriel stuck out his hand, and they shook on it.

Half an hour later, Andrew stood by the window in Gabriel and Olivia's Green Drawing Room and watched the carriages roll by at a distance. 'What time is it?'

'Almost five,' Gabriel replied from where he sat by the unlit hearth with Olivia.

'Maybe she changed her mind,' Monty said from somewhere behind him. 'Women are apt to do that from time to time...or so I hear.'

'Do not tease him,' Olivia chided. 'Can you not see he is in no humour for such an exchange?'

'He hasn't been for ages. Why is that, do you think?'

'Montague.' The reprimand came from their mother this time, and it thankfully made his brother stop talking.

Never in his life had he anticipated and dreaded something at the same time the way he did Charlotte's arrival this evening to meet his family. They would eventually be living apart. It should not matter what his family thought of her. While Gabriel was surprised by the news and warned him unnecessarily of the dangers of revealing what he did to Charlotte, he had received no reaction at all from his mother. She only enquired what he intended to do. There were no questions about how it happened. There was no request to tell her about Charlotte. There was nothing. And for a woman who would ask him twenty questions before the soup course was served at dinner, this left him the most unsettled.

Turning from the window, he caught Olivia's sympathetic gaze.

'I don't think this was a wise idea,' he said to her.

'It's too late now,' Gabriel replied offhandedly. 'You must agree, your life would be more agreeable should we all approve of her.'

'I don't approve of a woman trapping a man into marriage,' Monty offered. 'Should you need an escape, I offer you the spare room in my set.'

'She didn't trap me,' Andrew retorted. He wasn't giving up his set at Albany. Gabriel knew. The others didn't need to. Not yet.

Olivia tried to change the direction of the conversation. 'Tell us what she is like.'

'Since she captured Andrew's interest, I imagine she is fond of boxing. What do you think, Monty?' Gabriel asked, baiting their younger brother for that bet.

'And brandy,' Monty added with a broad grin, 'or perhaps gin.'

'She might spend her days racing horses. A member of the Four Horse Club, perhaps?'

The idea that they were poking fun at Charlotte's expense tied Andrew in knots, even though he knew Gabriel was trying to win the bet. His right hand curled into a fist.

'I've heard there are women in the countryside that are quite unconventional and have taken to boxing themselves,' Monty said through his smile. 'I would not be surprised if Lady Charlotte—'

Andrew charged at Monty and Gabriel jumped up. He came between them and pushed Andrew back by his shoulders so the punch he threw missed his younger brother's face by mere inches.

'Lady Charlotte Gregory, Mrs Robert Sommersby, and Lady Juliet Sommersby.' The voice of the footman at the doorway silenced the fight going on in the room.

They all froze in the absurd tableau and turned to the three women who stood in the doorway. The tips of the fingers on Charlotte's right hand were raised to her neck. Mrs Sommersby, who was standing to Charlotte's left and bearing a strong resemblance to their nanny, looked as if she wanted to scold all of them. And the younger woman to Charlotte's right, who he assumed was her sister, was shooting daggers with her eyes at Monty, who was staring back at her with his eyebrows up near his hairline. If he was uncertain if their tussle had been witnessed, their reactions confirmed that they had.

He shook himself out of Gabriel's hold and adjusted his collar as he walked over to greet Charlotte. How did one welcome their fiancée, whom they were forced to marry, in front of their entire family for the first time?

He pasted on a smile and bowed over her hand. She curtsied in return and introduced her Aunt Clara and sister Juliet to him. The assessing appraisal her sister gave without trying to be inconspicuous let him know her family would be judging him tonight, as well. He had done the honourable thing. He was marrying her sister. What more could she want from him?

Olivia joined them by the doorway. With her presence beside him, the moment felt less awkward and he didn't feel as if he were in a rowing boat without an oar.

She introduced herself and invited them into the room, guiding them through the protocol in the situation. Andrew presented them to Gabriel first and he knew his brother was taking notice of every small detail about each woman even while he was respectful and reserved.

His mother was next. He could barely take his eyes off her when he introduced Charlotte. It surprised him how much, at that moment, he wanted his mother to like a woman he didn't even love.

'Lady Charlotte,' she said, 'I understand you are the Earl of Crawford's oldest child and your other sister is the Duchess of Skeffington. Your late husband was the third son of the Earl of Haslington, I understand. He served admirably under Wellington and was killed at Waterloo.' Her gaze travelled down Charlotte's grey gown. 'You have my condolences.'

It appeared his mother had spent a very busy day gathering information about his future wife. No wonder she hadn't asked him anything about Charlotte.

He was relieved to see Charlotte's composure, considering his mother was not exuding any of her usual warmth, as she gave her a respectful curtsy. 'Thank you, Your Grace.'

'I expected to see the Duchess here today,' his mother continued as she looked over at Andrew and held his gaze for a few seconds too long. Over the years, she had advised him about the Duchess of Skeffington's interest. 'Is your sister ill?'

It was the first time since she'd arrived that

Charlotte looked uncomfortable. 'She had a prior engagement.'

For a brief moment Andrew thought he saw sadness in her eyes. Was her sister too scandalised by Charlotte's pregnancy to support her? Families should stand together in times of crisis. His always had. It hadn't occurred to him that not all families might react the same way. Had their indiscretion created a wedge between Charlotte and her sister? At least he had every member of his family there to support him. Charlotte had arrived at his brother's door with just one sister and an aunt.

It was obvious her parents had died at some point. How many times had she suffered through the loss of someone close to her? He couldn't allow himself to be added to that list. The faster they married and the faster they separated, the easier it would be for Charlotte if something happened to him. Their relationship could not develop into anything more than it already was. He would not be responsible for causing her any more pain. However, as much as he came to that realisation, he still found himself stepping up beside her as she faced his mother.

Thankfully the conversation changed as his mother tilted her head at Mrs Sommersby and narrowed her eyes. 'Clara, is it not?'

'It has been a long time. I did not think you would remember me.'

A smile finally lightened his mother's expression. 'I have fond memories of my first Season and recall some of the times we spent together whispering behind the columns of Almack's.'

Hopefully that memory was a sign that this dinner would not turn into a disaster after all.

Charlotte sat staring at the turtle soup still in her bowl and debated if she should take even one spoonful. Her stomach had been in knots since this morning when she received the invitation to dine at Winterbourne House from Olivia, Duchess of Winterbourne. It was a polite note congratulating her on her engagement to Andrew and suggesting the families meet over dinner. Because Olivia did not know who else was privy to the news of the sudden engagement, she asked Charlotte to extend the invitation to any family members she wished.

When Charlotte wrote to Lizzy, asking if she would like to attend, the letter was returned to her unopened. If Lizzy had refused to attend because it was an engagement dinner, Charlotte would have understood. But the letter was returned with its seal intact. Lizzy no longer cared for anything Charlotte had to say. It was crushing. Not only had she lost Jonathan, but she had lost the love of her sister as well. The only good that would come out of any of this was the child she was carrying. The child that hour by hour was becoming more real in her mind. It no longer was this terrible thing that had thrown her life into turmoil. It was a baby. Her baby. And Andrew's.

She stole a side glance at his ruggedly handsome face as he sat beside her in the grand dining room of Winterbourne House. Would their child resemble him? Would it have brown eyes with flecks of gold, as his did? Or thick light brown hair that always looked slightly tousled? Sitting beside him with his confident shoulders and easy manner was helping her relax. But she still couldn't eat her soup.

'Do you not like turtle?' Andrew whispered, leaning towards her.

'I had one as a pet when I was a child,' she admitted low enough so only he could hear.

He wiped the smile from his lips with his napkin. 'Did it have a name?'

'Edgar. My turtle was named Edgar.'

'And was Edgar a fine turtle?'

'He was wonderful. I found him on a log by the pond on my parents' estate. He was just a small thing. No bigger than my thumb.'

'I can assure you, Edgar is not in that bowl.'

'I'm aware of that. He is buried by the folly on the estate, but members of his family are in here.' She stirred the contents around and scooped up some on her spoon. Then she let the liquid with bits of turtle slip back into the white bowl trimmed with gold.

'Do you think he had relations in London?' His mouth was near her ear and the deepness of his voice mixed with his warm breath near her neck sent tingles through her body.

'Doesn't everyone have relations in London?'

'Perhaps he did not like his London relations.' He peered over at his younger brother who was seated next to Juliet. 'Not all of us like ours.'

She had witnessed the brothers tussle with one another when they'd arrived and wondered what could have provoked men at their ages to raise fists to one another. 'Sometimes our relations can make life difficult, even when they don't mean to.' She thought of Lizzy and it came out on a sigh.

'That's why I think Edgar would recommend that you try the soup.'

He made her smile. It was the first time she had felt like doing so all day. He always seemed to have some kind of effect on her. Either it was raising her spirits with his good humour or raising her temperature with his heated looks. Even just sitting beside him was making her insides flutter and they weren't even touching. Heaven help her if his leg inadvertently moved against hers. At the moment, his smile was bringing back memories of kissing his soft, yet firm lips. She feared, if his leg brushed against hers, her body would recall the other intimate activities they'd shared. Now was not the time to recall any of that. She should simply be waiting for the footmen to remove the pet soup from in front of her. Now was not the time to wonder what his lips would taste like if they could somehow manage to steal a kiss without any of their family members noticing.

Once more she glanced at him, wondering what it was about this man that captivated her. While he was attractive, she knew there were other men she had met over the years who were more handsome than Andrew. Yet in all her life, she had never met anyone who had the kind of effect on her that he did.

'Have you given any thought as to where you'd like the wedding ceremony to take place?' Olivia broke in, reminding her of the reason they were dining together today. She felt her smile slip. All of this was done out of obligation. He had never intended to see her again.

They hadn't got that far in their discussion yesterday and, as she went to look back at Andrew, she caught the watchful eyes of his mother— eyes that were the same shade as all three of her sons. There was no expression on the Dowager's patrician face as she sat regally with her diamonds sparkling in the candlelight. And she didn't bother to look away as if she was embarrassed to be caught staring at Charlotte.

Andrew straightened up in his chair and took a sip of claret. 'I thought Charlotte and I would discuss it once we obtained the licence.'

'Weddings take planning, Andrew. Arrangements have to be made. Unless you are heading off to Gretna Green.' There was a teasing smile on Olivia's lips that reminded Charlotte of the looks she would sometimes share with her sisters.

He was kind enough to leave the choice to her. 'Do you have a preference?'

It wasn't as if it was going to be a real marriage. The less they pretended this was not a marriage of convenience, the better she would be in the end when they parted ways. He had been gracious to her so far. She would let him decide. 'Do *you* have a preference?'

He shook his head.

'Might I suggest St James's,' Olivia offered, sitting back so the footman could remove her empty bowl that once held Edgar's kin. 'I'm certain Gabriel can arrange something with the Bishop even though it is rather sudden. We were married there and it is a lovely church.' She looked at the Duke, who was seated at Charlotte's left at the head of the table, and the love between them was evident in their shared smiles.

His Grace turned to Charlotte and sat back. 'I sense my wife will arrange all of this for you if you don't speak up, Lady Charlotte. I'm certain you do have some preference. Would you like to marry in St James's with all the fanfare?' His gaze darted to Andrew before it settled back on her.

All discussion around the table stopped and everyone was looking at her. She had no friends in London. The only people in Town she cared about were sitting at this table, except for Lizzy, who hated her.

There was a lump in her throat. Her beloved sister would never attend her wedding. They had been there for each other through every important event in each other's lives. But that was over now all because for one brief moment when Charlotte had wanted to feel desirable again.

She did not need strangers gawking at them. She needed to put the wedding ceremony behind her as quickly as possible. 'In truth, I hoped for a more private occasion. Small and not quite so grand.' And one that didn't feel so much like a wedding ceremony.

Andrew pushed his muscular leg gently against hers, sending a wave of warmth up her thigh.

'I agree. There is no need to invite extra attention,' he said.

Thank God.

He rested his hand on her knee. It might have been done in a reassuring gesture, but Charlotte couldn't help wishing they were alone.

'You may use my home for the ceremony, if you wish.' Her aunt's voice broke the spell his touch was casting on her. Aunt Clara gave her a kind smile, reminding her that she still had family who loved her. 'It is modest, but will suit your purpose. And if you so desire, you may remain there to stay for the rest of your time in London. I imagine Albany is not a conducive residence for a newly married couple and Juliet and I will be leaving Town after the wedding breakfast. It would be a shame for the house to sit idle when it can be of use.'

As the footmen entered with large platters of delicious-smelling meats and vegetables, Charlotte looked at Andrew. He was studying her. Would the brother of a duke think it was beneath him to get married in her aunt's house? Would he prefer to get married in this grand home instead, with its multitude of gilded rooms?

He answered for the both of them. 'That is very kind of you. We would be honoured.'

The Duke cleared his throat and arched his brow at Andrew's younger brother, Lord Montague. Apparently, they did not think Aunt Clara's house was an appropriate location for the ceremony.

'What is so amusing?' The annoyance in Andrew's tone was distinct.

The Duke raised his glass of claret to Lord Montague. 'Would you care to tell him?'

All three brothers bore a striking resemblance to one another with their light brown hair and brown eyes with flecks of green and gold. Lord Montague appeared a few years older than Juliet and more mischievous than his brothers. You could see it in his eyes.

'I bet Gabriel twenty quid you would be married in the ring at Jackson's.'

'You honestly thought I would do that? Truly?'

As if he really did believe Andrew would be married in a boxing ring, Lord Montague bobbed his head from side to side. 'I did place the bet.'

A boxing ring? They thought Andrew would want to be married in a boxing ring? Who would do such a thing? Why would someone even consider that an appropriate place to exchange wedding vows?

On the other side of the table, Juliet rolled her eyes. Exasperation was evident in her expression as she reached for her wine and took a long drink. Andrew, on the other hand, appeared to be trying to hide his smile in the rim of his glass.

When dinner was over, the men remained in the dining room for their after-dinner port and the women went to retire to the drawing room to wait for them. But before the women reached the drawing-room door, Andrew's mother made her way to Charlotte's side.

'Lady Charlotte, I don't know if you've heard

of Olivia's love of art. Perhaps you would be interested in taking a tour of her gallery with me. The works displayed there are remarkable.'

Butterflies crashed inside her stomach and she wished she hadn't eaten so much food. It was too soon to find out what Andrew's mother thought of the scandal she had brought to their door. The dinner had been delicious, aside from the soup, and Andrew attentive. So far it had been an enjoyable evening. Something told her that might be about to change.

Summoning her courage, she tried to smile. 'That would be lovely.' Or torturous…she would find out soon enough.

They walked silently side by side until they came to a long room at the back of the house that looked out on to the gardens. It was a lovely, quiet space that Charlotte would have enjoyed spending time in by herself. Gilded frames filled the walls with pastoral scenes as well as portraits of noble men and women.

As they proceeded further into the room, the Dowager stopped before a particular set of paintings. 'These horses were painted by Mr George Stubbs. Olivia purchased them for Andrew a year ago. He liked them well enough, however he could not find sufficient room for them, so they hang here instead.'

The collection of four paintings in gilded frames were of fine muscular horses and seemed to fit what she knew of her future husband. 'I can see why he would like them.'

'As can I.' Her attention was on Charlotte and not on the wall. 'I believe Andrew could have made room for them in his home, but he didn't see how his life would be richer with them there. I love my son, Lady Charlotte, but he shuts himself off from much of the world. I don't know why. I just know he does. I hope you will find a way for him to change that and perhaps find some room to hang a few new things.'

The analogy between the paintings and Charlotte had not escaped her notice.

'I will try, Your Grace.' She didn't have the heart to tell her Andrew had already informed her there was no room for her and their child in his life.

She hadn't been particularly close to her own mother. She wasn't a warm woman. Charlotte tried to recall a time when her mother had openly expressed her love for Charlotte or any of her sisters. She couldn't recall even one time. At least his mother admitted the emotion existed.

They strolled leisurely back to the drawing room and, by the time they reached the threshold, the men were right behind them. And when it was time to leave, Andrew escorted them out to their carriage while offering Charlotte his arm. The muscles of his arm under the sleeve of his formal black tailcoat were hard and she couldn't help but curl her fingers around to feel his bicep under the guise of adjusting her hand. There was a strength about Andrew, not just from his body, but from his manner. Charlotte wished she could capture some of his strength to store away for herself for the times she particularly needed it.

He assisted Aunt Clara and Juliet into her aunt's carriage before turning back to Charlotte. Instead of helping her immediately inside, he held her back for a moment. The warmth from his ungloved hand on her bare arm had her wishing she could press her body against his. Their eyes held for a few moments and she had the strongest urge to kiss him.

Until he dropped his hand and cleared his throat. 'I shall have the licence in two days. Shall we marry on Wednesday?'

Four days. In four days, she would be legally bound to him. He would hold all the power over her. Control her money. Own her property. In four days, she would be his wife.

'Do not fear for your future, Charlotte. My solicitor will be filing my Will tomorrow. You and the child will be provided for should anything happen to me. And your house, all the property and income from it shall remain yours.'

It was surprising he had thought of providing and protecting her so soon after their engagement. He was not going off to fight a war, and by the way he carried himself he appeared to believe he was invincible. Yet he considered she was well versed in the uncertainties of life and wanted to put her at ease.

'Thank you. And I will inform my aunt of the wedding date.'

Would he kiss her goodbye? They were engaged to wed. It would not be unheard of. And she longed to feel his lips brush against hers.

His gaze dropped to her grey pelisse. It appeared he wanted to say something, but then thought better of it. They stared at one another for a few more moments, as if each was waiting for the other to decide how they should part. If they were a couple who were marrying for love, he might have leaned down and kissed her. Instead he bowed politely and assisted her into the carriage. The reality of their situation made her heart drop as they rolled away from the house.

'Lord Andrew appears to be a lovely gentleman and I find I rather like most of his family,' Aunt Clara said from where she sat across from Charlotte. 'I know this is not what you would have chosen. I know you had no intention of marrying again. And I know you have chosen to remain in half-mourning to honour Jonathan's memory. But you are to be married to Lord Andrew now. He is an honourable man. It's time you put those gowns away.' The advice was given gently, as if she was trying her hardest not to offend Charlotte.

Put them away? Her chest tightened with the rocking of the carriage. She hadn't considered having to dress differently as Andrew's wife. She liked her gowns. She knew how to face the world as a widow. How did she face the world as Lady Andrew Pearce?

'I know a wonderful couturier here in Town. Why don't we go there tomorrow? I'm sure she must have at least one gown that she can alter in time for your wedding. And then we can see about having additional gowns made for you. It will be my wedding gift to you.'

'That is too generous. I can never accept a gift like that.' She looked over at Juliet, who seemed to be lost in thought as she stared out the window at the passing houses in Mayfair.

'I want to do this for you, Charlotte. You would not deprive me of the joy of seeing you dressed in happier colours, would you?'

When Jonathan was killed, she hadn't wanted to be a burden on anyone. Proving to herself she could live independently and not have to marry again had given her the courage to go on, when all she wanted to do was crawl into her bed and remain there for months. Admitting to herself that she needed help wasn't easy. Asking for help was even harder. But her aunt's offer would cer-

tainly help, especially since she did not know the
exact state of Andrew's finances.

So much of her new life was unknown.

Chapter Seventeen

The morning of their wedding, Charlotte stood in her bedchamber at Aunt Clara's home, staring down at the yellow-silk gown as if she had somehow switched bodies with Juliet.

'You look lovely,' Juliet said with a big smile from where she sat on the edge of Charlotte's bed. 'I've become so accustomed to seeing you in greys and lavenders that I'd forgotten how you glow when you wear other colours.'

'It feels so bright.'

'It's yellow.'

'It feels wrong.'

'It won't for very long. He seems like a good man, Charlotte. I was prepared to not like him. However, Lord Andrew appears very attentive to you. He does not seem condescending or cruel. I think you will have a good life with him, if you allow yourself.'

But she would not be spending her life with

him. They would just be together for a short while. That thought should have made her happy. She had never wanted to marry again. Andrew knew that. And yet...

'Jonathan loved you, Charlotte. He would have never wanted to see you unhappy. He would have never wanted you to stop living your life because he sacrificed his.'

'I don't know how to honour his memory any more. I don't know how to still love him and be another man's wife.' She toyed with his ring that she still wore around her neck.

'He fought to save you, Charlotte...to save us all. You honour his memory by living a full life. Give yourself a chance to be happy. You don't have to love Lord Andrew, but you can still find happiness with him.'

'I wish Lizzy were here. I wish...'

'Lizzy will find her own way through this.'

'She will never speak to me again.'

Their wedding banns weren't posted in a church and an announcement was not yet placed in the papers. All three letters she had sent Lizzy came back unopened. Did she even know Andrew had asked her to marry him?

'Have you told her?' she asked Juliet.

Her sister looked down. 'She knows you will be married today. She knows that you wanted her here.'

'But she cannot forgive me.'

There was sadness and pity in Juliet's eyes as she shook her head. 'I've tried to talk with her about it, but each time I mention your name, she changes the subject. I'm sorry, Charlotte.'

Her heart hung heavy in her chest.

Juliet stood and walked over to her. 'You have Aunt Clara and me. We love you.' She kissed Charlotte's cheek and hugged her tight. 'This is the beginning of a new life for you. Do not dwell on sad things. Soon you will be Lord Andrew's wife and you will be a mother. You will have the child you never thought you could have. That in itself makes this a joyful day. I will wait downstairs for you. Lord Andrew's family have already arrived, as well as Father Vincent. When you are ready, the service can begin.'

With one more crushing hug, Juliet left her alone, closing the door behind her.

Charlotte placed her hands on her stomach to steady her nerves and thought of her child. Andrew had given her this gift, even if he hadn't intended to. No gift was greater than the child growing inside her. Juliet was right. He was a good man. There were only two of them saying their vows before the vicar. It was time to put away her last reminder of Jonathan. She owed that to Andrew. But it wasn't easy.

The signet ring that was given to Jonathan by his father was brought back from Belgium by Wellington and he had presented it to her when

he called on her to offer her his condolences.
She had worn it on a ribbon around her neck
ever since. It was the only physical proof she
had that he was not returning home. When she
first received news he was killed, she thought
it had to be a mistake. A man in his position
would not have been killed in battle. He was not
a foot solider. He was protected. And she waited
for his miraculous return. Wellington came to
speak with her and gave her the details of how
Jonathan had died. But it wasn't until he gave
her Jonathan's ring that she finally accepted he
would never return.

Charlotte looked down at his ring and knew it
was time to put it away. With shaky hands, she
removed it from around her neck, kissed his ring
and placed it in her jewellery box.

It was time to begin her new life.

Andrew's eyes shot to the drawing-room
doorway the minute Lady Juliet Sommersby entered, and his heart began to pound in his chest.
She didn't bother to look his way, but walked
directly to Father Vincent and whispered something in the man's ear. Had Charlotte left? Had
she escaped through her window and taken a
carriage north, leaving him to wonder what had
happened?

He'd dreamed last night that she had left him
and he hadn't needed to marry her. In the dream,

he was searching for her in a dark, thick wood. He could not let her go. It should have been what he wanted. It would have made his life easier. Yet every time he saw movement by the door, he prayed it was Charlotte.

'It is only her sister,' Monty said from beside him, adjusting the collar of his tailcoat. 'You can go back to breathing.'

'I am breathing. I have been breathing.'

Gabriel's attention shifted between Monty and Lady Juliet. 'It has just occurred to me, Montague, that Andrew's soon-to-be sister is named Juliet.'

Monty was becoming visibly uncomfortable under the scrutiny. 'So?'

'So, you're Montague and she is Juliet.'

'And you're an ass.'

'Wrong play,' Andrew muttered, keeping his eyes fixed on Lady Juliet who was walking towards him.

'Yes, I believe that line comes from *Much Ado*,' Gabriel said with a laugh.

The conversation stopped when she joined them. There was a shadow of apprehension in her eyes. He didn't know if it came from approaching the three of them together or at what she was going to have to tell him about Charlotte. All the nervousness he had been feeling when he first woke slipped back to grip him.

'My sister will be coming down shortly, Lord Andrew.'

Words might have been spoken after that, but all he could focus on was that Charlotte was still upstairs and not on her way out of Town. He could breathe deeper now.

'Thank you for coming to tell me.'

'She was having a problem with her dress, but it's all fixed now.' Lady Juliet's hair was brown, where Charlotte's was black, but he could see the resemblance when she smiled.

It took seventeen more minutes before Charlotte stopped at the threshold of the room. And when she did, he almost didn't recognise her. She wasn't in lavender or in grey. She was wearing yellow, just like the day they had breakfast at Toby's, and she looked stunning. The silk of her gown shimmered in the muted sunlight and it draped low on her shoulders, exposing her smooth, flawless skin. From the first moment he saw her weeks ago, he had found her tempting. But this version of her, removed from the traces of gloom of the half-mourning she always wore, almost brought him to his knees.

Not caring about what the protocol was, he strode across the room, grabbed her by the hand and pulled her out into the corridor, pushing the drawing-room door closed behind them with his foot. A sense of urgency drove him and he spun her around so that her back was against the wall-papered wall and he was crowding her with his body. Resting his right forearm on the wall above her head, he dropped his gaze from her surprised expression to her shoulders and then settled on her breasts—breasts that were rising and falling along with her rapid breathing. Her lips had him recalling the reckless abandonment of their passionate night together. This attraction he had for her was beyond reason.

'You look beautiful,' he said, meeting her watchful gaze.

She placed her right hand on his chest. At first, he thought she would push him away, but then she slid it up to rest it on his shoulder. A scorching trail of fire moved in its wake. Still holding his gaze, she curved her lips into a smile. 'Thank you. You look very handsome.'

Those pillowy lips called to him, and he lowered his head so their mouths were a few inches apart. 'I don't care that people are waiting for us. I need to kiss you.'

He claimed her lips and pushed his body into her soft curves. The kiss was meant to appease his desire—instead the taste of her mouth and the warm, wet softness of her tongue was making him hungry for more. He pressed his forearm harder into the wall, as her hands moved to pull him even closer by the small of his back.

Father Vincent was on the other side of that

door, along with members of their families, waiting for them. They were waiting for them to exchange vows so that they could go about the rest of their day, but he didn't care. They could go on waiting.

This was safer. This was what he and Charlotte knew. This unbridled passion that had been simmering between them ever since they met was what defined them. What would define them when they were husband and wife? It was something he had considered during the last few days and it left him unsettled. He prayed neither of them would come to regret the marriage. After all this, he didn't regret their night under the stars. And he very well should.

Knowing they couldn't walk back into the room the least bit dishevelled, he resisted the urge to cup her breasts and broke the kiss. Charlotte blinked a few times as if she, too, needed to find a way out of the passionate haze that had settled between them.

Once more, he looked down at her gown. 'I didn't think I'd ever see you like this again.'

'It was time.'

He searched her eyes for regret, but didn't see any. 'I thought you might have reconsidered,' he said, a bit hoarse.

'Is that why you kissed me?' It was said in jest, but she might have hit the mark. 'I'm sorry I kept you waiting.' Her fingers were drawing small circles on his lower back and he wondered if she was even aware she was doing it.

'Seeing you like this was worth the wait.' He never thought she would try to reach out to him like this. He never thought she would stop missing the man she married. Did this mean she had?

'We should go inside,' she said with a smile. 'If we stay out here much longer I fear they will think we have changed our minds.'

'Or gone to Jackson's to get married there.'

'While I've never entered an establishment such as that, I confess it does not sound very romantic.' That familiar blush deepened and spread across her cheeks as if she realised she had referenced this day as a love match and not what it really was.

For her sake, he chose to ignore it. 'I think it could be,' he replied in all seriousness.

'Then I am grateful Lord Montague hadn't brought the suggestion up before my aunt had offered us her home for the ceremony.'

Stretching out his arm, he gestured down the corridor towards the entrance hall. 'There still is time. All we need to do is grab the vicar.'

'And if we arrived in the middle of a match?'

'Then we would place our bets, make a few quid and get married all in one day.'

'I truly hope you are joking.'

The wary expression on her face boosted his mood and he gave a snort of laughter, which in turn made her laugh. It was an unexpected thing for both of them to find levity on a day like this—on a day when he should have been finding comfort in a case of brandy.

'If ladies such as yourself were allowed inside, then I might suggest we leave now to do the deed.'

'I don't know if I am relieved or intrigued. What does an establishment where men go to voluntarily beat each other senseless look like?'

'Some day, I shall tell you.'

'In detail?'

'In detail.'

'I will hold you to that.' She removed her hands from around his waist and patted his chest, right above his heart, as if she had just realised she had still been holding him. 'I think it's time.'

Their lives were about to change. She knew it. He knew it. They couldn't delay it further.

He held out his arm to her. 'We shall face this together. The three of us.'

Chapter Eighteen

Father Vincent could have been reciting a list of expenses for running his local parish for all Charlotte knew. Standing in front of the hearth with the fire inside crackling and popping, she couldn't stop glancing at the man beside her and thinking about the words he said to her.

'We shall face this together. The three of us.'

The three of us.

This was the first time he had mentioned their child since the day she told him about it—the day he said they should live apart. He stated he would provide for them both and that he intended to visit regularly so the child would know him, but this was the first time he made it sound as though they would be a family. And they would be, regardless of where he lived.

There was no doubt in her mind that when he would be around, he would be a good father. She had watched him with his nephew Nicholas.

The six-year-old had even decided he wanted to stand near Andrew's side during the ceremony, mimicking his uncle's perfectly erect posture. It might be because Nicolas obviously idolised him, but Andrew didn't seem to mind his close proximity, and she found that endearing.

The words of the vicar all blended together until it was time for them to recite their vows. The words fell from her lips easier than she had anticipated. Last night she had dreaded reciting them. But today, as she stood beside Andrew—a man whom she did not love, but genuinely liked and respected—the words just tumbled from her lips. The thin gold band she now wore was of his choosing and soon he would leave her to live the life she wanted. She would be able to return to her home, where she could raise their child and try to mend her relationship with Lizzy. That was what she wanted, wasn't it?

She was still asking herself that very question, hours later, when she was walking through the small formal garden at the back of her aunt's house. Even the birds that flew above her in the early evening sky were of no help in finding an answer.

As she strolled slowly back to the house, she spied Andrew standing alone on the terrace, watching her with his arms crossed and his hair tousled by the soft breeze. The night was warm and he was just in his shirtsleeves and black waistcoat, the very picture of relaxed, masculine strength. And the sight of him left her whole body hot and wanting.

He was her husband now. There was no scandal in making love to him and it was her wedding night. Had he come out of the house to find her?

As she made her way up the terrace steps, he silently watched her progress. It wasn't until she was at his side that he uncrossed his arms.

'You've been out here for over an hour.'

'I like walking in the evening air. I find it helps me sleep.'

'I understand you instructed my valet that we would be sharing a bedchamber.'

'Yes, I thought... I thought—'

Reaching out, he took her left hand and rubbed her gold wedding ring. 'I do not sleep well. I haven't for ages. Often times I will wake up in the middle of the night and it will be hours until I can fall back to sleep, if in fact I do. I would hate to disturb your sleep, especially now with the child.'

There were times like this that the circumstance of their marriage was glaringly obvious. They had not married for love. This was about giving their child a name. It would never be a true marriage.

'Forgive me. It was presumptuous of me.'

He raised her hand and pressed a soft kiss across her knuckles, just above her wedding ring. Her body came to life at the touch of his lips.

'There is nothing to apologise for, Charlotte. Had you relegated me to the stables, an apology would have been in order, but not now.'

His teasing comment alleviated some of her embarrassment and made her smile. 'The stables are too far.'

'How lucky for me.' He guided her hand to the crook of his arm and they stood side by side staring out into the garden and watched the sky turn a deeper shade of orangey-pink.

'Did you find a room to your liking?' she asked, still staring straight ahead because looking at him like this, while they were all alone and she could feel the heat from his body, was making her insides flutter.

'I have not seen it yet. I told him to place me in a bedchamber next to yours.'

'Oh.' It came out on an excited breath.

His warm hand guided her chin gently towards him, and he turned his body so he was facing her. 'Were you aware that I adore how tall you are?'

'You do? Why?'

'So that I do not have to bend down so far to do this.' He lowered his head, and his soft tongue traced the fullness of her lips.

She opened her mouth to him and their kiss

was surprisingly gentle and slow, as if they had all the time in the world together. Which they didn't—but they did have tonight.

'We should have checked for lurking gardeners,' she said in almost a whisper, pressing herself into him.

'Perhaps we should go upstairs.' Eyeing her hair, he released one jewelled comb, then the second, and finally the last. They were a wedding gift from him and she adored them.

Her hair cascaded down around her shoulders and the heavy weight brushed against her skin as he placed the combs into the pocket of his waistcoat.

'Are you trying to be scandalous, Andrew?'

'We are so good at it. I see no reason to stop now.' His gaze moved over her hair before settling on her eyes. Desire reflected back from the depths of his. Threading the fingers of both his hands into the hair at the back of her head, he took her lips once more. But this time in a more urgent kiss.

She gripped his waistcoat at the small of his back, afraid if she let go she might fall. With every sweep of his tongue, her legs grew weaker and weaker.

'I've had you once outside, it's time I take you in a proper bed.' As the sky darkened, she could make out the devilish look in his eyes. He looked dangerous. He looked as though once he got her in bed, they would not be coming out for days.

She released her grip and took a step back. 'But you don't know where my bed is, do you?'

Slowly, he shook his head.

She took one more step back to separate them. 'Then how will you find me?'

Picking up her skirts, she ran for the house with Andrew not far behind. Once she rounded the corner in the entrance hall, she skidded on the slippery marble floor as she made her way for the stairs. If she had any chance of reaching the top before he did, she would have to take the shallow steps two at a time. Luckily her legs were long and she easily made it to the top. The sound of his heavy footfalls behind her had her sprinting towards her bedroom. She wasn't certain if she was running to reach it first or because she wanted to get them both in her bed as quickly as possible.

Pushing open the door, she was relieved to find the room empty, but the sight before her left her frozen in her tracks. Seconds later, Andrew skidded to a stop behind her. Their heavy breathing mixed together and filled the room.

There were no words that could describe the sight before them of her bed. Or maybe there were too many. Astonishing. Unexpected. Mortifying.

'Did you have your maid do that?' he asked with astonishment.

She thrust her bottom back into him and nudged him out into the corridor, quickly shutting the door behind her. When she spun to face him, she knew she was blushing and, in the candlelight of the corridor, she knew he could see.

When he opened his mouth to speak, she raised her finger in warning. 'Do not say a word.'

'But—'

'Not one.'

He bit his lip to stop himself from smiling, but it wasn't working. She could still see his lips curving up at the ends.

'We will go to your room,' she stated firmly.

'So that *is* your room.' Amusement danced in his eyes.

'Yes, it's the one I've been using since I came to stay with my aunt, but I did not do that. I did not have my maid do that.' But she was certain Aunt Clara instructed someone to.

He picked her up by her biceps and moved her aside as if she weighed nothing more than his nephew. Before she was able to stop him, he opened her bedchamber door and stepped inside. She ran behind him.

A fire was already lit in the hearth, casting the room in a warm, flickering glow. And on her bed—all over her bed—were red rose petals. There had to be hundreds of them scenting the room.

Andrew's eyebrows were somewhere up near his hairline as he surveyed her bed before turning to face her. 'I can say with all certainty that I have never seen so many rose petals in one place in all my life.'

She tried to smile, but her lips were too stiff with embarrassment. 'Certainly that can't be true.'

Running his hands through the petals and watching them drop back down, he parted his lips in fascination. 'Oh, it's true. Who—?'

'My aunt. Or her maid. It doesn't matter, I am certain this was Aunt Clara's idea.'

The allure of watching the rose petals drift down from his hand was still holding Andrew's attention. Not sure what to do, Charlotte shifted on her feet and then reached for the corner of the coverlet.

He took hold of her wrist. 'What are you doing?'

'I was going to wrap up the coverlet and shake it out the window.'

'Why?'

'What else should I do with them?'

That devilish look was back in his eyes, making her catch her breath.

'I have a few ideas.' He released her wrist and gently pulled her towards him by the neckline of her gown. Looking down, he took his time un-buttoning his waistcoat before he peeled it off his body. Next, he undid the knot of his cravat and unwound it from his neck as if he were unwrapping a present for her. With his cravat gone, his shirt fell open, giving her a glimpse of his smooth muscular chest. The shadows from the firelight played with lines of muscles that stretched from his ribcage to the angles of his face. When he looked up at her through his lashes her mouth went dry, but when his gaze dropped from her eyes to her breasts, he was the one to wet his lips.

She was afraid to move. Afraid to break the spell he had over her that was causing her body to tingle in the most intimate places. When he reached behind his head and pulled off his shirt with one hand, she had to grab on to the bed post to steady her legs.

The corner of his mouth crooked up a fraction and he took his finger and trailed a line from her collarbone over the top swell of her right breast and rested in her cleavage. In a tantalisingly slow movement, he slid his middle finger from the swell of one breast, across the swell of the other and back again. The entire time, he didn't say a word.

It was becoming difficult to take a steady breath and she would have given anything to slip out of her stays. As if he read her mind, he spun her around by her waist and pressed his already hard length into her bottom. He took her hair and pushed it over her shoulder before he undid all the buttons on her dress. It slipped easily from her shoulders, falling down around her feet in a shimmering heap. Holding her hands, he assisted her in stepping out of it.

When she straightened up, he pulled on the string of her stays, looking at her as if he would devour her. His mouth found her nipple and he tongued it through her chemise before sucking it into his mouth. Carried away by her own response, she threaded her fingers through his hair and tugged. A soft moan slipped from his lips as he pulled his head away.

'I need to see all of you this time.' His deep voice sounded even huskier.

She looked over at the bed of rose petals and wanted to cry. All she wanted to do was feel him inside her. When she looked back at Andrew, their eyes met as he kicked off his shoes.

He reached for her chemise by her hips and lifted it over her head. She should be embarrassed. She should want to hide from him. But the curse he uttered while his gaze raked over every inch of her had her feeling desired and emboldened, so she undid the buttons on the fall of his trousers. He practically tore them off along with his stockings before he picked her up and placed her gently on the bed. Rose petals flew in all directions.

He stretched himself over her. The touch of his hand was almost unbearable in its tenderness as he traced the line on her collarbone and down between her breast, before trailing down even further. They had all the time in the world and Andrew appeared intent on taking advantage of every second of it. When he slid two fingers inside her, it was impossible to take a deep breath, and she arched her back at the delicious feeling. She wound her arms around his waist, wanting to feel even closer to him. Not wanting to let him go.

Could she say it? Could she be that forward?

'I want you, Andrew.'

His fingers slipped out of her, spreading her wetness along the way. 'Now?'

'Now.'

She barely got to finish the very short word before he leaned his torso over her and thrust himself inside her. Her head flew back while she cried out from the sensation. He claimed her mouth in a hungry kiss that told her she was not alone in her intense desire. She dug her nails into the curve of the muscles in his arms and held on, needing him to ground her. She felt absolutely defenceless against the onslaught of emotions rising inside her.

Andrew found a rhythm that suited them both,

at times urgent and then slowing down to long leisurely thrusts. His fingers were tangled in her hair when he pulled his head away and stared into her eyes. There was an unspoken moment that passed between them—a moment where it felt as if they were the only two people in the world and were intent on spending the rest of their lives together. But as suddenly as she felt it, it quickly passed and was replaced by the need to give each other the most pleasure. He leaned down and kissed her once more and before long they cried out their releases in unison, as if their bodies were acknowledging how perfect they were for each other, even though neither of their hearts could see it.

Chapter Nineteen

Andrew collapsed next to Charlotte on the bed while they both were having a hard time catching their breath. The circles of red petals were stuck to his skin that was damp with sweat. Suddenly, the recollection of their child made him roll to his side and look down at her. 'Did I hurt you? Did I hurt the baby?'

Her eyelids fluttered open and her dark well-arched brows furrowed. 'You have done no damage to me. And I think the baby is fine. It's still too small. Look, my stomach doesn't yet have a bump.'

He looked down at her flat stomach and placed his palm upon it. Their child was in there. He rested his ear against her soft skin to listen for any sound.

She trailed her fingers through the strands of his hair. 'Olivia recommended her physician to me and I saw him yesterday.'

'Why did you not tell me?'

'I didn't think it was something you would want to know. He said, if we wanted to, we could continue to make love until the time I deliver. It will not harm the baby.'

That bit of information told him that she wanted to keep having sex with him for the time they were together. They didn't have very long. From now until they parted ways, they should have sex every night. Or every morning. It didn't matter which. Maybe both.

'Do you hear anything in there?' she asked, pulling him out of his thoughts.

He wasn't sure what a baby would sound like inside its mother, but he listened closely. 'Just some gurgling sounds. Do you think that's it?'

'I don't know.'

'Do you feel anything moving inside you?' It seemed logical that she might, but he honestly didn't know if mothers ever did. He knew his nephews were noisy and moved around a lot as babies, but it was possible when they were growing inside Olivia they were still and silent.

There was a pause, as if Charlotte was analysing what her body was experiencing at that exact moment. 'No. I don't feel anything.'

'Do you think it's a boy or a girl?'

'Each day my opinion changes,' she replied as she softly rubbed the strands of his hair between her fingers. 'What do you think?'

'I assume it's a boy. My family comes from a long line of boys. I don't think any Pearce man has conceived a girl in hundreds of years.'

Her hand stilled in his hair. 'That can't be true.'

He looked up at her. 'It is. The last girl born a Pearce was in the sixteenth century.'

'Humph.' She went back to gently stroking his hair. 'What would you want to name it if it's a boy?'

Andrew hadn't ever given much thought to what he would name a son. He had never wanted one. Or a daughter. 'I think Edgar is a fine noble name,' he replied with a teasing smile. The sound of her laughter drifted to his ear. 'Do you have an idea what you would want to name it?' The idea that she would want to name it Jonathan brought bile to his throat. He held his breath and waited for her response.

'I thought we would name it Andrew, after you.'

The gesture humbled him and he kissed her abdomen and hoped his child felt it.

'But since you suggested Edgar…'

He poked his finger into her side and was rewarded to find she was ticklish.

'And if it's a girl?' she asked. 'I understand the likelihood is small, however if it is indeed a girl what would you like to name it? Do you have any dead pets you're fond of?'

'Not any that were girls,' he replied. 'What about you?'

'I'd like to name her Elizabeth.'

'After your sister?'

'Yes.'

'Why was she not here today?'

Her hand stilled once again. He picked his head up to look at her and saw sadness mixed with something else in her eyes. Something that resembled guilt.

'She doesn't approve of this...of what happened between us, does she, Charlotte?' He knew her sister had had an interest in him, but he had found her shallow and too preoccupied with position and wealth for his taste. She was a duchess. Did she truly fear her position in Society was in danger because of their child? He had married Charlotte. The scandal had been averted.

'She...she...' Charlotte looked away and closed her eyes, as if she was trying to block out where she was.

'That's it, isn't it?'

'Must we talk of my sister now? Here?'

His family had always banded together during difficult times. Facing problems together they were stronger. He had never thought her family would not feel the same when faced with a scandal. And yet, Charlotte still wanted to name their child after her sister. They must have been close at one time.

Andrew lowered his head back down, not liking to see Charlotte sad and wanting to erase this moment of causing her pain. 'You may name the baby whatever you like.'

There was a long pause. He thought she hadn't heard him.

'So, I can name him Andrew Edgar?' she teased.

He smiled and sent a kiss to their child. 'If you like. Although we might want to avoid telling our child he was named after a turtle.'

'It will be our secret.' She picked rose petals off his back and tossed them to the floor.

Then, just as he thought she had picked them all off, the pad of her fingers began tracing a line on his side below his ribcage close to his hip. As her fingers gently moved back and forth, he knew she had discovered one of his many scars.

'How did you get this?' she enquired, craning her neck to see it in the firelight.

'Fencing,' he lied and wondered how many more lies he would tell her in their lifetime. If she knew he had been in a knife fight it would stir up questions he wasn't willing to answer—not truthfully anyway.

She continued to trace the raised scar that was his largest, as if taking a tactile measurement of it, as silence stretched between them.

'Do you fence often?' There was a catch to her voice that made him think that, unlike his past lovers, Charlotte would not be an easy woman to convince.

'Occasionally.'

'Well, with a scar this size, it's possible I've found the one thing you do not excel at.'

The competitive nature inside him was at war with his rational mind. He had won that knife fight. How he wished he could tell her that.

Charlotte moved her hand up his side and once again ran her nails softly across his back, scrubbing away the reminder of the time he was attacked outside the tavern in Dover. She was bound to see his other scars. He could always blame them on his time in the ring. Not only was it a way to hone his skills with his fists, over the years boxing had always proved an ideal way to explain his other injuries.

It was becoming difficult to keep his eyes open. He glanced at the clock on the mantel and was surprised to see that it was only nine o'clock. This was much too early to go sleep. He hadn't fallen asleep this early since he was Nicholas's age. But the warmth of the room, the quality of the mattress and Charlotte's gentle caresses were lulling him to sleep.

There was only one woman in the world for him. He knew that now and could never imagine wanting anyone else. But their separation was necessary. He couldn't allow them to develop deep feelings for one another. If they did and something happened to him, there was no telling what another loss would do to Charlotte. He wouldn't risk hurting her like that. And he could never be an effective operative if he was distracted worrying about leaving his wife and child. Living apart, without any chance of falling in love, was best for both of them.

Even now, sleeping in the same bed together would be a mistake. It was too dangerous and would create too many questions. It was one of the reasons he chose to live in Albany. The restrictions on women being on the premises made it an ideal place to call home.

The nightmares of pulling the trigger on his Uncle Peter had haunted him since that fateful night. He was only able to sleep a few hours, and waking up in a cold sweat with your heart pounding wasn't conducive to going back to sleep. Charlotte didn't need to be exposed to that. And how would he explain the gun he slept with under his pillow?

His own room wasn't far away. He should go there.

Just as soon as she stopped caressing his back...

Andrew tried to open his eyes, but his eyelids were so heavy. There was a different scent in the air, not like the familiar smell of ash from a fire that had been burning all night and had recently gone out. This smell wasn't smoky.

A hand dropped on his chest.

On instinct, he rolled to his side, pinning the body beside him down and holding the owner's wrists above their head with his right hand. His chest was heaving with fear and his left hand dived under his pillow in search of his gun. It wasn't there. Where the hell was it?

When his vision cleared, he saw Charlotte's wide eyes staring up at him with fear. Immediately, he released her. He tried to help her into a sitting position, but she knocked his hand away.

'My God, Charlotte. I'm so sorry. I forgot where I was.' He knew the power and strength he had. He knew he could have easily broken her wrists or injured her in some way. His instincts from years of protecting himself had screamed he was in danger and he needed to subdue his potential attacker. That was why falling asleep with a woman was a bad idea.

The clock on the mantel said it was seven. How was that possible? The last time he had looked it was nine. That was almost twelve hours. He never slept more than a few hours a night. The languid feeling that he had when he first started to wake up was gone. Every muscle in his body was strung tight as he watched her rub her wrists.

He was afraid to touch her now. He wasn't afraid he would hurt her. Knowing now that it was Charlotte, he knew he never would. However, he was afraid she would once again push him away.

'What is wrong with you?' she asked, her tone filled with anger.

'Please forgive me. I am so sorry. I told you we shouldn't sleep together. I told you it would be best for me to have my own room.'

'Because you said you had trouble sleeping at night and wake frequently. Not because you'd try to kill me!'

At her words, the blood drained from his face, and his body ran cold. It was impossible to swallow and every instinct he had was telling him to run. This was why men like him should never marry. But it was too late now.

'I wasn't trying to kill you. I was disorientated. I've never slept in the same bed with anyone before. I'm sorry. I'm so sorry.'

Criss-crossing her legs, she pulled a pillow from behind her and hugged it to her chest. 'Tell me why that happened. Tell me why your first instinct upon awakening was to defend yourself from an unknown enemy.'

She understood exactly what had happened. Perhaps because she was the wife of a soldier. But he couldn't tell her the truth. He couldn't tell her about his years of work that at times included fighting for his life. His father had told him countless times to suspect everyone and trust no one.

For a moment, it was years earlier and he was back in the garden of their safe house in Richmond. Flashes of lightning were exploding in the sky around him. Rain was pouring down in sheets as he ran towards Gabriel's anguished cry. When he came upon him, his friend Matthew's lifeless body was cradled in Gabriel's bloodied arms.

The last time he'd seen Matthew alive was when they'd parted ways in a tavern before Matthew joined Peter for the journey up north to investigate an uprising about Catholic emancipation. Now Peter was standing over Gabriel with a gun pointed at his chest. A minute later Peter cocked his pistol and Andrew shot him. The reality of it, all these years later, still made his blood run cold. Gabriel managed to cover up the nature of the shootings and they had been blamed on an attempted robbery. The kind of trust answering her question required was something he couldn't afford to offer her.

He scrubbed his hand across the light stubble on his cheeks. She was still waiting for his answer. He would have to lie and blame his reaction on his pugilist training. She couldn't know that his instincts to defend himself began when his father had one of his finest operatives train

Andrew and Gabriel in various forms of self-defence when the boys were only ten and eleven years of age. At the time, they were unaware their father was grooming both of them for a future protecting the Crown. That was only revealed to them seven years later. But for over twenty years his instincts had been honed for self-preservation. It wasn't something he could shut off at will, even if he wanted to—which for his own safety would not be wise.

'You know I like to box. When you're standing in the ring you become so focused. It's as though you are looking at things through a pipe and all you can see is what is directly in front on you. Everything else is blacked out. Your sole focus is on survival—on not being carted out looking like a bloody mess. I've boxed for years. I've trained and worked at it with a determination to be the best I can be.'

Her gaze shifted from his face to his shoulders, then landed on his biceps. The fear was gone from her eyes and replaced with her undivided attention.

'The more you box, the more your brain and your muscles react by instinct. If someone is trying to plant me a facer with their right hand, I don't have to think that I should block them and give them an upper cut into their stomach. I just do it. My body takes over before my mind tells it to. That's why I'm so good at it. That's why I win as many matches as I do. I have quick reflexes.'

'You're saying that is why you held me down?'

'I'm saying my body saw you as a threat. I've never woken up beside someone before. My instinct screamed I was in danger and that was how I reacted. Please believe me when I say that if I knew it was you, I never would have reacted the way I did when you put your hand on me.'

'You did that because of how you were trained to fight in the ring?' She was eyeing him with obvious curiosity.

He was able to nod and swallow the lump in his throat.

'Then I agree, Andrew. We shouldn't sleep in the same bed. Soon we will be living apart. You won't have enough time to get accustomed to sleeping beside me. It would be safer this way.'

He held his hand out to her. Without hesitation, she placed her left one in his. The gold ring reflected the morning light.

'I am sorry, Charlotte. Truly I am.'

'You really have never slept in the same bed with anyone before?'

'You're the first,' he replied with a shrug.

'Humph.' There was a small smile on her lips when she looked away. 'I hope all that boxing is worth it. You are depriving yourself of a wonderful experience.'

'Apparently, I am, since I slept for ten hours.'

The very idea of it was ludicrous. 'However, boxing is not only a sport I enjoy, it is one of the ways I've become financially solvent so I do not have to appeal to my family for funds.'

'I don't understand. Do you make money on your boxing matches? Do people pay you to box? Are there wagers?'

That made him laugh. 'No, I am a silent partner in a boxing saloon on Bond Street. I've helped the gentleman who runs the establishment by providing him with additional financial help. In return, he pays me a percentage of his revenue. I also have shares in two taverns in Richmond and a coffee house in Islington.'

Three of the gentlemen had worked for Gabriel. When they decided to end their careers in espionage, Andrew had helped them establish the coffee house and taverns so they could provide for themselves.

She moved closer. 'So, you are part-owner of a boxing saloon. Is that the one your brother thought you would want to get married in?'

'It is. I spend a great deal of my time there.'

'Then not only could you tell me what a boxing saloon looks like, you could show me.' There was a spark of excitement in her eyes.

'I could. I could show it to you any night you like after closing, or any morning before it opens for the day. I have the keys.'

'What time does it open for the day?'

'Eleven.'

She was practically bouncing on the bed as she poked his side. 'It is half past seven now.'

'Yes, and I have the oddest desire to go back to sleep after this morning's excitement.'

'Well, not in here you won't. Take me now.'

For the first time since he had woken up, he realised he was naked and she was not wearing anything under that white sheet wrapped around her curves. Crawling over her like a lion, he made her drop back on to her pillows.

'I would like nothing better.' He dipped his head down to her neck and placed soft kisses along her skin before trailing his lips to the swell of her breast. Kneading her soft flesh with his hand, he gave it a gentle squeeze before sucking the tip into his mouth.

Her back arched off the mattress and she let out a moan before pushing on his shoulders. He lifted his head and met her half-opened eyes.

'I meant take me to see the boxing saloon, not take me in my bed.'

'Can't we do both?'

'I suppose we can, but we should hurry before the saloon opens for the day.'

'You want to do this quick?'

As if she might be regretting her words, she chewed her lip. 'This time.'

'Ah, so you're already thinking about next time.' He cupped her breast again. 'I think I can accommodate your request this time. Next time we will take it slow. Or perhaps we can do it again rather quickly in the dressing room of an empty boxing saloon.'

Chapter Twenty

Tʜey had been married for only two weeks and Charlotte was already accustomed to her husband's behaviour. For a man who had lived alone, Andrew was remarkably easy to live with. They discovered they both woke up early and, while he hadn't slept in her bed again since their wedding night, he did manage to crawl into hers around the time she woke up each day, delaying her morning walk in the park and his morning ride.

They both read the same papers and both were not fond of sugar in their coffee or tea. He was gone most of the day, handling his business affairs, which suited Charlotte just fine since she wasn't accustomed to having a husband underfoot. However, each night he'd return home and they'd spend hours enjoying dinner together, walking through the garden and engaging in stimulating conversations.

She was also enjoying the time she was spending with Olivia, who had also remained in Town despite the Season ending. Apparently, Gabriel also had things to attend to in Town that kept them out of their country home in July. It was wonderful to be able to ask her questions about the changes she could expect in her body in the coming months. And since Olivia had delivered her second only five months ago, the memory of that birth was still fresh in her mind.

Thankfully, Andrew wasn't treating her like a rare piece of porcelain because of her condition. Around him, she never felt helpless. He even agreed to teach her how to box. And she was certain they were scandalising her aunt's staff when he agreed to do so, out in the garden.

Andrew had led her to a small grassy area lined with thick privet hedges and a garden bench that Charlotte had discovered was an ideal spot for reading. The sun was out and the breeze that was rustling through the leaves was warm enough for Andrew to go outside in just his linen shirt and his blue trousers that were tucked into a well-worn pair of topped boots. He had rolled his sleeves up and Charlotte was finding it difficult not to stare at the muscles of his forearms. It was an odd part of his body to set her pulse racing, however, she was finding it difficult not to keep looking down at them.

'Charlotte, if you want to learn to throw a

punch, you need to pay attention to what I'm saying.'

'I am.'

'No, you're not. I want your eyes on me...on my eyes.'

'Oh, very well.'

When she looked up at him, she was met with his amused expression.

He shook his head. 'Now show me again how to make a fist.'

She curled her hand into a first, remembering to keep her thumb on the outside, just as he instructed her.

'Good, now hit my hand.' He held up his right palm with his fingers extended straight into the air.

'I can't hit you.'

'Of course you can. Just punch my palm as hard as you can.'

She threw her hand into his and had the satisfaction of hearing a loud smack. His hand barely moved.

'Harder, Charlotte.'

'That was hard,' she insisted.

He arched his brow. 'Think of something that makes you really angry. Think of how you feel when I take the last bits of the crispy bacon at breakfast.'

She threw her hand into his, harder this time. His hand jerked back an inch.

'You can do better than that. Think of something that makes you furious…something that you wished you were able to address, but you can't…something that is out of your control.'

She thought of all the letters that she had written to Lizzy that were sent back unopened. She thought of how if only she was given the chance, she'd be able to make her sister understand and maybe forgive her.

The force of her punch was so strong that it threw Andrew's hand back and he shook it out.

She grabbed his wrist and looked at his hand. 'Did I hurt you?'

'Yes,' he said with a laugh. 'But you were supposed to. How did that feel?'

'Brilliant!' All this time thinking about Lizzy and worrying that she would never speak to her sister again had been eating her up inside. That punch made her feel a little better.

'Would you like to do it again?'

She threw another punch at his hand, this time with all her might. The sound of someone clearing their throat startled both of them and they turned to find one of Aunt Clara's footmen standing nearby holding out a calling card to Charlotte.

'Elizabeth, the Duchess of Skeffington, is here to see you, madam.'

Convinced she had misheard him, Charlotte took the card with her sore hand.

'Shall I tell her you're receiving?' He glanced at Andrew before looking back at her for some indication.

For weeks, she had tried to speak with Lizzy. Now that she was here, Charlotte's heart began to pound as she wondered what had finally brought her to her door.

Andrew stepped closer and brushed a way-ward curl away from her forehead. He had been with her when some of those letters were re-turned. Not once had he asked her about them, but she knew he was attuned to how sad she would get each time she received one.

The footman cleared his throat. 'Madam?'

'I will see her in the drawing room. See that tea is brought there and let her know that I will be in to see her shortly. I just have to tidy my-self up.'

With a nod and a nervous glance at Andrew, he went back down the gravel path to the house.

Andrew lifted her hand—the one that she had used to punch him—and kissed her knuckles. 'I assume by your expression you were unaware she would be calling on you today.'

'She has returned all my letters. She has never even read them. Perhaps she has come to tell me to stop writing to her.' Charlotte rubbed her stomach, trying to sooth the nerves that were jumping around in there.

'If that were the case, I would think she would

send you a note and not have travelled here to do it.'

Unless she felt the need to rail at Charlotte some more… She still felt horrible at destroying her sister's hopes of marrying Andrew, but there were still times she wondered if he would have pursued Lizzy if they had not met.

'Would you like me to remain by your side while you meet her? Perhaps if I lay the blame for the child at my door, you will be able to mend your relationship.'

He was being lovely. She placed her hand on his chest, just above his heart, and tried to absorb some of the calmness coming out of the steady beats.

'While I appreciate the kind gesture, I think it would be better if I speak with her alone.' She knew seeing them together would be difficult for Lizzy and they would never be able to discuss what had really caused a rift between them if Andrew was present.

'Very well. I'll be down in the kitchen having them chip away some ice for my hand.' A teasing smile lifted his lips before he kissed her temple. 'I know you have great affection for her. However, I am not pleased with her for causing you any pain, but for your sake I hope you and your sister are able to mend this.'

Deep down Charlotte knew this might be her only chance. If she couldn't get Lizzy to understand now, time would make it harder and harder to fix this and easier to remain estranged.

Charlotte's heart was pounding with apprehension as she walked into the drawing room and found her sister standing in front of one of the long windows with her arms crossed, staring pensively out at the garden.

'Hello, Lizzy.'

As she turned her head, Lizzy's eyebrows rose when her gaze dropped to Charlotte's dress. 'You're wearing green.' The surprise that was apparent in her voice was enough to make her turn her entire body to face Charlotte. 'When did you stop wearing your mourning gowns?'

'On my wedding day.'

Lizzy looked back at the window, but it was evident she wasn't seeing past the glass panes.

'I had begun to give up hope we would talk again,' Charlotte said, stepping further into the room, not sure if she was stepping into a lion's den. 'You returned all my letters.'

'I wasn't ready to read them.' Her attention was back on Charlotte and it was difficult to determine how she was feeling from her stoic expression.

'And now?'

Her sister scanned the open doorway behind Charlotte, while she rubbed her chest above the neckline of her grey and white muslin gown.

Lizzy had not removed her lavender pelisse, although it was unbuttoned. Hopefully this meant she had intended to spend more than a few minutes in the same room with her sister.

'Now I find I want to see how you are faring.' She gestured towards Charlotte's flat abdomen as if she couldn't bring herself to mention the baby that was the result of Charlotte and Andrew's one night together.

'I've arranged tea for us. Will you stay?'

Lizzy hesitated before walking towards the unlit hearth and taking a seat on one of the sofas. Charlotte wished she knew if the visit was one of true concern for her well-being or just morbid curiosity. Thankfully the tea arrived, breaking the awkward moment and giving Charlotte something to do. She handed Lizzy a cup of tea with milk and two lumps, just the way she liked it, and began to pour her own.

'Lady Margaret Dawson passed yesterday, delivering her sixth child.'

That was not news that was particularly comforting to hear at this moment of Charlotte's life. The statement hung in the air while Charlotte wondered if her sister realised how frightening news like that could be for a woman who would be giving birth.

'You have my condolences. I know she was a friend.'

'She was. Thank you.' There was sorrow in

Lizzy's eyes as she took a sip of tea. 'I understand you were married here.'

Charlotte glanced up from pouring tea into her cup. 'I was. Our aunt was kind enough to offer it to us.'

'Which room were you married in?'

Afraid her hands would shake because she was leery of how the conversation might turn, Charlotte rested her cup and saucer on her knee. 'This one.'

Her sister surveyed the room. 'It's an interesting choice for a wedding location. I understand from our sister that his family was in attendance along with Aunt Clara and Juliet, but no one else save the vicar.'

'We… I wanted something small.'

'I would have chosen St George's or St James's.' She eyed the room again and then her gaze landed once again on Charlotte's muslin gown and her forehead wrinkled. 'You've taken off Jonathan's ring.' It was stated as an observation, not an accusation.

Charlotte hadn't thought about that ring since she locked it away. As if she could still touch it, her hand went to her chest, where there was a sudden pang of guilt. 'It was time to put it away.'

'I'd been telling you that for years,' Lizzy said over the brim of her teacup. 'You never listened to me.'

'I would still be wearing it if it weren't for…'

She put her lips together because she didn't know what else to say. She knew Lizzy had been picturing what her own wedding to Andrew would have been like.

'You don't look as though you're carrying his child.'

Was she accusing Charlotte of fabricating a baby so Andrew would be forced to marry her? 'I understand in another two months or so I will begin to show.' It was hard not to sound defensive.

'What does it feel like?'

Oh, God, did Lizzy want to hear what it was like to be married to Andrew? It was wonderful. He was wonderful. But that wouldn't help mend fences with Lizzy. Or had she meant carrying the child? 'I suffered with some minor illness early on. It seems to have subsided now.'

Lizzy put her cup down on the small round table beside her and leaned forward. 'I recall how green you were in the carriage that day. Do you truly feel better? Margaret had suffered through sickness with each of her children. This last had been especially difficult for her.

There was concern in her sister's voice. It almost brought tears to Charlotte's eyes.

'Yes, although if I smell chocolate, I want to vomit.'

A small laugh escaped Lizzy's lips before she

pressed them closed. 'Can you feel it moving inside you?'

'No, not yet. I think it is still too small.'

She nodded as if she hadn't considered that. 'Are you planning on delivering the child here or in Cheshire?'

'The Duchess of Winterbourne has introduced me to her physician. I understand he is very reputable and she has kindly offered to stay with me on their estate in Kent for the months surrounding the birth. I can alter the date of the birth if I choose when I return to Cheshire to ensure there is no speculation about the cause of my marriage.' Since Andrew would not be living with her, she was giving this consideration.

'Princess Charlotte had a well-respected physician attend to her. You know what happened to her.' She looked down at her hands and her shoulders dropped. 'I fear for you.'

It was as if Charlotte's heart leapt at the declaration. Was it possible that she hadn't lost Lizzy for ever? Was it possible they could be as close as they once were? 'I will be fine. You have nothing to fear.'

'But you can't say that for certain.'

'No, I cannot. But I won't live my life afraid that death is around every corner.'

There was a profound sadness in Lizzy's eyes. 'I've missed you, Charlotte. Terribly.' She extended her hand across the space between them with her palm facing up.

Instead of taking her hand, Charlotte moved beside Lizzy and wrapped her in her arms. 'I have missed you, too. I never meant to hurt you. Had I known...' She looked into her sister's large liquid eyes. 'This isn't what I wanted. You should have been the one to get married. My future was behind me.'

'Are you in love with him?'

She didn't want to talk to Lizzy about Andrew. And she didn't know how she felt about him. Each day they were together, she consciously avoided analysing why she liked being around him more than she liked when they were apart. Could one heart hold love for two men, even if one of them was gone? She had never thought that was possible. And trying to determine if it was only made her head hurt.

What she did know was that he made her happy and now, sitting across from Lizzy, that notion burned in her gut. Her sister looked so sad and alone. It broke Charlotte's heart to know that she had done that to her. She had taken away the chance at the one thing her sister thought would bring her happiness.

'I loved Jonathan, Lizzy. I do not love Andrew. We had to get married. There is a difference. From the time I realised I was carrying this child, I've been asking myself why did this happen now. I had prayed for years for a child when I was married to Jonathan. When he was killed, I mourned losing him and the child I would never have with him. This child should have been his.'

Lizzy's eyes were red and she began to sniffle. Charlotte grabbed her napkin off the upholstered bench of the sofa across from them and her eyes met Andrew's stoic expression as he stood in the doorway.

He held her gaze for a few heartbeats and then turned to walked away.

A cold chill ran through her body. Part of her wanted to run after him, but she didn't know what she would say. Knowing he had heard her filled every space of her heart with anguish.

Chapter Twenty-One

Andrew sat on a bench in the garden, hunched over and staring down at the grass between his boots, where a short while ago he had been laughing with Charlotte. His chest ached and it was hard to swallow. He was an ass. As much as he vowed to himself that he wouldn't get close to her, he had. He cared for her and wanted to have a life with her.

This child should have been his.

They didn't belong together. She was never his and never would be. He would always be a poor substitute for the one man she had ever loved—would ever love. That would never change.

There was no sense in denying he was falling in love with her. He thought about her more than he should and would rather be here teaching her how to plant a facer than in Gabriel's study discussing threats to the Crown. She had disrupted his orderly life and he hadn't stopped her.

It was time he drew up a new plan.

The sound of slow footfalls crunching on the gravel path should have had him looking up, but he couldn't be bothered. It wasn't until Charlotte's green slippers came into view that he finally raised his head. She brushed a wayward strand of his hair out of his eyes and clasped her hands together in front of her. For someone who appeared to have mended her relationship with her sister, her expression was very grave.

'Were you able to get some ice for your hand?'

He looked back down and dug out some grass with the tip of his boot. 'The iceman hadn't been around today.'

Birds started chirping in the tree behind him. 'Does it truly hurt?'

He never thought leaving her would hurt this much. He never thought his heart could hold this much pain. 'It won't hurt for ever.' At least he hoped it wouldn't, but he wasn't entirely certain.

'May I sit down?'

The wooden bench wasn't very big, but he made room for her by sliding to the end. He knew what he had to do, but every time he opened his mouth to say it, his chest would tighten and his throat would dry up. Finally, he found his voice. 'London is horrid in the heat.'

She clasped her hands together on her lap. 'It is—however, it's rather comfortable here in the shade.'

'But not everywhere you go do you find comfort in the shade.' Closing his eyes, he rubbed his chin and then turned to face her.

There was a look of regret in her eyes mixed with sadness. Had her visit with her sister reminded her how much she regretted having to marry him? It appeared that way.

'I loved Jonathan, Lizzy. I do not love Andrew. We had to get married. There is a difference.'

He would always remember those words. The grim sound of her voice while she said them would haunt him for a long time. It shouldn't matter to him. But those words, said by the woman sitting next to him, sliced him to pieces like no knife could.

He took a deep breath and braced himself for what he had to do. 'London in the summer is no place for you. You should go back to Cheshire.'

'You want us to go to Cheshire?'

'No. I think *you* should go.'

Charlotte couldn't unclasp her hands if she tried. Her entire body stiffened with his words. He wanted her to leave?

'I don't mind the warm weather and I find I actually prefer London when the Season is over. There are far fewer crowds and no social obligations.'

'It is not good for you or the baby.'

'It won't be that much different up north.' It

was too soon. They were just settling in together. Two weeks. They had only been married two weeks!

'Charlotte.' His stern tone startled her with its sound of reproach. 'This needs to end.'

Her stomach dropped. 'What?'

He scrubbed his hand across his mouth and looked over at her, all the while keeping his body angled forward. 'Why are we doing this? Why are we pretending this marriage is more than it really is? We were married because of a child. Both of us have lives that we want to live and those lives take us to two different places. There is no reason either of us should be inconvenienced this way.'

The smallest tremor shook her body. He was doing this because he heard her tell Lizzy they hadn't married for love. It wasn't a lie. But that didn't mean she hadn't come to care for him. That didn't mean that she wanted to live apart.

But apparently, she had reminded him that he did.

Butterflies were crashing in her stomach while her chest was so tight it was a wonder she could breathe. She was losing him and she didn't know what to say to stop it from happening.

'Why should we prolong the inevitable?' His voice faded in the hushed stillness between them. 'Why should you remain here in London with me?'

Through the jumble of her emotions, she tried to determine why she didn't want their time together to end so soon. She had no words to describe what it was she felt about him or why she wanted to be with him. She only knew she did. But he was asking her for a reason and she didn't have one to give him, not one that she was willing to admit to him or even to herself. And the fact he was pushing her for an answer she didn't have was making her feel as though she was in a small room with no way out.

'You don't have to accompany me,' she said in a rush. 'I am capable of returning home on my own.'

She had just mended her relationship with Lizzy. Her sister's words when she was leaving were still fresh in Charlotte's mind.

'I'm sorry. I realise you didn't do any of this to purposely hurt me.'

For the past three weeks, Charlotte believed that if Lizzy would only speak to her again, this hollowness inside her would go away. But it was still there. And, it felt even bigger now.

He turned away and stared at his foot digging into the ground, pushing dirt and grass up on the black leather. 'I will accompany you to Cheshire.' More dirt slid across the leather. 'As the new master of the house, I need to become acquainted with your staff. I expect I'll stay for a day or two before I return to London.'

At least this time when he left, she would know he was going. Not that it would make adjusting to his absence from her life any easier. Her mouth was so dry it was difficult to speak. 'Shall I send word to you when I arrive in Kent prior to the birth?'

He continued to look down at the ground, and she almost thought he hadn't been paying attention to what she said, until he gave her a nod.

'Very well then, if this is what you wish.'

He kept digging his boot in the dirt.

There was no sense in sitting beside him when she was on the verge of tears. She was too proud for that. 'I should go inside and write to a few people to let them know I am leaving.' Her voice cracked when she said it, but she couldn't help it.

Chapter Twenty-Two

A soft breeze blew in through the long open widows of the billiards room at Toby's house as Andrew prepared to take his shot. The suggestion to play billiards was his, since it was the closest thing he could do with Toby to help him try to forget that he was leaving Charlotte in less than an hour. He would have preferred to go a few rounds with Toby, but that would likely end with his friend bloodied and bruised, and he didn't think Ann Knightly would appreciate that.

'It's taking you an awful long time to line up that shot,' Toby said.

'You're standing too close.'

'I'm on the other side of the table.'

For good measure, Andrew flicked his wrist to indicate Toby should move. It didn't matter if Toby stood in another room, Andrew's attention would still be drawn to the murmur of female voices travelling into the room through the open windows. And no matter how much he strained to listen, he couldn't hear what they were saying.

'Have you always been this bad at billiards? If I had known, I would have asked you to play more when you visited here last.'

'You're trying to distract me.'

Toby lowered his cue like a walking stick and leaned his lanky frame on it. 'No, I'm not. I am glad you did stop here before you left for London, though. It's nice to see you again.'

'You're only saying that because you're winning.'

'That might be true.'

When Andrew looked up from surveying the potential shot in front of him, he caught the look on Toby's face. 'If you would stop talking, I could make my shot.'

'Sorry.'

It was a warm day and both men had removed their coats. Andrew had rolled his sleeves up and the felt of the billiards table was warm against his skin. Getting ready to take his shot, he moved his head from side to side.

'With all the creaking, you sound like an old man.'

'Blast it, Toby, will you just stop talking.'

'Sorry.'

The sound of the voices outside grew from a murmur to a faint whisper. All he was able to make out was 'London' and he wasn't even sure who said it. Toby lowered himself so he was out of view of the table. Only the top of the billiards cue was visible.

Andrew leaned as far as he could over the table and saw the top of Toby's head. 'What the devil are you doing down there?'

'Sitting. Waiting for you to make that shot is exhausting.'

Letting out a groan, Andrew got back into position, lined up his shot and missed the ball entirely.

'Is it my turn?'

'Yes, come back up. It's your shot.'

When Toby stood, he surveyed the table. 'The ball hasn't moved.'

'Just don't...'

His friend held up his hands and walked around the table to study his shot. 'It will be nice to have you near now. We were thrilled to hear you and Charlotte met up unexpectedly in London and weren't surprised when we learned of your wedding.' He caught Andrew's eye before he looked back at the table. 'It was apparent the two of you liked one another and I won't mention that you looked as though you wanted to bed her the moment you laid eyes on her.'

'That is my wife you are speaking of.'

Toby looked back to Andrew. 'I mean no disrespect.'

'Then I suggest you find something else to

discuss. Or better yet, stop talking and take your shot.'

'I could analyse my shot for an hour and it still would be less than the time it took you to make your last one.'

Andrew moved his hands in a rude gesture which made Toby laugh.

'I do have one question for you,' Toby said, looking back down at the table. 'Why are you leaving so soon? You just arrived. Now you are going back to London and Charlotte is staying here.'

'I have business to attend to and I cannot take time away from it to be here.'

He knew it was a worthless excuse. It didn't matter. His marriage to Charlotte and the reason he was leaving was no one else's concern.

They had barely spoken since he had told her she should return to her home. Throughout their journey north she stayed inside her carriage and he rode his horse. Each time they stopped along the way to dine and rest the horses, they ate in silence. And when they stayed overnight in the inn, he arranged for separate rooms. They were travelling together as strangers, instead of husband and wife. It was better this way for her. It was for the best she did not love him. He led a dangerous life. She didn't deserve to lose another person she loved.

He thought leaving her would be easy. It was

what he had wanted. But each time he told himself it was time to go, he would find another excuse to stay. This time he vowed to himself this visit to Toby's would be the last thing he did with her. God willing, the next time he would see her would be in Kent for the birth of their child.

How he wished he had one last chance to place his hand on her stomach and try to feel any indication his child was inside and well. He didn't doubt she was carrying his child. Charlotte would never have lied about such a thing. But there was yet to be any kind of physical evidence it was in there. It still didn't quite feel real.

Voices drifted once more into the room and he went to the window to see what Charlotte was doing. He spied her walking among the roses in the garden with Ann Knightly. The straw bonnet she wore obscured the view of her face—a face that he knew would be haunting his dreams for a very long time.

Charlotte was coming to hate the smell of roses, but to be polite to Ann she was admiring the newest bushes that her friend had added to her garden.

'Aren't they lovely?'

No, they weren't. They were making her melancholy because they brought back memories of her wedding night with Andrew—a night that she once cherished and now, in the last few days, just brought her pain.

'Your Aunt Clara always liked roses. They remind me of her.'

'They once reminded me of her as well.' Until she walked into her room on her wedding night. Now, they brought her back to when Andrew had laid her on a bed of them. She glanced over at the house that was not far away and wondered what he was doing inside.

'It's a shame he has to return to London so soon,' Ann continued, 'but I agree with him, summer in the country is lovely. And I'm sure he will be returning as soon as his business affairs are settled. It is so nice to have you back here close to me.' She took Charlotte's hand and gave it a gentle squeeze.

From the corner of Charlotte's eye, she spied movement on the terrace and watched Toby and Andrew slowly walk towards the stable. It was time for him to go and her heart slipped in her chest. They hadn't been married very long, but she knew she was going to miss him.

She walked to the front of the house with Ann, as if it were a funeral. The last time Andrew left Cheshire, he hadn't said goodbye to her. That might have been preferable to what she was faced with now. When he suggested they go to see Ann and Toby before he left, it saddened her to think their last moments together would be shared with their friends. But now she was grateful for their company, since they could do most of the talking. She didn't know how to say goodbye to him.

As the men approached, Andrew held the reins to his horse, Eclipse. His strode towards her with that commanding presence he possessed and his long brown coat was blowing behind him with every step. The brim of his hat was low, blocking out the midday sun from his hazel eyes. This would be one of the last images she would have of him for months.

They stopped a few feet from her and he bade farewell to their friends. When he finally turned and looked at her, it was impossible to read his expression. There was no coldness in his eyes. They were just devoid of any emotion. Although she did see the muscle in his jaw tighten for a fraction of a second. When Toby and Ann stepped away from them, he walked closer to her.

'If you need anything at all, do not hesitate to write to me,' he said, scanning her face. 'I have left instructions with Mrs Hatch that if anything should happen to you and you are unable to write for assistance, she is to summon me at once.'

'I know. She told me. She thinks you will be a fine master of the house.'

'That's because your housekeeper knows I am leaving her in peace and won't be interfering with her work.' His gaze dropped to her midriff where their child was growing and his voice changed to a whisper. 'When will you tell everyone?'

'In a few weeks, it will be time. Would you please write to me when you arrive so that I know you've had a safe journey?'

The faint look of surprise followed by a warming in his eyes changed his unreadable countenance. 'If you like.'

He took one step closer so only a foot of air separated them and raised his gloved hand as if to stroke her cheek, before he lowered it when it was halfway there. 'Goodbye, Charlotte.'

Even though he said he would be meeting her in Kent months from now, it felt as though this would be the last time she would see him. 'Goodbye, Andrew. God speed.' It was a miracle she was able to speak past the lump in her throat.

He mounted his horse and tipped his hat to her. As she watched him gallop down the road without looking back, she tried to press his image into her memory.

'He will be back before you have even had a chance to miss him,' Ann said, coming up to her side. 'You will see.'

She was missing him already, and she knew for certain it would be a very long time before he came back here. And then it would only be to see their child. He didn't want to stay with her.

It was time she accepted that and stopped looking at an empty road. Taking Ann's arm, she returned with her to the garden, fighting the urge to turn back once more.

'You don't know how happy I am for you, Charlotte, that you found love again.'

Love? She wasn't in love with Andrew. She felt a deep affection for him. The human heart was incapable of loving two people. Her feelings for Andrew were different from those she had felt for Jonathan. When Jonathan had left her for his campaigns, she would always fear for his safety. That was her overriding emotion. But watching Andrew leave made her feel as if some light had gone out in her life. As if she had felt the sun on her face for the first time, only to have the sky darken with storm clouds. That wasn't love. Was it?

A dull ache was spreading in her chest, and Charlotte knew if she didn't distract herself somehow, she might break down in tears in front of Ann. 'It feels as if I have been gone for years instead of weeks. What news have I missed?'

'Here's something of interest. Mr Hunt will be addressing a meeting near St Peter's Church in Manchester soon. We've always wanted to hear him speak. Toby and I will be going. You should come with us.' She bumped her shoulder into Charlotte's. 'Don't look so sad. You'll see your husband again soon.'

If only that were true.

Chapter Twenty-Three

Andrew sat in Gabriel's study, his body humming with anticipation for a new assignment. Since he had been back in London, he had conducted numerous interrogations, trailed Lord Halford for five days, and met with an informant on information regarding a threat to Prinny. All of it had been relatively safe and civilised, and he wasn't sure if that had been Gabriel's intention. Now he was hoping Gabriel had something more exciting for him to do.

Last night he received word to call on his brother promptly at nine, which told him that he would be briefed on a new mission. It was just what he needed to keep his mind off the mess his personal life was in. Whatever this mission was, it was big enough that Gabriel needed three of his operatives to accomplish it.

'This is something we need to look into,' Gabriel said, sliding a piece of paper across his large mahogany desk towards Andrew, Spence and Henderson.

All three leaned forward in their chairs to get a better look. As was standard procedure when they all met together, the shutters were closed on the windows in Gabriel's study even though it was a warm day in late July, so they were forced to read the notice by the light of an oil lamp. The notice was a response to an advertisement that had been placed in a Manchester paper. Manchester was close to where Charlotte lived. What was his brother up to?

The paper stated that a meeting set for the ninth of August near St Peter's Church in Manchester had been deemed illegal by the local magistrates and anyone that did attend was doing so at their own peril. When Andrew looked up from reading the paper, Gabriel was watching him closely.

'I received this notice yesterday. Recently, it was announced Henry Hunt was invited to speak at a public meeting by the Manchester Patriotic Union,' Gabriel explained, sitting back in his chair, the leather creaking with his movement. 'He was to address the crowd on how to quickly obtain radical reform in the House of Commons and then they were to elect a representative to look out for their interests. It appears the magistrates in the area were concerned and decided to stop the meeting before people even had a chance to gather.'

Andrew felt his brow wrinkle in disgust. He understood the concerns of the people in those northern towns. He saw the conditions many were living in. Poverty was not reserved for Seven Dials here in London. If they were looking for ways to better their lives and those of their children, and have sufficient representation in the House of Commons, they should be able to do so.

'On what grounds can they prevent them from assembling?' Spence asked, his brows drawn together.

'On the grounds that it is illegal for them to elect a representative. They must have consulted with someone who has knowledge of the law, because they have moved their meeting to the sixteenth and will not be having an election this time. Now there is nothing the local magistrates can do to stop them from gathering in St Peter's Field.'

'How does this concern us?' Henderson asked from beside Andrew. Her brown hair was held up with some combs and, from her attire, one would think she was there to apply to be a nanny for his youngest nephew.

Gabriel glanced at Andrew before turning his attention to Henderson. 'We know about the unrest in this country. And, while I agree with the need for better representation for those people in the House of Commons, I also understand that along with those who seek a peaceful resolution to these problems, there are those who have a more radical violent view on how to achieve them. Those are the people we need to concern ourselves with. We must protect the Crown above all else and it's imperative for us to see if threats against Prinny and George exist among those who seek reform.'

'You think there are people who believe their only chance at reform is if some harm befalls the monarchy?' Spence asked, shifting his wiry frame in his chair.

Gabriel leaned forward and rested his forearms on his mahogany desk. 'I can't afford to ignore the possibility. That's why I'm sending the three of you up to Manchester to hear Mr Hunt speak on the sixteenth.'

Andrew looked across at his brother and noted Gabriel was focusing his attention on Spence and Henderson. He knew enough not to look at Andrew. If he did, he would be able to tell that Andrew wanted to throttle him. It had been a conscious decision on Andrew's part to throw himself into his work so he wouldn't have time to think about how much he missed his wife. Now, his brother was purposely sending him to an area that was a short ride away from her.

'Why me? I just came down from the north.'

Andrew could hear the frustration in his own voice and felt Spence's eyes on him.

'That is precisely why you need to go. You are more familiar with the area and you will be able to advise these two how to look as though they belong.'

'Spence knows the area as well.'

Gabriel ignored him. 'The three of you will leave on the twelfth. James is arranging rooms for you in Manchester.' He eyed Andrew. 'Unless you would prefer to stay in Cheshire.'

'Manchester is fine,' Andrew growled back.

'Excellent. Take note of any rumblings you hear that could lead to violence against the Crown and pay close attention to the people who appear to be the ones who instigate the crowd. Oh, and you two will pose as husband and wife.'

Henderson rolled her eyes and gestured towards Spence. 'For once, couldn't I be his sister?'

'You look nothing alike,' Gabriel replied, stating the obvious.

'Damned ginger,' she mumbled under her breath to Spence.

'The local magistrates will not be informed you are there,' Gabriel continued. 'I do not want their anxieties interfering with your unbiased observations. If you get into a fix, rely on each other. That is all of it. You can go now.'

Andrew wasn't going anywhere. He needed to have a word with his brother.

Henderson and Spence nodded their goodbyes before leaving the two brothers alone.

'You look as though you could use a brandy,' Gabriel said, sitting back in his chair and cocking his head to the side.

'It's too early for brandy—however, if I could darken your daylights it might improve my humour.'

'Come now, there is no sense in hitting me. You'll only travel to Manchester with a sore hand.'

'My hand will improve by then, my humour will not. Why are you doing this to me?'

'I wasn't aware I was doing anything more than giving you a mission.'

'A boring one.'

'To you, maybe.'

When that excuse didn't seem to work, he decided to confront Gabriel with the truth. 'I am trying to forget my wife. You have made that objective harder to achieve by placing me just miles from her home.'

'*Your* home.'

'It's her home. It's mine in name only.' Andrew raked his hand through his hair. 'Send someone else.'

Gabriel cross his arms. 'No. You were the one who took it upon himself to survey the area for

dissonance when you were instructed to distance
yourself from your work. You were the one who
had been following the stories in the newspapers
about Mr Hunt's speeches. You need to go to
Manchester.' He leaned forward and his exasper-
ated expression softened. 'Before anything, you
are an operative in this organisation. You need to
place duty before all else. You need to be able to
block out thoughts of your wife, of your child, of
everything related to you in order to be effective
at what you do. How can I trust that you will return to me from a truly dangerous mission, un-
harmed, when you can't put aside thoughts of her
on this one, because you are merely close by?'

Andrew dropped his head back and stared at
the coffered ceiling, hating whenever his brother
was more perceptive than he was.

'I have not asked what has caused this rift
between you and Charlotte. It is your marriage,
not mine. But unless you can find a way to move
past your emotions about it, I cannot send you
out on anything that might place you in physical harm. My affection for you is too great to
risk losing you.'

Gabriel was studying him intently, making
Andrew feel as though he was seated across
from their father and he was once again a young
man who had just come back from his first mission. At that moment, with that expression on his
face, Gabriel even bore a striking resemblance

to the man whose portrait hung above the fireplace in that very room. Andrew looked over at it and was met with their father's eyes.

'He was very proud of the work you did for him,' Gabriel said.

Andrew let out a small breath. 'He is looking down thinking I've let a woman lead me around by my nose.'

'You haven't. You are here trying to find your way around your feelings for her. You fell in love with her, didn't you?'

Andrew dropped his head back once again. 'I think I did. I tried not to, but…'

'It's not something you can control, Andrew. It just happens. There is no rhyme or reason to it. I take it Charlotte does not reciprocate the feeling?'

'Charlotte is in love with her husband…her dead husband. There is no room for me in her heart.' He scrubbed his hands across his eyes, wishing he could wipe away his feelings for her as easily.

Gabriel let out a sigh. 'I am truly sorry. I wish there were some words of wisdom I could give you on how to stop loving her. In time, her feelings may change.'

Andrew was not going to wait around for something that would never happen. It would just be too painful. He was much better with distance between them.

'I will prove to you that my duty comes before all else.'

And prove it to myself in the process.

He would go to Manchester, listen to Hunt speak, and study the crowd for potential dangerous radicals. He would not go anywhere near Charlotte's village—or Charlotte. Even though he knew he would have to remind himself of that vow every moment until the day he walked on to St Peter's Field.

Chapter Twenty-Four

The midday sun was shining so brightly, Charlotte had to adjust her straw bonnet as she walked alongside Ann and Toby towards St Peter's Field to hear Mr Hunt speak. She had read in the papers about the number of people that would come to hear him, but she never imagined what it would feel like to be in a crowd of people this large. There were people walking in front and behind them as far as the eye could see, all dressed in their Sunday best as they were advised to do. The organisers wished to show the local magistrates this would be a peaceful meeting of people coming together to hear what they could do to help repeal the Corn Laws and find ways to achieve better representation. This would not be a riot.

'I am relieved it is a clear day,' Ann said from beside her, 'although I am not fond of the heat.'

A little girl in front of them dropped her tat-tered doll and Charlotte picked it up, dusted it off, and handed it to her. The girl's mother smiled her thanks.

'I'm sure it feels even warmer because we are in the middle of such a crush.' If today would keep Charlotte's mind off wondering where her husband was and what he was doing, she would gladly endure the heat. Not a day had gone by since he'd left that she had not thought about him. And each night as she lay in bed, she wondered if he was happier without her. In her heart, she knew she was miserable without him. Today might help keep her mind on other things. 'Do you think we will be able to hear him?'

'We can try to make our way to the stage— however, I don't know if that will be possible,' Toby offered in almost a shout so he could be heard from Ann's other side above the chatter of the crowd.

'It might not have been wise for you to come with us,' Ann said, threading her arm through Charlotte's. 'In your condition, this might prove too much for you. Are you certain you will let me know if you get too tired and need to leave?'

She had told her friends about her pregnancy a few days earlier and Ann, whose only child was away at Eton, had been continually recalling her own experiences eight years earlier.

'I am fine,' Charlotte reassured her. 'However, should I feel faint, I will be certain to let you know.'

'Charlotte feels faint?' Poor Toby looked panic stricken.

'No. She said if she does.' Ann patted his hand reassuringly.

'Toby was so attentive while I was carrying William. You will see when Andrew returns. I'm certain he will be the same.'

The hole that had opened in Charlotte's heart when he'd left her widened.

'Just imagine,' Ann continued, 'when he sees you for the first time since receiving your letter with the news.' She rocked her shoulders slightly in an excited fashion. 'You will have such a lovely time celebrating.'

Charlotte had to look away so Ann wouldn't see her watery eyes. The idyllic scene Ann described would not be part of Charlotte's memories years from now. Her memory would be of telling Andrew she was carrying his child and him storming out into the rain in Hyde Park. It was better if she focused on that memory and not the one of him kissing her stomach as they lay in bed together on their wedding night. It only made her miss him more. She quickly wiped her wet cheek before turning back to her friend. 'Look, we have finally reached the field. What time is it, Toby?'

'Half past. Mr Hunt should be arriving soon.'

'Do you see the stage?' Charlotte sprang up on her toes and looked ahead of them.

'I believe it's in that direction, but I doubt we will be able to make our way there. I think I see a good spot for us to stand over there,' he replied, leading them to the left.

Andrew had agreed to stay near the back of the crowd that gathered to hear Mr Hunt speak, while Spence and Henderson had stationed themselves close to the stage. He had never been in a crowd this large. Thousands of people were pouring on to the field from the adjacent streets. And the thought of the damage a crowd this size could do should they turn violent had him on edge. It was instilled in him from the time he was young to expect the unexpected and, this morning when he got out of bed in the inn, he had a feeling that something of note was about the happen.

Luckily, Andrew found it easy to start conversations with the people around him who were all excited with the prospect of Mr Hunt helping them achieve better representation and improve their economic condition. He hadn't seen even one person carrying sticks or rocks, or other implements that could be used to instigate violence. Women and children were even in attendance. And so far, he hadn't heard any mention of King

George or Prinny. Maybe today would be just a pleasant day outside in the sunshine.

'Charlotte!'

The name was called out by a man somewhere to his right and Andrew turned so quickly to follow the exclamation it was a wonder he didn't hurt his neck. His hope at catching a glimpse of his wife was dashed the moment he saw a little girl run into the arms of an older gentleman for a firm hug.

He had been doing very well at not thinking about her when they'd walked here from the inn. This was the first time in hours she had crossed his mind and he told himself it was only because he had heard her name. There wasn't time to think about her further because the sounds of music and shouts coming from Deansgate indicated Mr Hunt and his party had arrived. From where he stood he could see a band turning in, followed by several men holding flags, and then Mr Hunt and his party. As they made their way through the crowd to the stage, one universal shout of huzzah arose from the crowd.

When Mr Hunt reached the stage, he took off his white hat and began to address the crowd. They watched him silently, straining to hear his every word. There was a sense of respect in the air that you could almost feel.

Suddenly, a noise followed by a murmur rose through the crowd by the church. From where

he stood, Andrew could see a party of cavalry-
men in blue and white uniforms trotting with
swords in hand around the corner of a garden
wall. They reined up in line in front of a row
of new houses. They were a formidable sight.
One that pricked Andrew's senses. If the magistrates saw fit to have the yeomanry present to
ensure order on a crowd this size, Andrew could
understand. But from their seat on horseback,
Andrew knew they had no intention of remaining there quietly. The crowd was peaceful and,
from what he had observed over the hours he
had spent amongst them, they had every intention of remaining that way.

His instincts about the men on horseback
proved accurate when, without warning, they
waved their sabres over their heads and, striking spur to their horses, dashed forward into the
crowd, slicing at people that were in their way.
Shouts and screams rose up around Andrew as
people began to run. The cavalry was attempting to make its way to the stage, but the compact
mass of people impeded their progress. Their sabres shone in the sunlight, covered with blood
from the bare held-up hands, limbs, and heads
they hacked. Piteous cries and heartrending sobs
filled the air, along with sounds of hoofbeats.
People were running in all directions—men,
women and children. He tried to make his way to
the stage to get to Spence and Henderson when

a number of cavalry officers decided they could reach the stage from that route, as well.

Andrew pushed his way through the crowd pressing towards him when his gaze landed on a tall woman dressed in white not far from one of the soldiers on horseback and he froze. It was Charlotte. She spotted him at the exact same moment and a cry of his name roared from her lips as she ran from Toby and Ann's side towards him. He thought he must be hallucinating. It wasn't until she reached his arms and held on tight that he was certain it was her.

He tried to shield her from the crowd with his arms. Scanning the masses for a safe way out, he caught Henderson's eye some distance away as she pulled Spence back by the hand and pointed to Andrew. His ginger-haired friend looked at Charlotte and then tipped his hat to Andrew before he pulled Henderson towards a group of cavalry men who were arresting Hunt.

'What are you doing here?' Charlotte yelled as Toby and Ann ran up to them.

'We have a carriage,' Toby shouted. 'Follow us.'

Andrew nodded before tightening his grip on Charlotte's hand and charging with her through the crowd. A thundering sound followed them and grew louder as if the horse that was making the sound would roll over them like a wave. A horrible pain sliced through Andrew's right arm and Charlotte screamed beside him as a man on horseback rode past them.

Through the tremendous pain Andrew kept running, knowing he needed to reach Toby's carriage and get Charlotte to safety. Their hands, clasped tightly together, were warm and wet with his blood.

Within ten minutes St Peter's Field was empty of the chaos, but littered with personal objects and bodies of the wounded and dead. Andrew could see it at a distance as he sat inside Toby's carriage while his friend's driver was preparing the horses and he was instructing Charlotte how tie one of her long gloves around his arm as a tourniquet.

Chapter Twenty-Five

It took Charlotte three tries to open the door to her house because her hand was shaking. Andrew, standing beside her, was of no help. His eyes were closed and he was in obvious pain. If only he hadn't instructed Toby and Ann to go home. She could have used their help right now.

Andrew needed her physician. Doctor Colter would know what to do. But when she suggested they ride directly to him, Andrew insisted they couldn't spare the time to go that far.

'Wells!' she screamed, calling for her butler as she pushed open the door.

The thin man who was old enough to be her father came running into the entrance hall as white as a sheet. The last time she'd screamed for anyone in this house was the moment she had found out Jonathan had died.

'I need you to fetch Dr Colter. Tell him we

need him immediately. The master of the house is injured.'

The man's eyes widened at the sight of blood soaking Gabriel's entire sleeve and a good part of Charlotte's white dress before he rushed towards the front door.

'Wait!' Andrew bit out through his teeth. 'Charlotte, if we wait much longer to remove this tourniquet, I will lose this arm.' He turned back to Wells, who was frozen in the doorway with fear in his eyes. 'Is there brandy?'

Wells nodded, seeming afraid to speak. She couldn't blame him.

'Thank God,' Andrew muttered on a sigh. 'Two bottles of it. And a needle with lots of thread. In the drawing room. Now!'

Without waiting for a reply, Andrew took to the stairs with Charlotte fresh on his heels. Sunlight streamed in from the open window as he stumbled on to the yellow-brocade window seat. Charlotte ran and knelt beside him.

'Take off my cravat. You're going to help me stop the bleeding.'

'No. No. We need a physician.' Her hands were trembling so much she didn't think she would be able to untie the knot.

'There isn't time. We are going to do this together.'

She unwound the linen from his neck and prayed he wouldn't die from all the blood that had been seeping out of his body. When he left it was as though a light had gone out in her world and no matter what she did or who she saw, that light would not come back—until she spotted him amidst the chaos at St Peter's Field. She couldn't think any more about why he was in Manchester and hadn't come to see her. She needed to stop him from bleeding.

Mr Wells came running back into the room with two bottles of brandy, two stemmed glasses and her sewing basket.

Andrew had lost his hat in the tussle and sweat was dripping down his temples. 'I'll need clean linen we can rip into strips.' His voice was strained, but he was composed.

Once more he had her butler running for the door.

'You need to untie your glove. Once you do, my arm will begin bleeding again.' There was clear determination in his eyes. 'We are going to save my arm. I need you to believe that.'

How much blood did one body hold? He had lost so much already. It was hard to slow her breathing, but she was going to do everything she could to help him.

'How do we even stop the bleeding?' she asked.

'I'll know once I look inside the wound.'

Breathing through her mouth, she unknotted the glove he had instructed her to tie tightly on his arm over an hour ago. Blood gurgled to the surface and covered her hands as she helped him slip out of his coat and waistcoat. When she removed his shirt, he held his breath as she pulled the linen gingerly away from the wound.

'Press my shirt into it as hard as you can and hand me a bottle of brandy.'

She pushed his shirt down over the wound and handed him one of the green-glass bottles.

He took a long drink and wiped his mouth with the back of his hand. His ragged breathing was evident with the rise and fall of his bare chest. 'We need to clean the wound. Remove the shirt.'

Just as she opened her mouth to call out for someone to bring water and soap, Andrew poured the brandy over the wound and let out a terrible inhuman sound that bounced around her body. Brandy and blood ran off his arm on to the wooden floor. When he spread the six-inch wound apart to look inside the bloody mess, she ran to the window and sucked in some air.

'Bone seems intact,' he ground out over her shoulder.

With one last deep breath, she closed her eyes. *I will not be sick. I will not be sick.*

'Charlotte, grab a needle and thread. You have to stitch my arm up.'

I'm going to be sick. I'm going to be sick.

'Charlotte!'

She turned to find him staring at her. Blood was continuing to soak his shirt while he held it to his arm.

'I cannot do this alone. The gash is on my right arm. I will never be able to thread the needle and use my left hand to sew.'

'Surely someone else—'

'No, I need *you*. If we don't do this now, I will eventually bleed out.'

Mr Wells ran back in, looking green, with a bunch of clean linen in his hand. Charlotte grabbed it and shooed him out of the room. It took her a few tries to thread the needle, but she finally managed to do it.

'Pour brandy on it.' His voice wasn't as commanding as before and he was blinking as if trying to stay awake.

She couldn't imagine how badly the brandy was burning his arm. He had drunk a considerable amount from the bottle in his bloodied hand and there was only an inch or two left when she took it from him. As she poured the remaining brandy on the needle and thread, he grabbed the other bottle from the table and swayed before steadying himself enough to sit down on the floor and lean back on the wall between the windows.

Without a word, he motioned for her to come closer. 'When I remove this, pinch the wound closed and sew deep.'

That was it? That was all the instruction she was given? How did one sew flesh?

'Vomit away from me, Char.'

She met his half-lidded eyes and a faint smile curved his lips as if a full smile was too much effort. He wasn't the only one who needed brandy. She took a swig from his bottle and handed it back. It burned her throat and made her eyes water, but hopefully it would steady her nerves.

'I can do this. I can do this.' She didn't care that she was talking out loud. He had asked her to do this, so he would just have to listen to her try to convince herself she could.

'It's like mending gloves. I'm just mending gloves.'

Bloodied gloves that had muscles that flexed each time she stuck a needle in them.

'Doing fine,' he slurred as he continued to drink from the bottle.

Dear God, she should have made him lie down. What would she do if he toppled over in the middle of a stitch? He couldn't fall asleep. Or pass out. She needed to keep him awake.

'Why were you at St Peter's today?'

'To hear Hunt.'

'You told Toby and Ann you were planning on seeing me when you left there today. That wasn't true, was it?' She held her breath, waiting for his reply.

'No. No, it wasn't.'

Hearing he had not wanted to see her made a painful knot form in her chest. But she needed to finish sewing him up and she needed to keep him talking. 'How do you know how to take care of this?' she asked, motioning towards his arm.

'Training…for the field.'

'What field?'

He took another swig of brandy. 'I've done it.'

'Done what? You've sewn up a wound?'

He was looking at her through one eye when she glanced up. 'Spence. Knife fight. Couldn't do it himself. Bloody imbecile.'

'Knife fight? Why was he in a knife fight?'

'Crown. Always for the Crown.'

'Someone you know was in a knife fight for money?'

He let out a small breath that under different circumstances might have been a laugh. 'Not that Crown.'

He wasn't making sense and both of his eyes were closing. She only had a few more stiches to go.

'Hurts,' he groaned.

The sound of his pain brought tears to her eyes and broke her heart. He was a good man. He had done nothing to deserve this. 'I know it hurts. I'm almost finished.' She tried to soothe him with her words and clear her blurry vision. 'See. Just like mending gloves. You'll be fine.'

'No, my heart. It hurts. I…'

Her hand stilled on the final stitch and she looked up at him.

He licked his lips. A sheen of sweat glistened on his bare chest that was rising and falling unevenly with his erratic breathing, and his eyes were closed in agony. 'I shouldn't love you,' he breathed out. 'Don't know how to stop. Need to leave.'

His head lolled to the side.

Her world tilted.

'Andrew? Andrew!'

Seeing that his chest was still rising and falling, she raised the back of her hand to her mouth to stifle a sob. The coppery scent of his warm, wet blood filled her nose.

He loved her. She never thought she would ever hear those words again. And coming from Andrew—the man she...she... Oh, God! Tears fell. She loved him. Her heart had hurt for so long, she had stopped listening to it. But now it was screaming at her to hold on to him. She would not let him leave. Not this time. She loved him and was miserable without him. They belonged together. She just needed to finish stitching him up and tell him.

Chapter Twenty-Six

Andrew could feel himself being pulled out of a deep sleep and was grateful for the soft mattress his body was melting into. He wasn't sure which hurt more, his head or his arm. As he slowly opened his eyes to the darkness, he was beginning to think it was his head.

Months ago, waking up to find himself in unfamiliar surroundings would have set his pulse racing, but this time it helped that he recognised traces of Charlotte's perfume in the air. He took a deep breath, finding comfort in her scent.

The mattress dipped beside him. With the scratch of flint against steel, she lit a candle and secured it in a holder on the table beside the bed. There were shadows under her eyes and concern etched on her brow. The last time he had seen her, she was covered in his blood. Now she was wrapped in a pink dressing gown and her long black hair was twisted into a braid. This was much better.

She rested her warm palm on his forehead. 'Still no fever. That's a good sign.'

'Where am I?'

'My bedchamber. I had the footmen bring you here after I cleaned you as best I could. I thought you'd rest more comfortably in a bed instead of on the drawing-room floor. After the sun comes up and you've rested some more, I'll call for a warm bath for you. How are you feeling?'

'Sore. And my head hurts like the devil. My arm aches, but I still have it. And I didn't die. Thank you. I wouldn't be lying in this bed intact if it weren't for you.' He wished he could have held her hand to offer some reassurance and remove the creases from her forehead. But he needed to start trying to lock away his feelings for her. He would leave when the sun came up. He had to. 'What time is it?'

She walked with the candle to the clock on the mantel and then came back to sit on the edge of the bed. 'It's almost two.'

'Why do I sleep for so long when I am in your bed?' he asked, rubbing the sleep out of his eyes.

'I believe this time you had a very good reason. Do you remember anything that happened?'

'My head is not that muddled with brandy that I could forget being hacked with a sabre.' It was a struggle, but he managed to sit up.

'And do you remember what happened after that?'

There was a catch to her voice he hadn't missed. 'Most of it.' Apparently, he must have passed out, which was something he had never done. He could only remember Charlotte's first few stitches into his arm. He didn't recall her finishing or anything after that. Drinking to excess was dangerous. Things could be said. Secrets could be spilled. That was why he never did it—until now. But the gash was too long and too deep, and he had needed something to numb the pain.

She toyed with the fabric in her lap, but continued to look at him with concern. 'Why were you so insistent I should be the one to stitch you up? Why did it have to be me?'

He couldn't tell her that looking at her kept him calm. He couldn't tell her that if something were to happen to him, he wanted her face to be the last one he saw. He couldn't tell her any of that, so instead he gave her another reason. 'I knew you could do it.'

'I thought you were in London. Why were you in Manchester?'

'I saw an announcement in the paper about the meeting. You seemed impressed with Mr Hunt. I decided I wanted to hear what he had to say. Why were you there? You could have been injured or killed. That was no place for you.'

'Had I known it would turn violent, I never would have gone. I am not a proponent of violence to achieve reform. This was to be a peaceful gathering to hear constructive ideas. Everyone was told to arrive sober and come without any implements that might be misconstrued as weapons. And yet they came at us with sabres drawn, hacking through a crowd of innocent men, women and children. Did you see the children?' There was anguish in her eyes.

'I did.' And it made him sick. 'I don't know why it started.'

'Neither do I. But those people were unarmed. *You* were unarmed...except for the knife in your boot.'

There was a watchfulness about her that told him she knew that knife was just the beginning of the secrets he held. Damn! She knew something.

'Where are my trousers?'

'They were laundered and have yet to dry. One of the footmen was kind enough to offer you a pair of his breeches for now. Would you like me to get them?'

'Yes, please. I need to get out of bed and stretch. It will help with the long ride back to London if I move now.'

There was a slight hesitation before she reached behind her and handed him the breeches from somewhere at the foot of the bed. She helped him into them since his right arm was still sore. They were a bit snug, but they would do for now. As they sat beside one another on her bed, he could see their faint reflections in the darkened windowpanes.

She looked down towards her lap. 'I wish you wouldn't leave.'

His heart stopped at her words. He didn't want to leave her either, but he knew it was what he had to do—for so many reasons. 'I cannot stay.'

It looked as if she wanted to say something, but was unsure how to begin. She picked at the fabric of her dressing gown. 'You said some things before you passed out.'

Damn! There were so many things he could have told her. There were so many secrets he had. 'I drank quite a bit of brandy. I'm sure what you heard were drunken ramblings.'

She went still and suddenly seemed so sad.

'What did I say, Charlotte?' He walked to the window and lifted the sash, needing to feel the cool night air and hide his unease.

'Do you... Do you work for the Crown?'

Andrew spun back around and stared at her. 'What?' He prayed he sounded convincing.

'You spoke of a friend who was injured in a knife fight. You said it was done for the Crown. I've been thinking about that...and about your reaction to waking up with me the morning after our wedding and the knife I found in your boot today.' She was studying his reaction.

He had never been asked that question and was trying to think of what to say.

'Just tell me. There are too many things that make me believe you do. The way you thought Aunt Clara was kidnapping me when she approached you on Bond Street. Your scars. How you knew what to do to address your wound. One does not get a wound like that in a boxing match. All of that tells me there is more to you than you show the world.'

His head and his heart were both telling him he could trust her, but this was something his own mother didn't know about him.

'I will never betray your confidence, Andrew. I saved you. Does that mean nothing?'

It meant everything to him. And telling her the truth, or some part of it, was probably better than any speculation she might make. He knew how important it was to control information.

'Very well, I will tell you some things, but what I say to you now must not leave this room.'

'Of course.'

He walked closer, standing less than a foot in front of her. 'Much of my life is lead in secret. I cannot reveal who I work for, just that I do protect the Crown.'

She looked up, closed her eyes and let out a breath. 'Thank you for confiding in me. I do not need to know who it is. Jonathan would be gone for months. We never discussed battle plans. I knew he was protecting this country. I didn't need to know exactly how. I will not pry into your work. I understand there are things you would need to keep from me.' An expression that resembled hope crossed her face. 'Is this why you insist we live apart?'

If she knew all the things he had done, she would beg to live apart. Any caring thought she had about him would be replaced by contempt and fear. Maybe that would be easier on his heart.

He ran his hand through his hair. 'There are things about me…things I've done… I've had to make choices.' This was the first time he would admit out loud what he had done to his uncle and guilt was spreading through his body like frost on a windowpane. 'I've taken someone's life. I am the type of man who can kill another.' He rubbed his hand over his eyes, afraid to see her disgust. Surely now she would not want him to stay.

'Was it done indiscriminately?'

'No.'

'Was it out of hatred or malice?'

He shook his head. 'They were about to kill someone else and I couldn't let that happen.'

He looked up and saw compassion in her eyes, as if she understood how much he had struggled with that decision over the years—how standing a few feet away and killing his uncle had changed him. 'This person was someone I once cared for. I should have thought of another way to stop them. But I didn't. Instead I stood there and pulled the trigger on my gun.' The pain and guilt he had carried around with him for years cracked through his voice.

'You did what was necessary to protect someone else. It doesn't diminish my feelings for you.'

Her feelings? While he had no doubt she cared about him, she would always want her dead husband and not him. He needed more than that from her and being around her was a painful reminder. 'Now that you know my secrets, I trust you to keep them after I've gone.'

'I still don't want you to leave. I will not interfere in what you do. If you need to live in London, then we shall live in London. I just want us to live together during the times you are not away out of necessity.'

'We can't, Charlotte.'

He did not want her. It was crushing Charlotte's heart. Were his words of love last night just the ramblings of a drunken man? Was it a lie?

She had no pride left. He meant the world to her. She would tell him how she felt. If he didn't feel the same, then at least she would know she had done everything she could to save her marriage. She had to try.

'I love you, Andrew.'

His eyes widened before his brows drew together. 'I have no doubt you care for me—'

'Care for you? I love you.'

'As one does a friend.' He took a step back. 'While our friendship will serve us well in dealing with one another, it is no reason for us to live together.'

'Is that what you truly believe?'

'I can't live with you.'

'But you love me. You said it last night.'

He closed his eyes and dropped his head. 'I was drunk.'

Her heart was breaking. Did he not love her? He had brought light and life back into her world and reminded her what a strong woman she already was. With him she had found joy again. Had she given him nothing in return? Had her presence had no effect on him at all?

Tears were filling her eyes. She was the only one who felt happier when they were together than when they were apart. He probably never even thought of her when he was gone.

'Don't cry, Charlotte. This is what's best for both of us.'

She wiped at her eyes and shook her head. This might be what was best for him, but it was not what she wanted.

'I can't live with you, Charlotte. I can't live with you knowing every day you wish I were someone else. I can't live with you knowing you wish that child growing inside you belonged to another man. I can't do it. I am not that strong. And in the end, you will thank me for it.' He walked around her and stood by the bed, looking down at the rumpled sheets.

'But I don't feel that way.'

'I heard what you said to your sister when she came to see you. You saw me and yet you didn't deny or try to explain those words.'

'Because I didn't know what to say. My heart hurt for so long that I had stopped listening to it. I never believed I could fall in love again—that a heart was capable of falling in love more than once. But now I know, I love you.'

He shook his head and looked away.

She walked up to his side and gently guided his chin so he was facing her once more.

'And I was afraid. You said you wanted us to live apart. You always have. I was afraid to care for you so deeply when the feeling would not be returned. But I fell in love with you anyway. More than one loves a friend. I love you more than anything. And you not loving me will not change that.'

He looked down at her abdomen, then up into her eyes. 'But you will always love Jonathan more. You will always wish that our child was his.'

'It did make me sad that I did not have a child with Jonathan. But this child that I am carrying is yours and you have to believe me when I say I don't want it to be anyone else's. I want this part of you. I want you to be this child's father... to be my child's father.' She blinked back the tears. 'I am sorry that I hurt you. So very sorry. My love for you isn't any less than the love I had for Jonathan. It is just different. In such a short time, you have brought light into my darkness and all I know is that I am much happier when I am with you than when I am not. And maybe that makes me selfish for wanting this. For wanting you when you do not feel the same way. For that I am sorry. All I know is I don't want to lose you. I don't want to live without you.'

He wiped the tears from her cheek. 'I wanted to hear that you loved me for so long. I thought hearing those words would make things better—now I don't know if I feel worse. I love you. I do. And hearing you say you love me is something I never thought possible. But I wish I could offer you a stable life. To be able to say I can stop my work for the Crown tomorrow and be the gentleman farmer you deserve after all your loss. I want with all my heart to tell you I can do that, but I can't. I can't give up this thing inside me that is a burning need to protect the stability of this country.'

'I'm not asking you to.'

'You've already suffered through losing one husband. What if you lost me, too?'

'You don't think I'm strong enough? You don't think that if something happened to you I would find a way to go on and raise our child without you? You are sentencing me to that life regardless if you are here or not. I love you. That is not going to change whether you are here beside me or whether you live in London and I am here. We have a choice. We can grab every moment we have with one another and hold on tight for the times we are apart. Or we can live apart as if the other is dead while we are still alive.'

'I saw how Jonathan's death affected you. You were in mourning for four years when I met you!'

'Clothes! I wore mourning clothes! Is that what you are afraid of? I shall don those weeds should you leave me now for London. I will wear them every day you are gone to mark how my heart breaks for the loss.'

She fisted her hands at her side. She would not let him go. Not this time. Especially knowing he loved her. *He loved her*... How could a person move from sorrow to joy in mere minutes?

'I am stronger than you think I am, Andrew. I have a strength inside me the likes of which

you have never witnessed, so do not tell me I am
not strong enough to survive your death should
it come to that! And for good measure, I think
I'll die on you first just for spite!'

'I have no doubt that you would.' His countenance softened. 'Come here.'

She took a step closer and he wrapped her in
his arms. Each held on as if they were in need
of an anchor in a storm.

'I don't want you to regret that you ever met
me.' His voice was husky and low, as if it were
difficult to speak.

'The only thing I'll regret is letting you go.
Don't go, Andrew. Don't leave us.'

'You're speaking for our child now?'

'He needs you, too.'

'For years I've known that one night can
change your life for ever. But you have taught
me that one night can also change your heart.'

'So, you will stay?'

'If you will have me.'

Hot tears streamed down her face, and she
stepped back to look at him. 'I have never wanted
anything more.'

Epilogue

London—November 1819

Charlotte stood in the sun-filled drawing room of her new London town house, staring at four paintings of horses she had retrieved from Olivia's house the day before. She wanted to surprise Andrew when he came home from his current assignment in two days. He had been gone for five days and it felt like five weeks.

Decorating their new home overlooking St James's Square had proved to be an enjoyable way to pass the time and she wanted to get these paintings that Olivia had purchased for him a year ago hung before he arrived home. The order the four of them should be arranged in was proving troublesome. Should the one with the red jockey go on the top right or bottom left? She took a step back and tilted her head. Lizzy was much better at this than she was. She was the

Sommersby sister who possessed a talent for decorating. Charlotte would send a note to her if by evening she still wasn't satisfied with the arrangement.

The sound of footsteps on the wooden floor behind her let her know Wells had entered the room with her tea and biscuits. They would help sustain her until she dined at Olivia's hours from now.

'Thank you, Wells. You may leave them by the sofa,' she called out, her eyes still on the paintings. She wanted them to be just perfect for him.

The soft clattering of her cup as Wells lowered the tray to the table was followed by his footsteps approaching her. Andrew's mother had told her she would call on her this week to see the house. He might be coming to inform her of her arrival. The poor man still appeared a bit flustered when he had any contact with the members of Andrew's elevated family.

Just as she was about to turn around, two arms came around her waist, startling her so thoroughly she rammed her right elbow into her assailant's side. A loud curse filled the air and the arms that were around her dropped away. She spun around, recognising that voice instantly.

'Andrew, you're home!' Charlotte threw her arms around the neck of her hunched-over husband who was gripping his side. 'Oh, God, I'm so sorry.'

'How foolish of me to assume, coming home to my wife, I'd receive a more welcoming greeting,' he ground out in pain.

'I thought you were your mother.'

His brows drew together and he looked at her as if she had lost her mind. 'You intended to injure my mother?'

'No. No.' She let out a laugh and covered her mouth. 'Of course not. I thought you were Wells coming to tell me your mother had come to call, but then you put your arms around me and... Here, let me help you to the sofa.'

He managed to straighten up and stretched out his side while trying unsuccessfully to hide his smile. 'I am fine. There's no need to fuss over me.'

'Perhaps I enjoy fussing over you.'

'Why don't you offer me a kiss instead?' He raised his eyes and tried to appear innocent. No matter how hard he tried, Andrew never looked innocent. Maybe because she knew the things he liked to do to her on their bed.

She took a step closer so they were mere inches apart. 'You're certain I will not injure you further?'

'I'm willing to take the chance.'

Wrapping her arms around him, she leaned in and pressed her lips to his. It was a slow, thoughtful kiss, one that she hoped conveyed just how much she missed him and how happy she was to have him home.

Andrew would never grow tired of kissing his wife. The slow languid kiss they were sharing filled his heart with happiness and was just what he needed to forget the trying days he'd spent trailing a useless lead. He still loved what he did, but he loved coming home to Charlotte even more.

'I missed you,' she said, placing her forehead against his.

'And I missed you.' He kissed her again before stepping back to look at her.

She was glowing, wearing a long-sleeved cinnamon-coloured gown with a bright smile.

'You look beautiful.'

That blush that he adored so much swept over her cheeks. 'If I'd known you'd be arriving today, I would have worn a better gown.'

'I like this one. The colour suits you. I would have arrived home earlier today, but I had to stop to get something on Bond Street.'

'You went to Jackson's before coming here?' The hurt was evident in her tone.

'Not Jackson's. I went to shop.' He walked out and came back in with a large box. 'Open it.'

She took it and placed it on the sofa. Her body appeared to be humming with excitement. 'This is far larger than the last one you brought.'

When he was away for an extended time, he liked to bring her small gifts when he returned. 'I wanted you to have this before you left for Kent.'

Her brow wrinkled and she looked back at the box.

'Open it.'

She lifted the lid. 'Oh, Andrew.' She let out a breath and ran her fingers gingerly over the red velvet before she took the cloak out of the box. Immediately she threw it around her shoulders and pulled up the hood. The ermine-fur trim framed her smiling face. 'How does it look?'

'You look lovely. Do you like it?'

'How could I not? It is gorgeous.' She continued to stroke the fur trim that went all around the garment. 'Juliet will not be getting her hands on this when she is in Kent for Christmas. This I will not share.'

'Your sister agreed to spend Christmas with us?'

'Yes, she has finally agreed to visit us with Aunt Clara, although I honestly have no idea why she was so hesitant to spend the holidays with us. We've always spent Christmas together and she does seem to like your family.'

'Most of them anyway,' Andrew said with a grin. 'I don't think she is very fond of Monty, however.'

'Nonsense. She hasn't been around your

brother long enough to form such a poor opinion of him and I'm sure he is not the reason she didn't want to spend time with us.'

Andrew wasn't convinced. 'Did she ask if he would be there?'

Charlotte appeared to be recalling the contents of her sister's letter. 'She did.' Her brow wrinkled.

'And what did you tell her?'

'That he would be in attendance along with the rest of your family.'

'And her reply to you?'

She stopped stroking the fur of the cloak. 'She said she wasn't certain if they would be able to travel that far from Bath in December to join us.'

'You see.'

'That can't be the reason. In any event, they will be spending the holidays with us, which fills me with happiness. Lizzy is still so muddled in her own affairs with the new Duke that she will not be there, but promises to visit as soon as she is able.' Charlotte went back to petting the cloak. 'I shall wear this Christmas Day to church.'

'Wear it before then. I had them line it in wool to keep you warm all winter.'

She sashayed up to him, making Andrew laugh, and showed him her appreciation with a long deep kiss.

'I shall be the envy of all the women I meet.'

Gabriel was much better with fashionable

things than Andrew was. It had taken him over an hour to choose the cloak. 'You think I made a fine choice?'

'I was referring to you. All the women will envy me because I have such a thoughtful husband.' Her eyes widened and she turned around towards the fire burning in the hearth. 'I almost forgot, I have something for you.'

'You do?'

'Yes, come here.' She pulled him by the hand to the hearth and gestured to the wall. 'Look.'

His four paintings by George Stubbs were hanging on the wall, two on each side of the fireplace that had her prized arrow on the mantel. 'How did you know?'

'Your mother showed them to me the night I met her.' She took a step forward and cocked her head. 'I'm still not certain I like the red jockey on the upper right. What do you think?'

'I'm coming up behind you,' he announced with a grin before he slid his arms around her and rested his hands over the bump where their child was.

She leaned her head back next to his.

'Do you even like horses?' he asked. 'I mean, like them enough to have them hanging in our drawing room?'

'Don't you? I think I rather do. They remind me of our home in Cheshire.'

He kissed her temple. 'Thank you. I love them.'

'But you still haven't told me if you like the red jockey on the right side.'

'Perhaps we should ask our daughter.' He dropped to his knees in front of her and rubbed her stomach.

'I thought you thought it was a boy.'

'Today, I think it's a girl.'

'For someone so certain it would be a boy, you have been changing your mind an awful lot lately.'

'Perhaps I like the idea of a small version of you running around our house. So why don't we ask her if we should keep the red jockey where it is.'

Her stomach pushed against his hand, making it move, and Charlotte let out a gasp.

Andrew's heart stopped and he froze. 'What did I do? Should we get the physician?'

'No. You didn't do anything. It's the baby.'

'Has that ever happened before?'

She shook her head and let out a soft laugh. 'Olivia and Ann both told me this would happen. I just never expected it to feel so…so…'

'Painful?'

'Odd.'

Her stomach rolled under his hand, moving it again.

'Yes, odd is the right word for it,' she said.

They looked at one another with silly grins. Their child was in there. He was going to be a father. In his head he knew he was, but it had never felt quite real. It somehow felt as if Charlotte had just gained weight. But now...now he could envision it. Soon they would have a child in this house. One that would run around these rooms. One that he could teach to ride a horse. And build houses out of cards. And throw on his shoulders for walks around their garden in the summer.

He stood up and pushed Charlotte's hood back, bringing the sunlight streaming in from the windows on to his wife's face.

'Thank you for this,' he said. 'Thank you for all of this. I thought I was condemned to a life without love and the comfort of a family of my own. I thought I was broken, for what I had done, but you put me back together, piece by piece with your kindness, your strength and your understanding. I'm thankful every day for the love you've given me.'

She brushed the hair from his forehead and he kissed her palm.

'I should be thanking you. I thought my life was over four years ago. I was merely existing, not living. You brought light into my world when for so long I had been moving through darkness. You've showed me what it means to truly live life and enjoy every small moment. When I look at you, my heart bursts with all the love I feel for you and I am thankful every day that I met you and that you liked fireworks.'

He wrapped his arms around her. 'Especially fireworks in Cheshire, seen from a secluded hillside.'

Charlotte leaned closer. Her lips were a mere breath from his. 'They are my favourite ones.'

Instead of agreeing, Andrew closed the distance between them and his lips met hers for a soul-searing kiss.

* * * * *

Author Note

The idea for this story came to me while I was helping two of my dearest friends get through some difficult times in their lives. I wanted to write a story about hope—a story that would remind people that it's never too late to find love.

If you've read my other books you'll know that I like to use nuggets of history in my stories. The meeting in Manchester that Andrew and Charlotte attended is known today as the Peterloo Massacre and was held on the sixteenth of August 1819. During that summer Henry Hunt, who was a proponent of working-class radicalism and known as the Orator for his rousing speeches, was invited to address the crowd at a rally of the Patriotic Union Society in Manchester. He believed in annual Parliaments and universal suffrage, and favoured a tactic known as 'mass pressure' which he felt could achieve reform without insurrection.

The crowds that turned out to hear him that day were enormous. There are accounts that sixty thousand to one hundred thousand people were there. Since the press frequently mocked meetings of working men because of their ragged appearance and disorganised conduct, the organisers instructed people attending to practise cleanliness, sobriety, order and peace. All weapons were to be prohibited throughout the demonstration.

Local magistrates, some fearing a riot would take place, sent the local yeomanry to arrest Mr Hunt and the other speakers and to disperse the crowd. When the cavalry arrived, they charged into the crowd with their sabres drawn. Fifteen people were killed and four hundred to seven hundred were injured either from attacks by the cavalry or by the stampede of the crowd as they ran to get away.

Mr Hunt was arrested and sent to prison. The massacre was given the name Peterloo by the *Manchester Observer*—a combination of the name of St Peter's Field, where the massacre took place, and the Battle of Waterloo, which had taken place four years earlier.

During the following months it appeared the country was headed for an armed rebellion. There were aborted uprisings in the autumn and in the winter the Cato Street conspiracy plot to blow up the Cabinet was discovered and stopped.

By the end of the year the government introduced legislature, later known as the Six Acts, to suppress radical meetings and publications.

If you're interested in learning more about the Peterloo Massacre, Henry Hunt and other historical details found in this book, please visit my website at lauriebenson.net and click on the link to my blog. You can search *One Week to Wed* for relevant articles. And while you're there please subscribe to my newsletter for information about forthcoming books.

I hope you've enjoyed reading *One Week to Wed*, which is the first book in my The Sommersby Brides series. To find out when Juliet and Lizzy's stories will be released, visit my website.

COMING SOON!

We really hope you enjoyed reading this book. If you're looking for more romance, be sure to head to the shops when new books are available on

Thursday
26th July

To see which titles are coming soon, please visit
millsandboon.co.uk

MILLS & BOON

MILLS & BOON

Coming next month

THE CAPTAIN CLAIMS HIS LADY
Annie Burrows

Lizzie felt her cheeks heating as her thoughts, and her tongue, became hopelessly tangled. How she wished she had more experience of talking to men. Well, single men, who'd asked her to dance with them, that was. Then she might not be making quite such a fool of herself with this one.

'I will make a confession,' Harry said, leaning close to her ear so that his voice rippled all the way down her spine in a caressing manner.

'Will you?' She lost her ability to breathe properly. It felt as if her lungs, now, were as tangled as her thoughts.

'When I looked in upon the ballroom, earlier, and saw how few people were actually dancing, and how many were watching, my nerve almost failed.'

'Well, it is just that there are not that many people here who are fit enough to dance. But they do enjoy watching others. And then…'

'Giving them marks out of ten, I dare say,' he finished for her.

'Yes, that's about it. And I'm terribly sorry, but—'

'Oh, no,' he said sternly. 'You cannot retreat now. We are almost at the dance floor. Can you imagine what people will say if you turn and run from me?'

'That you've had a narrow escape?'

'That I've had…' He turned, and took both her hands in his. 'Miss Hutton, are you trying to warn me that you are not a good dancer?'

She nodded. Then hung her head.

She felt a gloved hand slide under her chin and lift her face. And saw him smiling down at her. Beaming, in fact. As though she'd just told him something wonderful.

'I have no...' she tried to wave her hands to demonstrate her lack of co-ordination, only to find them still firmly clasped between his own. 'And people do try to get out of my way, but...'

'I can see that this is going to be an interesting experience for both of us,' he put in.

'And for the spectators.'

'Yes,' he said, turning and leading her on to the dance floor where she could see the dim outlines of other people forming a set. 'Let us give them something worth watching.'

Continue reading
THE CAPTAIN CLAIMS HIS LADY
Annie Burrows

Available next month
www.millsandboon.co.uk

Copyright © 2018 Annie Burrows

LET'S TALK
Romance

For exclusive extracts, competitions
and special offers, find us online:

📘 facebook.com/millsandboon

📷 @millsandboonuk

🐦 @millsandboon

Or get in touch on 0844 844 1351*

For all the latest titles coming soon, visit
millsandboon.co.uk/nextmonth

* cost 7p per minute plus your phone company's price per minute access charge

Want even more
ROMANCE?

Join our bookclub today!

'Mills & Boon books, the perfect way to escape for an hour or so.'

Miss W. Dyer

'Excellent service promptly delivere and very good subscription choices.'

Miss A. Pearson

'You get fantastic special offers and the chance to get books before they hit the shops'

Mrs V. Hall

**Visit millsandbook.co.uk/Bookclub
and save on brand new books.**

MILLS & BOON